FALLING

STEFAN MOHAMED is an author and occasional poet. He lives in Bristol, where he does something in editorial. Find out things you never wanted to know about him at www.stefmo.co.uk

Also by Stefan Mohamed

NOVELS
Bitter Sixteen (Salt 2015)
Ace of Spiders (Salt 2016)
Stanly's Ghost (Salt 2017)

NOVELLAS
Stuff (Salt 2014)
Operation Three Wise Men (Salt 2015)

FALLING
LEAVES

STEFAN MOHAMED

LONDON

PUBLISHED BY SALT PUBLISHING 2018

2 4 6 8 10 9 7 5 3 1

Copyright © Stefan Mohamed 2018

Stefan Mohamed has asserted his right under the Copyright, Designs
and Patents Act 1988 to be identified as the author of this work.

First published in Great Britain in 2018 by
Salt Publishing Ltd
International House, 24 Holborn Viaduct, London EC1A 2BN United Kingdom

www.saltpublishing.com

Salt Publishing Limited Reg. No. 5293401

A CIP catalogue record for this book is available from the British Library

ISBN 978 1 78463 142 0 (Paperback edition)
ISBN 978 1 78463 143 7 (Electronic edition)

Typeset in Neacademia by Salt Publishing

Printed and bound in Great Britain by Clays Ltd, St Ives plc

Salt Publishing Limited is committed to responsible forest management.
This book is made from Forest Stewardship Council™ certified paper.

For Cath

CHAPTER ONE

I WAS CRYING when I woke up. Already crying, I mean. I'd woken up and started to cry before, of course, overwhelmed by the shock of transitioning from an unpleasant dream to the cold dark of reality. Everyone has. But this was different. It was as though it had been going on for ages, and I had just walked in on myself and was now standing there awkwardly, trying to work out exactly what the fuss was about. And at the same time I was lying in bed, my baggy old Simpsons T-shirt sweat-moulded to my body, flailing around in a chaos of panicky limbs, overwhelmed by some strange, foreign grief.

The two Vanessas snapped together and I pulled myself up into a sitting position, shrugging off the out-of-body feeling as misfiring neurons, some weird quirk of dreaming. I tried to ground myself, to be where I was, in the bed, in the bedroom, in the flat, but I couldn't stop *shaking*, couldn't stop . . . *ugh.* I closed my eyes. I counted to ten, twenty, fifty. I paid a great deal of attention to my breathing. The trembling eventually subsided, but what I was left with was almost worse.

I felt *sad*, so terribly sad, and angry, and I didn't know why, and that made me angrier still. I opened my eyes, sniffing, wiping my nose with the back of my hand, and looked down at Stuart. He was slumbering still, snoring sporadically, alliterative arsehole.

No. That was a bad thought. Shouldn't think that thought.

I sat there and let myself cry quietly until the residue of the forgotten dream had faded. Then I looked at him again. Once upon a time he would have woken up the instant I had, maybe even a few seconds before, like he could sense what was about to happen, and his soft voice would have guided me back like a lighthouse beam and I would have let him cradle me until the crying stopped. To be fair, it had been a while since I'd had a nightmare.

Although that wasn't the reason he hadn't woken up.

I thought about the reason. The reasons. And I felt as though I should feel sad about it, sad that beyond the basic need for some comfort at this most vulnerable moment, I didn't actually mind all that much that he was still asleep. I didn't, though. I felt some other sadness. Some foreign interloper in my brain, pulling my levers.

I slid out of bed and opened the window. Breeze poured in and my body tingled and I watched a three-legged fox hobble wonkily across the road before being absorbed by the shadows between someone's dustbins. *Foxes know,* I thought, although I wasn't sure why.

I wanted to speak to Alice.

I wanted a cigarette.

I wanted a drink.

I wanted to listen to Elliott Smith.

These last two things I could do. I retrieved my bottle of Captain Morgan's from its home on the wrong shelf, that is the wrong shelf according to Stuart, because rum should live in a cupboard in the kitchen, or on the side with the other grown-up spirits, not in the bedroom among seashells and figurines and meaningful meaningless bits and pieces, *well that's just tough shit really isn't it,* and I went and sat in the kitchen and drank two rums with ginger beer and listened to half of XO. Halfway through 'Waltz #1' I had to turn the CD player off because I thought I was going to cry again. This wasn't exactly revolutionary, as I'd cried to this particular song approximately fifty thousand times before and undoubtedly would a further fifty thousand times in the future, but . . . no. It was different. It wasn't the song. And it wasn't Stuart or the flat or the bills or any of that. None of the real stuff.

It was the dream. Whatever it had been about, wherever it had taken me, whatever it had shown me, had left this behind, this awful feeling. I kept coming back to the word *residue* as I clenched and un-clenched my fists, getting increasingly frustrated. There was nothing concrete, no explanation or meaning, just a deep, heavy melancholy, an ache in my chest and stomach that I couldn't pinpoint or quantify. Origin unknown. Does not compute. Blue screen of death. Try un-plugging it and plugging it in again.

My hand, seeming to operate at least partly of its own accord, walked itself across the table and grabbed my notebook and a pen. Interesting. This had to mean something. Such items were never within reaching distance when you wanted them, not when you were me.

I put pen to paper, trying not to think.

Just let the words out.

'She died,' and everything stopped. The fly on the opposite wall, rendered gigantic by a lurid splash of lamp post light. The rubbish fidgeting in the night breeze. The breeze itself. The blood chugging thickly from the knife wound in her stomach.'

I stopped and read it back. My writing engine was rusty, to say the least, so I wasn't surprised that it was stalling after a single paragraph. I was also very bad at just letting myself

3

write, I always went back and edited, deleting and moving things around and cursing myself for the utter shiteness of my prose, before I'd even finished what I was doing, even though I'd been told so many times that editing should come later.

And what the hell *was* I writing? A graphic murder scene? Is that what I'd dreamed about?

Come on, Vanessa. Get it out, whatever it is.

'*She was intrigued, though somehow not surprised, to find that she had not stopped. Not entirely. Her thoughts, her memories, her awareness, continued to simmer, shiver and spark, except suddenly weightless, un-tethered.*'

Again, I stopped. The words were there. I could feel them in my brain and they definitely needed to come out. But it was like a frazzled mother coaxing an unruly teenager out of bed on a Sunday.

I put my hair up in a bun and chewed my lip. Maybe making myself look more writerly would help.

'*She floated free of herself, becoming a new component in the air above the girl's body, an abstract mass. The five physical senses blurred and combined into something else, a sight that was total and far-reaching, and the dank death smell of the alley that had caught like rotten gas in the girl's nostrils was no longer merely a smell but the idea of smell, both the actuality and the concept, exploded, like a schematic rendered in too many dimensions.*

'*She knew she should feel dizzy, but all she felt was absolute calm.*'

Had this been my dream? It really didn't feel familiar. It didn't connect with the sadness, which was still there, lurking, although less intense than it had been. This didn't even seem like something I would have written, neither in terms of style

4

nor subject matter. I didn't go in for this kind of trippy shit. Trippy shit was very much not on the menu for Vanessa these days.

'She observed the girl's body. It looked so very small from up here. So temporary. She could see the sticky wound, see through it, following the ripples from intention to action to consequence. She knew exactly what could have been done to save the girl, what could have been pressured, plugged, re-attached.

'She tried to sigh but instead she rippled, as though she was a patch of water catching a plummeting star, and then there was a sound like all the air escaping from the sky and she was everywhere. Everyone.

'She was the girl. Her family, her friends. The boy who had somehow made all this happen.

'She was everything that each of these people, these women, these girls, this boy, had ever felt and would ever feel.'

The machine died, or the mother gave up, or the teenager went back to sleep. I strained to force out a cursory ending, something to complete the thing, however naff and disconnected. But I couldn't. That was definitely it. Your girl was dry.

I put down the pencil and read it all back. It did not sit right. I'd hoped maybe I could coax out the dream, write my way to the source of this sadness, but this wasn't it. I hadn't written this from memory, trying to depict something I could see in my mind's eye. I could not visualise the girl, the women, the boy.

Well. I could visualise a boy, but I sincerely hoped that wasn't what my brain was getting at. That way lay madness.

I sighed. Oh well. At least I'd written something, for the first time in about fifty years. I let my hair down, poured a third rum and ginger beer to celebrate, drank half of it, felt sick, told myself to stop being such a wanker and went back to bed.

Stuart left early in the morning. I was aware of him whispering goodbye but I didn't move or say anything. He didn't kiss me. I slept again instantly and woke up properly at eleven when my alarm went off, but it was pointless as I didn't have to get up for anything until late afternoon, so I put on *Selected Ambient Works 85-92* and was asleep again before the end of 'Xtal'.

When I eventually rolled out of bed it was half one. I had a coffee, brushed my teeth, showered and looked at myself in the mirror, at the wet hair plastered against my head, neck and shoulders, dark blonde half-heartedly infiltrated by faded streaks of blue. Time for a change. I decided to call Alice before work and schedule une session de cheveux á domain.

The sadness had faded. In fact, all systems seemed to be operating within standard parameters. I meandered around, avoiding the notebook on the kitchen table, Facebooking and eating peanut butter on toast until I couldn't eat any more, which coincidentally was the same point that the bread ran out. I'd have to remember to get some more later. Stuart wouldn't say anything, but he hated it when I ate all the bread or used the last of the toilet paper or the last teabag and didn't replace them at my earliest possible convenience.

To be fair, on the scale of things Stuart got uppity about, that was a legit gripe.

I drank more coffee and listened to the rest of the Aphex album, then some Elliott, then some early dubstep, then some heavy classical, then a bit of Robbie Williams, the kind of jarringly eclectic improvised YouTube playlist that rarely went off at parties, and I rang Alice but it went straight to her voicemail. I left a long rambling message because I knew it would annoy her, and at five I left the flat to go to work.

It was two for one day at the cinema, which meant loads of stress and zero pissing about. I hadn't been here very long, having sacked off my umpteenth horrible bar job as soon as something different came up, and I quite liked it, although I was pretty low on the food chain and the pay was not what you'd call extravagant. I'd already established a good routine, though, and I didn't plan to be here for long. Some of my co-workers were twice my age or more and had literally been here forever, since the days of audience members running screaming from their seats, terrified that the train was going to come crashing through the screen into the theatre. It was all right for now. I got free cinema tickets. Could have been a lot worse.

Certain aspects could have been better, of course. Principally our rancid team leader, Mike, who would have benefited from a few more years in development before being released onto the open market. I was in his bad books because he'd made a drunken grope-y pass at me a few weeks ago at a team-building drinks meet-up, and I'd slapped him *really* hard and said he had the look of a potential child molester about him. I hadn't had the energy to report him, though, knowing that he was pally with the higher-ups, and as punishment for my rejection he kept assigning me jobs he knew I didn't like.

Today I was at the front desk, which involved interacting with a million plebs with no taste. They only ever seemed to watch Adam Sandler films. Always, without fail, even when none were showing, even when he'd taken a five-year break from making films, even when it was the one where he did the voice of an anthropomorphised fart slowly making its way through the body of a morbidly obese man played by Paul Blart, Mall Cop. It was like everyone was scared of exposing themselves to anything that might require the use of more than one braincell.

Not that I'm elitist or anything.

The first few hours passed by OK. I tuned out and thought about music, gizmos and guys I wouldn't mind getting my hands on, serving people on autopilot. And then, while I was talking to a nice but fairly vacant old lady, wearily explaining the plot of one of the dozen or so new Adam Sandler films we were showing, something about his soul getting trapped in a pair of ladies' underwear, I started to cry.

'Oh dear,' said the old lady. 'Are you all right, dearie?' Yep, she actually said dearie.

I couldn't answer, couldn't apologise, couldn't even make a joke about how upsetting I found the film. Could barely breathe. The grief was back, like a freezing anvil pushing my guts down down down, and with it came tears and harsh, racking sobs of an intensity I simply wasn't used to. It was so overwhelming that I had to get up, run away and shut myself in the store cupboard. It took several minutes to regain even a rudimentary level of speech, and once I did regain it I started muttering to myself, ignoring the frantic knocks and queries from my co-workers outside.

'For fuck's sake, Vanessa. Pull yourself together. When was the last time you cried like this? Yes. Exactly. And you had good reason then. Not some abstract feeling. *Pull yourself together.*'

I slapped myself round the face for luck and took lots of

deep breaths, and a minute or so later I felt composed enough to leave the cupboard. I walked past Sarah, Kizza and Mike, assuring them in a mutter that I was fine. As I rounded the corner in the direction of the toilets I actually heard Mike sneer something along the lines of 'time of the month, yeah'.

'You'll pay for that, you greasy little fuck,' I muttered as I stepped into the Ladies', although I was heartened to hear Sarah tell him that it had been a dick thing to say.

I looked at myself in the mirror. The red, salt-blotched puffiness was fairly cringeworthy, but at least I didn't look like a demented clown panda. I cleaned myself up as best I could, congratulating myself for scrupulously attending the 'less is more' school of make-up, and by the time I was done the sadness had completely vanished. Not only that, but I could barely remember how it had felt. All that was left was confusion, annoyance and embarrassment. I'd never been the type to break down in public, even with a perfectly good reason. This was just . . . nothing. It was pissing me off.

Sarah came in. 'You OK?' she asked hesitantly.

'Yeah.' I popped some chewing gum into my mouth. 'Thanks.'

'What happened?'

'I . . .' Well. What could I possibly say? Sarah was the only one of my co-workers that I considered an actual friend and we'd confided in each other before, but I didn't feel I could tell her I'd completely lost it over a dream I couldn't remember. So, shame rising like an iceberg, I lied. 'The old lady I was talking to reminded me of my granny. The one who died last year. It was weird.'

Now, a granny of mine had died the previous year, that much was true. And I had been severely broken up about it.

But at that point fact and fiction parted company, because apart from anything else, Granny Annie had been the sparkliest, sarkiest, most dynamic old girl you could imagine and she hadn't looked remotely like the lady I'd been serving. So I felt guilty, especially when Sarah gave me a lovely cuddle and lots of 'awww', but I managed to justify it to myself, just about, figuring that Annie would appreciate the need to save face in such a bizarre situation. She'd been a pragmatic old thing.

Once I felt fully composed, I returned to the floor. Unsurprisingly, I'd been replaced. I doubted Mike was feeling charitable, more likely he thought it was bad for business to have a hormonal loose cannon on the front desk, ready to go off in unsuspecting customers' faces at the slightest provocation. Whatever. It suited me fine. I just sneaked into a screen and went catatonic in front of a loud superhero film until the end of my shift.

CHAPTER TWO

'**D**O WE HAVE to listen to this?'

'*Fermé* that *bouche*, Loch Ness. It's my hair-cutting music. I need the groove.' Alice reached over to her phone and turned it up.

'You know I love repetitive electronic bleeps and bloops as much as the next gurning space case . . .'

'This is *techno*, child.'

'I stand by my definition.'

'Appreciate.'

'Merci non beaucoup.' Shit French. *Une specialite des Vanessa et les Alice.*

'I'm not changing it.'

'Look, I love *techno* as much as the next German person on roller skates in the 90s. But couldn't we at least have some slightly more interesting techno? This has been plodding along for about ten minutes.'

'It's a *groove*. You have to tune in. Do a bit of work. It's *mature* techno.'

'Old people techno.'

'*Refined* techno. The sort of thing you want me listening to when I'm going at your hair with sharp implements.'

'Noted. But . . . refined? Is this the kind of thing that soundtracks your days at *We're Literally So Fucking Now It's Painful* dot com?'

'Shut it, Nessquik.' Alice tugged sternly on a lock of

my hair. She loved coming up with new and stupid names for me, almost as much as I liked coming up with new and stupid names for the uber-slick modern culture hub where she worked, writing long discursive articles and launching super-literate *bon mots* into the Twittersphere. Alice's nicknames were always variations on a theme of Ness. Nessquik. Loch Ness. Wilderness. Bewilderness. Nessun Dorma. Nestling Between My Voluminous Breasts. And so on.

'Anyway,' she said, 'you were saying.'

'Oh God. Yeah. I can't remember it at all and it's *really* pissing me off. I never ever cry for no reason and I doubleplus never ever cry for no reason in front of fifty thousand people.'

'Maybe you've entered the menopause.'

'At twenty-three?'

'Could happen. I swear my sister's been menopausal since she was born.'

I'd never met Alice's legendary basket-case sister, but she sounded intriguingly nightmarish, much more so than my tediously nightmarish Bible-bashing one. 'Well,' I said, 'I don't think that's what's happening to me.'

'Nah, agreed. Unless . . . hot flushes, at all?'

'Nope.'

'So it must be something else that's on your mind. Stuart maybe?'

'Nurrrgh.'

'You've been finding reasons not to break up with him for an impressively long time. Maybe your brain finally broke.'

'Meargh.'

'See?'

I sighed. 'I know it's been building up . . . but no. I don't think it's Stuart. I know what my Stuart angst feels like. I could pick it out of an emotional line-up with a psychic blindfold on. And I *am* sad about it, don't get me wrong. He's lovely and it's shit that things have . . . decomposed. But this was different. I can't remember it completely clearly, which is also really weird, but this was like . . . *despair.* Actual despair.'

'Shit. How's that look?'

'Bit more off the fringe.'

Alice kept snipping. 'Maybe it's London.'

'What do you mean?'

'Living in London. Maybe it's getting to you. The overwhelming grimness of everything and everyone.'

'But I love London, you nitwit.'

'Nitwit yourself, you nincompoop.'

'It's not London. I have no idea what it is. Maybe I'm just going mental.'

'Maybe.'

'You're, like, the bestest best friend ever.'

'Kidding. Of course you're not mental. Although we should both put a quid in the Not Woke Jar for such ableist language.'

'I'll owe you.'

'You just . . . I don't know. Need something. But you're not sure what it is.' She snipped some more. 'So are you going to finish with Stuart or what?'

I wrinkled my nose. 'I should. God, I *have* to. It's definitely not working. And my reasons for staying are . . . really bad. Like, this calculating selfish bitch deserves the revenge porn bad.'

'That feels like hyperbole to me.'

'Je suis une hyperboler.' I sighed again. 'Je suis le *wimp.* I'm much better at being dumped than dumping, even if our relationship is about nine months past its sell-by-date. I should have ended it when we finished uni . . . but it was too *nice*.'

'Well, you know I've always put my tick in Stuart's column. But I'm not sure that "nice" is a word that dreams are made of.'

I nodded. 'Yeah. I *am* going to do it. And if you want to tick Stuart's column in the meantime, be my guest. Then I could be the wronged party and my conscience would be clear. I'm sure you and I could repair our relationship pretty quickly.'

'Ugh. Vileness.'

'Guilty as charged.'

'Right, how's that?'

'Perf. Well, by my standards anyway. I should probably find a hairdresser who doesn't have totally badass cornrows. Next to those, I look . . . well. Just a bit shit, really.'

'You want your hair like mine?'

'Are you offering? I thought you said I was five hundred per cent too white.'

'You are. So no, I'm not offering. We can't have *matching hair* anyway, you weirdo. That would be borderline . . . I dunno. "Incestuous" is totally the wrong word, but it feels like that level of *no*.'

'You're right, as usual.'

'Guilty as charged. Come on, let's purple this bitch up.'

I got home at five, went straight to the kitchen and made a cup of chai. Sweet steaming spicy comfort. I took it through to the living room and froze with the cup an inch from my mouth.

There was something in the corner of the room, slumped against the sofa. A human shape. It was white and featureless, like a clothes mannequin, but it looked soft, like flesh, like it would yield if you touched it . . . and there was a knife in its stomach. Blood slopped, gurgling, from the wound. I knew it was real blood. It had to be. It turned me to stone and I don't know how long I spent staring at it, numb and wishing I was blind, until I remembered how to close my eyes.

I counted.

One.

Two.

Three.

The room was so cold.

Five.

What came next?

Eight?

I opened my eyes, braced and ready for it to be standing there, face to lack of face with me, screaming with its lack of a mouth, but it was gone, of course, and the room was warm.

I returned to the kitchen and my eyes fell on the notebook. I put down my tea, picked up the notebook, tore out the offending page and calmly scrunched it into the tiniest ball I could manage. Into the bin it went. Then I sat down, forgetting my drink, and stared into space until Stuart got back.

'Hi,' he said, all lovely and tall and blonde and blue-eyed and oblivious. 'You're purple!'

'Hi. Yeah.'

'What's wrong?'

I looked at him. Really looked at him, for the first time in a while. 'I need to talk to you.'

Later on, when it was dark, I was still at the table, staring at my notebook. Stuart had gone to bed hours ago. Somehow I hadn't felt that I could follow him to the bed, the shared bed, so intimate a place now irrevocably changed. Not until he was one hundred per cent definitely asleep. Not after that talk. It could have been worse, to be fair; he'd been more upset than he'd let on during the endless conversation, but I think he knew it was all the truth. He understood. Neither of us had cried, but there had been a look in his eye, one I'm not sure he'd even been aware of.

I wrote a bad poem, tore it up, binned it with the other night's nonsense, flicked through the other pages. Idea after idea, some of them good, none of them finished, very few of them developed further than a couple of pages. I tried to expand a script whose opening I quite liked, but inspiration stubbornly failed to materialise. Helen and Charlie, despite some appealingly snappy dialogue, were stalling, refusing to come out of the kitchen. I didn't know where they'd come from, or where they were going, and with a dull throb of disappointment I realised that I didn't care. And if I didn't care, how could I expect anyone else to?

I sighed and closed the notebook and made myself a fiftieth cup of tea, to which I added a generous amount of honey with the wooden honey dripper Alice had given me. A present from a holiday. Always nice to be one of the people who gets presents from someone else's holiday. Watching the honey unwind, thick, sweet, decadent and amber gold, was a small, satisfying pleasure, like Amelie's bags of grain, and I stirred and sipped and enjoyed the way it made my blood bubble. It made me feel a little better.

All the same, when I did eventually head to bed, I conspicuously avoided even glancing in the direction of the living room. I felt guilty heading back to the bed, *his* bed, guilty and awkward, but I couldn't sleep in the other room as I'd originally planned. I just couldn't.

I knew I should have been panicking. I'd have to move out, and soon, and there was no way I could afford a place by myself. I'd have to find a house share . . . with *strangers*. A year ago, Vanessa would have been all over that new adventure. New faces, new opportunities for drinking and salty banter. Not now, though. When had the change happened?

Should have been panicking . . .

But I felt weirdly calm. It didn't seem to matter all that much, not compared to my impending psychotic break.

Don't think about that, I thought.

I could stay with Alice for a bit. Not long, but a bit. The one thing we couldn't do together was live. Travel, yeah. Hang out for hours on end. But living, day to day? That had almost destroyed our friendship once. I wasn't going to risk that again.

This train of thought led me to a memory. *That* argument. I could see it, hear it, with crystal clarity, like a video in my brain. Alice standing over the sink, the filthy sink, piled high with mould-colonised plates and bowls, every item of cutlery in the house encrusted with next-level gank, sobbing with rage and pain, staring at her bleeding thumb. She'd cut it while trying to unblock the plughole; as it turned out, the plughole was blocked by a sharp, broken fragment of her favourite mug, a mug with serious sentimental value, a mug that someone – not me, I swear – had used as an ashtray and then dumped in the sink. It was awful and I felt bad, but because I was hungover and grumpy and because it was Alice being all prissy about tidying up for the hundredth time, I wasn't sympathetic. Not like I should have been.

I was a dick, basically.

Even now, when we tried to laugh about that argument, it made me feel uncomfortable. We'd lived separately in third year and it had worked out brilliantly.

Sorry Alice, I thought.

I love you.

But you're a fucking nag.

That actually made me smile.

Maybe I really was going bonkers.

I was out of bed at eight and at work at eight-fifty. Stuart had already gone and I was ecstatic to discover that Mike was away today, and although I still had a lot to do, I didn't mind. It kept me distracted from unexplained emotional breakdowns and strange visions.

I kept order in two screens, silencing mouthy kids and phone wankers. It always baffled me when people paid large sums of money for cinema tickets and then spent the whole film loudly arsing about or texting. Surely there were places one could hang out and act like a prick for free? Kids today. I sort of understood the ones that sneaked in, but we were getting much better at catching them.

About the only thing I didn't like about enforcing the law in the screens was coming across frisky couples. I knew that Sarah took great delight in embarrassing anyone she caught perpetrating a sneaky handjob (or sometimes even the full two-backed beast) at the back of the room. She'd once told me she thought I'd have been the type to see the funny side, and I agreed, I *was* that type, but I just hated it. It was too cringeworthy. The first time it had happened to me I'd been too cowardly to say anything and had just left them to it. The second time I'd shouted and they'd shouted back as if I was somehow being unreasonable, and the guy was all red in the face and the girl's hand was sticky and to be honest, bugger all that drama. So since then I'd either ignored it or just turned the lights on and skedaddled sharpish. Luckily sexcapades mostly happened at night and I was only working until five today, so I enjoyed myself administering hearty bollockings to twatty kids and boosting pick'n'mix. Even fetching and carrying and till-related guff was better than seeing dead things, or finding sweaty perverts going at it on a carpet of discarded popcorn. Sarah and I had a mojito and a giggle afterwards and then I headed home and realised I'd managed to forget about Stuart, and felt bad.

I decided to put off going back to the flat – it wasn't home, not now – and went to the park instead. It was mid-May, warm, and the place was a gold-green glow of buds and bloom, and I sat on a bench by the pond and watched the ducks, geese and swans go about their secret society business. It was a lovely little park and I wondered why I didn't come down here more often. Oases like these were few and far between in London. *My old mate Londinium,* I thought, giggling to myself. I sat for a long time, thinking the thoughts of the lazy writer, that I'd love to capture this dreamy tranquility in a poem but knew I wouldn't bother, and justifying the fact that I wouldn't bother by thinking I *could never do it justice* and that there were fifty thousand perfectly good poems about sunshine and ponds and parks and darling duckies and what could I possibly add to the canon, and that sometimes a poem about a duck is, in fact, not about a duck at all.

And kicking myself for being pretentious, but not secure enough in my pretension to actually channel it into something.

And realising that this mess of thought, uninvited and unbidden, had sucked all the enjoyment out of sitting in the park. Nice one, Vanessa.

My phone rang as I was getting up to leave, and I answered with fresh joy in my voice. 'Auntie Paulie! How are you, my love?'

'Vanessa, are you sitting down?'

I stopped. She was about to tell me that something had happened to Mum. Or to Dad, alone and quiet in Scotland. Or my sister, impossible and pious in America. 'What's going on?' I said.

'You should sit down.'

I felt cold, but I didn't sit. 'What *is* it, Paulie?'

'It's . . . it's Mark, Vanessa.'

'Mark who?' I knew Mark who. There was no other possible Mark. But it didn't make sense. Why would she be calling about Mark? Mark was gone.

'He's here, Vanessa. He's at my house. He's alive.'

CHAPTER THREE

I LIE BACK *and sink down into the grass, one foot, two feet, three, four. 'Are you seeing what I'm seeing?'*

'I don't know,' he says. 'Maybe?'

'Those clouds. In the sky.'

'Yeah?'

'They're . . . they've become . . . you know Tinkerbell from Peter Pan?'

'The Disney one?'

'Yeah. Well . . . the clouds are . . . they're like her, fairies like her, but they're the size of skyscrapers.'

'Yeah?'

'Yeah. And they're . . . kissing.'

'Yeah?'

'Yeah. And one just winked at me.'

He laughs. 'Cool.'

'Are you seeing?'

'Not really . . . just colours. Nothing solid.'

'Yeah?'

'Yeah. How come you get lesbian fairies? That's way better.'

'Yeah.' I watch the fairies, bigger than dreams, kissing playfully, the top of my head touching the top of Mark's, and I don't think I've ever felt closer to anyone. 'Mark?'

'Yeah?'

'This is amazing.'

'Yeah.'

I was dimly aware that I was on my knees. The park had faded to a vague outline, a basic rendering of an environment, sound muted, air sucked inside-out.

'What the hell, Paulie,' I said, my voice low and grey, curdled. 'What the *fuck*. Why would you say that? That's not funny. That's horrible. Why would you say that to me? Why would you—'

'It's *true*, love, he's here, he's at my—'

'No. No, *no*, NO! It's not *possible!*' I was crying now.

'I know! I know it's not possible! But he's here! *He is at my house.*'

Why would she play a trick like this on me? My darling Paulie? It was too cruel. Too cruel. Mark was seven years gone. This was—

'Here,' she said. 'He wants to speak to you.'

'No! I—'

'Vanessa?'

The basic outline vanished. Even I vanished. Everything blank. Just my voice and his.

Mark's.

It was Mark's voice.

I stumble from Erin's front door, leaving the beats and smoke and giggles of the party behind, and walk up the road, hugging myself, staring at the stars, distorted into a bright blur by my stupid tears. 'Bastard,' I whisper. 'Fucking lying bastard.'

'Vanessa?'

I don't turn around. 'Go away, Mark.'

'Why?'

'I don't want to talk to anyone.' My voice is horrible. Low, grey. Curdled.

'Because of Dan?'

'Go away.'

He puts his arms around me and rests his chin on my shoulder. He's never hugged me like this. I shouldn't like it so much. I don't want it to be out of pity. I don't turn around. 'Please Mark. Leave me alone.'

'No.'

'Please.'

'Dan is nothing. You're so, so far above him.'

I can't answer.

I want him to make me turn.

I want him to kiss me.

But I know he won't.

'Vanessa, is that you?'

He sounded exactly as he had when I'd last spoken to him. Like he hadn't aged a day. Like this was seven years ago and we were talking on the phone and I was putting on a grown-up voice. He sounded scared and confused, but apart from that . . .

It couldn't be.

It had to be a trick.

'Yes,' I said.

There was so much relief in his sigh. 'It's you. Thank God. I . . . I don't know what's going on. I—'

'Mark!' Shrill. Jagged. Not my voice.

'Yes?'

'What's the last thing you said to me? Before . . .' *Before you disappeared forever.* 'Before. The last thing you said.'

I blow out the last, acrid remnants of the joint and toss it away.

'*You always smoke right to the end,*' *said Mark.*

'*So?*'

'*It's disgusting. Tastes disgusting.*'

I shrug. 'I like to get the most out of my joints. Unlike you, who tosses it away with about an eighth left in it. Wasteman.'

'*Shut up.*'

I check my phone. 'Ugh. Family dinner. I'd better go home and shower away the smell of druggie debauchery or Mother Dearest will have an epi.'

'*OK.' Mark shoulders his rucksack. 'What exam is it tomorrow?*'

'*English.*'

'*Tess?*'

'*Yeah.*'

'*Shit. Should have read it, really.' He smiles his famous smile and starts walking away.*

I call after him. 'You know she kills Dracula at the end?'

He laughs but doesn't stop or turn around. 'Oh yeah. Shortly after she finds out Mr Darcy's her father, right?'

'Something about Tess? Mr Darcy?'

I had become an attic with a draft whistling through it, hollow and numb, but tingling. 'Mark?' It was all I could say.

'Yes. Yes! It's me! For fuck's sake, Vanessa!' Mark never swore. Or at least, not when serious stuff happened. Swearing was for when he was being silly. 'Tell me what's going on! Is this a joke?'

'What happened? After you went home?' Now so tiny. Still not my voice.

'Last night?'

'No . . . I mean . . . yes.' Last night seven years ago.

'I . . . I don't think I got home. I don't really remember. I left you and then . . . I woke up in the bushes, just up the street. I figured I passed out from being stoned. Whitey or something. I went to my house and it was completely different, there was no-one in it and there was an extension, it had been re-painted. My phone didn't work. I didn't have a clue what was going on. So I came to Pauline's and she reacted like I was a ghost.'

'You are.'

'What?'

'I mean . . . you disappeared. You *disappeared*. Seven years ago.' I wished I was there to hold him, hug him as I told him this impossible truth, although I wasn't sure I'd be able to speak if I saw him, smelt him, felt him. Hearing him was bad enough. I pictured his eyes and his smell came unbidden to my nostrils. I felt faint.

'That's what Pauline said! But it's not *possible*! It's not . . . it's not . . .'

'Look at the calendar.'

'I did. Good Photoshopping. This whole thing is pretty impressive. Must have taken you weeks to plan it. Come on, Vanessa. What's the punchline? That I'm massively gullible? Come on . . .' With each word his tone was losing certainty. I couldn't speak and now he couldn't either. I heard him stumble and throw up and I couldn't even say his name to comfort him. I could hear Pauline's muffled voice, the sound of her getting water and paper towels, and I waited until she picked up the phone again.

'Vanessa? Are you still there?'

I had no idea. 'Yes.'

'I . . . I don't know what to do.'

'*You* don't know what to do?'

'I can't . . .'

'Just look after him!'

'You should be here.'

'I'm two hundred miles away!' I closed my eyes, counted, breathed. 'I can't . . . I . . . put Mark back on.'

A pause. 'Hello?' He sounded ghostly, far away.

'Mark. I need you to hold it together.'

'Vanessa, what do I do? What . . . where's Dad?'

He never said 'Dad'. Always 'my dad'. 'I don't know. He . . . he left town after you disappeared. I tried to keep in contact but he kept moving. I don't know where he is.'

'I need you. Please. Where are you?'

'I'm . . . I can't be there right now. I will be, as soon as I can. For now you need to stay with Pauline. Hold it together. I'll be there as soon as I can.'

'Please . . .'

'*As soon as I can.*'

I hung up and collapsed into myself. The world had re-appeared, I was no longer just a voice in a blank space, but everything had slowed to a sludgy crawl. I was there for a while, only dimly aware of anything, of people asking if I was OK. I managed to nod. I was almost impressed that I could do it, I was concentrating so hard on keeping my breathing level.

Mark.

I got up and walked. Back to the flat. One step at a time. As I walked, I dialled the cinema. It was as though someone else was operating my controls.

'Hello?' Mike.

'I have to go home.'

'Vanessa? You what?'

'I have to go home.' My voice didn't sound, or even feel, like it was in any way related to the rest of me. 'Back to Wales. Something's come up. I don't know how long I'll be gone. So I won't be coming in for a bit.'

'What's come up?'

'I can't say.'

'Is it a death?'

Jesus Christ. Tactful. 'No.'

I could see him shake his head. 'Not acceptable. I can't just let you vanish until you feel like coming back, without a proper reason. You're down to work all this week, who's—'

'Fine,' I said, in the same flat, nothing voice. 'I quit. You putrid little cunt.' And I hung up.

Mark.

Mark was back.

I got back to the flat. Stuart wasn't there. I fired up the computer and looked at trains. It took three to get home and the later I travelled the more difficult it was, but I couldn't just sit here all night. I'd never sleep. I'd go mad before tomorrow.

I booked my tickets, threw some things in a bag and went out again.

The sea unrolls like the sky's living reflection, greedily licking at the shore. I burrow into the sand with my toes and chew on my squashed ham roll, nostrils tingling with the cold, damp, salty air. 'Good, eh?'

Mark looks at me. 'What?'

'The sea, you div.'

'Oh. Yeah. Pretty good.'

'Where were you?'

'Far away.'

For a change. 'Penny for 'em?'

Mark leans back, twirling our only cigarette around his middle and index fingers. We managed to bring no tobacco and hardly any money, so he blagged the fag from one of the people we'd hitched with. We were saving it for when we were really desperate. 'I was thinking about humans,' he says.

'Humans'. He always said 'humans' instead of 'people'. 'Oh,' I say. 'Deep o'clock, is it?'

'Never mind.'

'No, no, I'm sorry. I'm sorry. I want to know.'

'Forget about it.'

I leave it, and we sit and watch the sea endlessly devouring itself.

I don't forget, though.

I sat on the platform, trying to keep still. I was doing a pretty good job. My body wanted to spasm, kick and punch the air, leap around, throw my head back, scream, lose all control. I was just sitting, staring.

My first train clanked into view.

'We should just hitch back,' says Mark. He looks nervous.

'Stop being a negative Nellie,' I say as the train pulls up. 'We can get nearly half the way on this.'

'But we've got no money. And the fine—'

'It'll be fine! Pun entirely intended.'

'Ha. Ha ha. Ha.'

'Sarky McGee. We'll get there with nary a hitch. Trust.' We get on and take a seat. I make Mark sit in the window seat. 'Now lean your head against the window and pretend to be asleep.'

'Vanessa—'

'Do it.'

He does it and I lean against him, put my head on his shoulder and close my eyes. He feels good to cuddle against.

We wake up just as the train pulls into Llangoroth station. My face is sleepy and triumphant. Mark nods, rubbing his eyes. 'Fair play.'

'Told you.'

Towers, bridges and industrial carpets bled into forests and fields and hills dotted with barns and animals. None of the feelings that usually accompanied this transition materialised. I didn't feel the prickly dread at the thought of seeing my mother, or the dull sinking feeling that I was travelling back in time to a place I no longer belonged, that I was getting further and further away from my real life, my world, leaving the present and future behind, that Llangoroth was just a model made out of the past. I wasn't really sure what I was feeling.

Maybe this was what madness was.

I hoped Pauline could make it all OK.

She always made it all OK.

Pauline opens the door, all wild hair and too many pendants, smelling of cake and incense, and her face erupts into a grin that would intimidate a Cheshire Cat. 'Nessa!'

'Hiya, Paulie.' We hug warmly and deeply. When she releases me she raises a quizzical eyebrow. 'And this would be . . .'

'Mark,' smiles Mark, a little nervously. He holds out his hand but Paulie rolls her eyes and pulls him into a hug, saying, 'Friends of Nessa get a hug.'

'OK,' he laughs.

Paulie leads us through to the living room and we sit down. Mark takes in the shiny black baby grand and the various exotic tapestries and throws. 'Drinks?' asks Paulie. 'Juice? Tea? Coffee? Beer? Wine? Whisky? Not that I should be offering fifteen-year-olds booze . . . naughty me . . .'

'Whisky for me,' I say. 'With honey.'

'Ah. Paulie Special, eh? Coming up. Mark?'

'A beer would be great, thanks.'

She gets our drinks. 'Paulie,' I say, 'Mark would like to skin up if that's OK.'

Mark looks embarrassed. Paulie smiles. 'A joint? Be my guest. As long as I get some.'

While Mark rolls, Paulie says, 'Well this is a delightful surprise.'

'Good,' I say. 'I've brought Mark for musical education.'

'Really?'

'Yes. He was raised strictly classical . . .'

'Ah!' Paulie nods approvingly. 'Who are your favourites, Mark?'

'Um,' says Mark. 'Tchaikovsky. Debussy. Chopin.'

'Paulie plays a mean Choppin,' I say, deliberately mispronouncing it because I know it aggravates them both. 'But that's beside the point. Mark – you don't mind me talking about you like you're not here, do you?'

'Yes.'

'Good. Basically, Mark was all classical all the time until high school, then he rebelled and went straight to hip-hop, punk and grunge. Nothing inbetween.'

'Nothing?' Paulie looks appalled.

'Nothing. So here we are.'

'Well, *you brought the poor lamb just in time.' Paulie walks over to the piano and cracks her knuckles. 'Now. Where to start . . .'*

'The way you wear your hat,' I murmured.

'Beg your pardon?' said the old tweed man sitting opposite me.

'Oh . . . nothing. Just singing.' Only I wasn't just singing. I was singing that first song that Pauline had taught Mark to play, as I watched and hummed tunelessly along. Mark could sing beautifully, if roughly, although he rarely did, and he picked up the chords quickly, absorbing them then reproducing them effortlessly through his slender fingers. The fingers of a woodland sprite.

'The way you sip your tea,' he sang in my head, echoing. 'The memory of all that . . . no, no, they can't take that away from me . . .'

I'm ready to leave for school. Way past ready, in fact. Mark's not texted back. I'm stressed enough about Tess of the pissing D'Urbervilles as it is without having to wait for cloud boy. There's no answer on his mobile or house phone, which is strange because his dad works from home. I hear my mother calling, ready as ever to make me feel worse, so I leave hurriedly. Fuck it. I'll go to school on my own. He'll meet me there.

Train number two was packed, as usual, and I stood up all the way, sandwiched between a chatty young couple in sportswear and a lazy-eyed man in a trilby hat. I had music on my phone but none of it seemed appropriate so I just stared into space and tried and failed to imagine what lay ahead.

I was jolted back to reality by my phone ringing. 'Hello?'

'Nessquik cereal.'

'Oh, hey Al bear. How are you?' I sounded normal. Funny.

'Fine,' said Alice. 'Long day. Which, considering it was a half day, was quite an achievement. What are you up to tonight? I'm meeting the SWLC and wondered if you were keen to have your intersectionality interrogated.'

'Actually, I'm on my way home.'

'Back to the sticks? Why on earth?'

'Some family stuff. Not bad. Just . . . need to go back. Be a few days, maybe a week, I'm not sure.'

'Are you all right? Do you need—'

'I'm fine. Really. I'll give you a ring when I get back, OK?'

'OK. Sure?'

'Sure. Thanks. Bye.'

'Ciao bella. Love.'

'Love.'

Train number three was delayed, so I sat on the world's most godforsaken platform for over an hour. It was barely a station, more a rickety bench and a sign, and it was dark, but at least it wasn't raining. I wished I had a cigarette, more so I'd have something to do with my hands than anything else. I knew better than to try and write anything. Who knew what kind of grisly murder scenes would emerge from my broken brain.

I texted Pauline with a progress update and she said she'd meet me at the station, but I texted back *no*. I didn't want her leaving Mark alone, and I couldn't handle seeing him as soon as I got off the train. I needed the walk to steel myself.

Train number three appeared.

'I don't know why I bother,' Mum says, sitting back in her chair, arms folded.

I want to say 'neither do I', but I force a reconciliatory smile. 'Oh Mum, don't, it's lovely, it looks lovely . . .'

'Here we go again,' says Izzy, in her most poisonous, pious voice. As if me refusing to accompany her Bible-thumping arse to church last night is still the issue, and not Mother Dearest's victim complex.

'Oh fuck off, Isobel,' I say, unable to hold it in. 'Just fuck off, will you?'

Isobel and Mum both get up and leave for their rooms. Perfectly synchronised. Almost worthy of a sitcom. I'm ashamed of myself for wanting to laugh.

Pauline shakes her head and raises her wine glass. 'Merry bloody Christmas. Pass the roasties, would you, Ness?'

I leave on Boxing Day. Thank God.

I hadn't seen my mother or sister since that awkward departure. I'd spoken to Mum on the phone but she'd stopped asking me when I was coming back next. Isobel was back in Chicago. I hadn't spoken to her, not feeling the need to be condescended to by a humourless, holier-than-thou hypocrite with a full-sized crucifix lodged up her Soddom and Gomorrah.

Thinking uncharitable thoughts about my sister actually made me feel a little bit normal. So much so that I almost missed my stop. I got off and stood on the platform, the old familiar place, smelling slightly of marijuana as it always had, ever since I was young, because there was a good place to hide just behind it. Same old badly-spelled homophobic messages on the wall. I nodded and tried to say something cynical like

'Home sweet home', but my voice didn't seem to want to work.

I wasn't going to see Mark, was I?

That was impossible. It was obscene and perverse and . . . and *blasphemous*.

It was a cruel dream.

I watched the train disappear before starting the long, short walk. I was glad it was dark. To get to Pauline's it was necessary to walk all the way through the centre of Llangoroth, and in broad daylight I would probably have met about fifty people I knew and had to stop and talk and explain and blah blah blah, and I could not have been less in the mood for that. So I kept my hood up and my head down and tried not to let the rush of memory and emotion bowl me over as I passed landmark after landmark. I went straight past the street where my mother lived. I hadn't yet decided what to do about seeing her, but I knew I definitely wasn't going there first.

The town was built on several hills and I had to go up one, down another and then up a third to get to my aunt's house. I went past all the same old pubs, risking a glance in the window of each and seeing all the same old drunkards, the same monosyllabic geezers and their gossipy wives, the same rugby and football lads. The only indicators that I hadn't literally travelled back in time were that the football lads were a bit taller, their hair was more sculpted and their polo shirts and jewellery were . . . well . . . *gayer*. There's simply no other way to describe the look. Ironic, seeing as how they spent most of their school days pounding on any boy who dared to have long hair or ride a skateboard, calling them *gayboy* or *gaylord* or *poof* or whatever. Nowadays the Village People would have thrown them out of the band for looking too camp.

I allowed myself a bit of a giggle at this, but it didn't sit

34

well, so I stopped. It was like trying to eat when you knew you needed to but your stomach wasn't keen. I hugged myself, gripping the straps of my rucksack, and mounted the last hill, up past the silent post office and the car dealership, and suddenly I was outside Pauline's house, staring at her front door with a feeling I was most unused to. I wasn't supposed to dread this door or what lay beyond it. It had always been my sanctuary.

I stared for a long time before I worked up the courage to knock. Pauline answered the door almost immediately and pulled me into a tight, intense hug. I couldn't hold it for long because I didn't want to start crying and I couldn't handle seeing and feeling her so scared and uncertain. It was too unlike the Auntie Pauline I knew.

'How are you?' I asked, stupidly.

'I don't know. You?'

'Yeah.'

'Come on. He's in the living room.'

She led me through, past the pictures and photographs I remembered and some new candles and hippie paraphernalia. She was so unlike my mother, I often wondered how they could possibly have emerged from the same womb. Although to be fair, I'd often had the same thought about me and my own sister.

I stepped into the living room and he looked up.

Looked at me.

Mark looked at me.

CHAPTER FOUR

H E STOOD THERE, a flesh memory, not a second older than he had been the last time I saw him. Maybe even younger. He was dressed in the same clothes, our old school uniform, that bastard navy-blue sweatshirt, his polo shirt untucked as always, same scuffed black trainers that should have been smart shoes. I couldn't move. It had to be a dream. It had to be.

No. Not even a dream could replicate him like this. Make his eyes exactly as bright and blue as they had been, his skin exactly as smooth, his hair exactly as ruffled. I could *smell* him, and the smell was right. Everything was.

Then he spoke.

He said 'Vanessa'.

And it was his voice, *his* voice, so young sounding, and I just nodded once, and then frowned, because something was different, something was, he was . . . *shorter.* He had *shrunk.* He—

'You've . . . grown,' he said. 'And your hair is purple.' He managed a bit of a smile, and at the first sign of that crooked smile I fell forwards and he fell into me and I hugged him to me so hard, *so* hard, as if by crushing him I could absorb him, make him part of me so I would never lose him again. We both sobbed. It was him.

Oh God.

It was *him.*

'What's happening?' he whispered.

'I don't know,' I was saying, barely conscious of how the words were being formed or what they were, 'but it's all right, I'll help you, it'll be all right, we'll get through it. God I missed you, I missed you so much . . .'

'What's *happening*, Vanessa?'

'Shh. Shh.' My initial eruption of tears had subsided but Mark was still crying, gripping me desperately, savage with fear and love. I let him hold on, let him pour it all out, taking deep breaths as he gasped, trying to compose myself. I'd been thinking about this. I'd known I'd lose it as soon as I saw him, but I also knew that I had to get over it as quickly as possible. I was older and wiser. I had lived for the last seven years, lived a normal life. He was my friend and he was young and he would be confused and frightened and I would have to be strong and help him. I would have to be the strong one now.

I thought these thoughts as I hugged him, repeating them over and over again, strengthening my resolve, letting my last tears fall, letting my breathing level out, trying to think clearly and simply.

Mark was back and I was going to help him.

That was all.

We eventually gave up trying to condense seven years' worth of stolen hugs into one. Fool's errand, really. I drew back and looked at him again, and he smiled again and this time it didn't hurt, it just filled me with relief. It made me want to smile back. 'You look really different,' he said.

'Well . . .'

'Yeah. Stating the obvious.' He looked at the floor, suddenly embarrassed. 'And I look the same.'

I laughed, even though it was probably a bit cruel. 'Kind of.'

'Do you want a cup of tea?' said Pauline.

Thank fuck for tea. 'Yes please. With honey.'

'Mark?'

'Same, please.'

Pauline disappeared into the kitchen and Mark and I sat on the sofa, not a little awkwardly. 'You never used to have honey in your tea,' I said.

'Just this once, I think it sounds like a good idea.' He was trying valiantly to sound casual and blasé, as if being displaced in time was something that happened to him regularly, but his voice shook, his voice that I remembered sounding so much wiser, so much more mature than mine, even though we were . . . *had* been . . . only a couple of months apart in age. Now it sounded so young, like it had barely broken.

'What do you remember?' I said.

'Exactly what I told you. I don't remember going home. Just leaving you. And then waking up in the bushes.'

'You didn't go home. I went to your house the next day when you didn't come to school and your dad said you hadn't been back at all. He thought you'd stayed at my house.'

'And you don't know where he is?'

'No. I think he wanted to disappear. I don't think he had anything to say to anybody. I saw him just before he left . . . he wouldn't say where he was going, told me not to try and find him.' I put a hand on Mark's knee. 'We'll track him down.'

He nodded. 'So . . . unless I'm dreaming, I suppose I fell into some sort of time hole.'

I smiled at that, and the smile quickly became one of those rogue grins that tugs insistently at your mouth, whether you

38

like it or not, and then the grin became a small laugh, which evolved into a bigger, heftier laugh, and then Mark caught it and suddenly we were pissing ourselves, doubled over, nearly crying again, but this time with joy. It took a while for it to die down. Pauline had been standing there watching for a good half a minute before we finally stopped. She was smiling as well, despite herself, and I couldn't believe how much better that made me feel.

'Something funny?' she said.

'Mark fell through a time hole,' I said. I barely got to the end of the sentence before I started laughing again. Mark hadn't stopped. Pauline joined in, setting the tray of tea down, and we all giggled away until we were panting and unsteady.

'Well, find me another explanation,' said Mark.

I shrugged. 'Time hole will do for now. Unless you're dreaming. But I'm pretty sure you're not dreaming. I'm definitely not.'

'I think I'd know if I was dreaming.' He frowned. 'I think.'

'So this is reality. That's a bit comforting.'

He sniggered. 'Yeah. Anyway. What have you been up to? It's all been me, me, me so far.'

'Mark—'

'No, really. Tell me.'

'Seven years of stuff?'

'Highlights.'

We drank tea and I highlighted. I skipped the aftermath of his disappearance entirely, feeling that a deep dive into my anguish and subsequent depression, and the appalling and destructive toll it had taken on my life, friendships, self-worth etc might not be what he needed to hear right now. Not even parts that I was sometimes able to laugh at now – like the habit I'd got into of locking myself in my room, putting on Lou Reed's *Metal Machine Music* at full volume and going catatonic until my family gave up banging on my door and left the house – seemed appropriate.

Instead I talked about the best bits of college – i.e. second year, because I'd been a bit of a disaster during first year – and university. And America. Mark was especially quiet when I spoke of things we definitely would have shared, but he wanted to hear every detail of my Stateside trip. I told him about Alice and I flying out and embarking on a prodigiously drugged-up weekend in New York, then heading to Washington, where we met up with some old college friends of Alice's and decided to be *cultured* and visit the Smithsonian, the White House and the Supreme Court, and getting terrifyingly lost in Great Falls Park, then heading to Chicago via Fort Wayne and going to Isobel's place and not even staying one night because of how obnoxious she had been. I told him about the hostel we'd found instead, the strange twins we'd met there, and Grizzly Dave, who it turned out went to our uni and now lived within walking distance of my flat in Surbiton. I told him about us deciding on a whim to go to a poetry gig by someone called Buddy Wakefield, who we'd never heard of but who'd broken our brains and hearts and whose words I now often used to comfort myself during bad nights. I told him about using the new pair of gorgeous red trainers I'd bought to fight off a guy who'd tried to mug Alice, about the Amtrak ride through Wisconsin, Minnesota, North Dakota – one endless field full of dying tractors – and Montana, about seeing the sun set over the Mississippi in a shower of burning blood, arriving in Portland, Oregon, home city of my beloved Elliott Smith, at nine o'clock in the morning and staggering out, trainlagged and mildly hallucinating, to be picked up by Alice's cousin Dean, who remains one of the finest humans I've ever met. He lived on his grandmother's farm a few miles out of Portland, and as I told Mark about it I remembered how much I'd loved that house, particularly the room I'd stayed in.

The incongruity of the room delights me. The lovingly hand-stitched quilt, each fragment of patchwork smelling of a different harvest, different traumas stifled with stitching, and the china oddities you're sure no-one actually buys, they just appear, and ancient lamps from the dawn of electricity, and sepia photographs of well-dressed people on the set of Gone With The Wind, *all that, like a time capsule, and on top of it the buzz of the air conditioning, a robot from the present intruding on the perfectly preserved past, a car left idling in the closet while horses churn up the dirt road outside. So frightfully romantic and eternal. I lie back and wish—*

No more wishing. He was here now. I told him about the rodeo Dean had dragged us along to, populated exclusively by tall guys in denim and girls who looked like Daisy Duke after a few too many hog roasts, the most redneck thing I'd ever encountered. Alice hadn't been super comfortable, unsurprisingly, so we'd evacuated early for copious drinking elsewhere. Then after Portland we'd spent a couple of days at the coast, where Alice had got laid twice and I'd sat on the beach and written nearly a quarter of a novel which I'd then left at the motel.

'You're joking,' said Mark.

'I'm so not joking that I might start crying.'

Mark made one of those *there's literally nothing I can say to that* faces. 'What did you do next?'

'Went back to Portland and flew home,' I said, feeling deflated by the memory of losing my novel and then feeling like the biggest douchebag imaginable for complaining, and for spinning this yarn, my fantastic trip, while Mark sat there, having missed out on seven years of his life. But looking into his eyes, I knew that he just wanted to hear my stories. I *knew*, because I knew him.

I still felt bad, though, so I skipped over the remainder of my life so far. 'So I came back, did my third year, scraped a 2:1 and am now in millions of pounds of debt that I will never repay. And I work in a cinema.' Except I didn't, because I'd quit, a decision whose repercussions had barely begun to make themselves felt in my head.

'A cinema? Cool.'

'Well. I sort of quit. But never mind.'

Mark sat back in his chair, sipping a second cup of tea that Pauline had just brought. He had his thinking face on, his deep mask. I waited for him to speak. When he finally did, it was the slow voice I remembered so well. The serious voice. 'I need to find Dad,' he said. 'Somehow. That's got to be the first thing. We never . . . we were never that close, you know that, but I need to find him. He needs to know that I'm not dead.'

I nodded.

'So how do you think I should go about finding him?'

'There'll be a way,' I said. 'I tried to keep up with him, but he really seemed to mean it when he said not to contact him. I literally have no idea where he is, whether he's even in this country, whether . . .' I stopped.

'Whether he's alive?'

42

'Mark . . .'

'It's all right,' he said. 'I've been thinking a lot, all day. Really hard. You know me. Shit happens and I get on with it. Like you.'

'This is fairly major shit, though, on a scale of shit to *shiiit*.' I resisted the urge to tell him that after he'd vanished, it had taken a *very* long time for me to get back to getting on with shit.

'Yeah. Well. I'm sure it'll hit me again later on today or tomorrow or in a week and I'll sketch out and throw a massive wobbly. But for now I need you to help me make a plan.'

'Of course.'

Pauline, who had been silent for a long time, said, 'Have you told Sheila that you're back, Ness?'

'No.'

'Are you going to?'

'I . . . I don't know. I don't know how long I'm going to be in town. If we're going looking for Mark's dad . . .'

'You should tell her. She's been pretty miserable lately.'

'So what else is new?'

'Ness . . .'

'No,' I said. 'Really. Tell me something new. I'm sick of having to coddle her and then getting nothing back.'

Pauline nodded. 'I understand. But, still. Go round there. Maybe she'll actually smile.'

'Yeah, and maybe I'll grow a tail and fuck myself with it.'

Pauline raised her eyebrows.

'Sorry,' I said. 'That was unnecessary.' I looked at the time. After ten. 'She'll be in bed now.'

'No she won't.'

'No, she won't. But I can't face her now. I need at least a

bit of a sleep under my belt before I go round there. Can I stay here?'

'Of course, you stupid girl.' Pauline shook her head and drew me into a hug. 'You think *you* find her difficult? I've been dealing with her my entire life!'

'I knoowww.' I let her hug me, let myself feel childish again for a few moments. Then my phone bleeped. A text from Stuart. Was I OK? Would I be back tonight? 'Shit,' I said.

'All right?' asked Mark.

'Yeah, I . . . just . . . nothing.' I quickly texted Stuart back with some nice simplifying lies. Hadn't he got my text before? Sorry! Stupid phones, eh? I'd decided to come home for a bit. Needed to sort my head out. Blah blah blah. Hoped he was OK. Non-specific apology. Bye. Kiss? No kiss? One kiss. One less than usual. That was etiquette, wasn't it? No kisses sent more of a message. One was fine.

Hopefully.

'I need to go to bed now,' said Pauline. 'I'm exhausted. Spare bed is made and I've made up a bed on the floor as well.'

'Thank you,' I said. 'Love you.'

'Love you too.' She gave Mark a hug and even though neither of them seemed to know what to say, I could see that it made Mark feel a little better.

'I'm going to need to sleep too, soon,' I said.

'Yeah,' said Mark.

We both yawned to make our point, even though we both knew we'd talk all night. Even if the circumstances hadn't been extraordinary, Pauline's living room just made you want to stay in it and talk and drink tea, with its soft embracing armchairs and sofa and Moroccan lamps and Indian throws

44

and incense and flowers and paintings. The word *cosy* had been invented for rooms like this.

But the circumstances *were* extraordinary, so we talked. And talked. And talked. And then it was half past three and we managed to drag ourselves through to the spare room, and I made a great effort to say 'I'm going to brush my teeth' and was proud that I was still able to form words with my mouth. Mark mumbled something indistinct from his pile of duvets on the floor.

I crossed the hall to the bathroom, a warmth I'd not known for years coursing through me, making my tired face smile. I'd never felt that warm and . . . *whole* with Stuart, not even when things were at their best. It had been lovely, but . . .

No. Not the time to feel guilty about Stuart.

Just time to bask in having my friend back.

I closed the bathroom door behind me and was immediately faced with the sink and the huge mirror that hung above it. As I looked at the mirror, the light started to flicker. *Onoffonoffonoffon.*

Off and the room was dark.

On and it wasn't me in the mirror. It was the mannequin.

Off and I could hear someone else breathing.

On and the mirror was just full of black.

Off and I couldn't even hear myself breathing.

On and I was there, hair jet black, screaming silently, bleeding from my eyes.

Off and there was something behind me.

On and it was me in the mirror, me, normal, purple-haired and pale-faced and frightened, but normal. Nobody behind me. The light stayed on.

I didn't move for ages. Finally Mark knocked gently on the

door and I jumped, feeling half my purple hairs turn grey. 'Are you all right?' he asked.

'Yeah,' I said, or at least I thought I said, because it wasn't my voice. It was the voice of a ghost. I didn't bother to brush my teeth, I just left the bathroom and returned to the spare room, where Mark had retreated into his nest of miscellaneous bedding. 'You were in there for like fifteen minutes,' he said.

'I'm a girl,' I said, climbing into bed. 'See you in the morning.'

'Are you sure you're all right?'

'Fine. Tired. Night.'

'Night.'

He switched off the light and we lay in the dark. I wanted to say once again how incredible it was to see him, even though I'd said it about fifty times during our long, long conversation. But I couldn't. All the warmth had gone. I was just cold, no matter how desperately I snuggled into my duvet. Cold, and frightened.

CHAPTER FIVE

I OPENED MY eyes. It was light and I didn't know where I was. Panic cut through grogginess like sun through cloud and I sat up in bed, looking around for something familiar. The painting of the flower garden on the wall. I knew that. Pauline's.

Pauline's spare room.

I looked down at the floor and Mark was sitting there, looking sleepy, hair all over the place. He smiled. 'I did that.'

'Did what?'

'Woke up and didn't know where I was. And even when I realised, I thought I was dreaming.'

I stared at him. He held my gaze for a few moments before inclining his head forward and raising his eyebrows comically high. 'Hello?'

'I'm not dreaming.'

'No.'

'You're . . . you're here.' I rubbed my eyes. 'This is going to take some getting used to.'

'Innit.'

That word, that one stupid word, brought back a hundred memories of pissing around at school and after school and at weekends, pretending to talk in gangsta speak, giving it all that. It made me smile. Mark smiled too. I wondered if he was as calm as he looked. He'd always been the master of appearing absolutely Zen, whether he really felt that way or not. It was

47

a strange mixture of nice and not nice to know that he was still as impenetrable as ever.

'What time is it?' I asked.

'Ten.'

'Fucking hell. I'm never up this early unless I have to work. And on a *Saturday*.' I propped myself up with pillows and hugged the duvet to me, luxuriating in that soft, just-woken-up warmth. 'How long have you been awake?'

'Not long. Maybe ten minutes.'

'Did you dream?'

'No. Did you?'

As I strained to recall, something else decided to surface in my mind's eye instead: what I'd seen in the mirror last night. It flooded in, callously sweeping away my just-woken-up warmth, making me shiver. 'Can't remember.'

He knew there was something. Mark always knew. But he didn't press it. Mark never pressed it.

'I'm going to get a cup of tea,' I said. 'Want one? I'll bring it.'

'Yeah. Thanks. I'll come if you—'

'It's fine. Honey today?'

'Go on, then.'

As soon as I left the spare room I smelled bacon and heard radio singing and real singing. It made me grin. Pauline was in her bizarrely-angled kitchen, where none of the cupboards were straight, none of the pictures were in line and none of the colours really matched, in her red dressing gown, frying bacon and singing along to something from the Eighties.

'Morning,' I said.

Pauline turned, her eyes exaggeratedly wide. '*Morning? You?* Dear God. If Mark's re-appearance was the first sign of the apocalypse, this *has* to be the second.'

'Hush.' I put the kettle on. 'Tea?'

'I've already had two coffees, thanks, love.'

'Little bit buzzing, are we?'

'*Alert*, shall we say. How's the young prince?'

She hadn't called him that since well before he'd vanished. It made me want to cry, and that made me want to slap myself. 'He's all right, as far as I can tell.'

Pauline left the bacon for a moment and wrapped me up in a hug. An everything-will-be-all-right hug, the kind in which she specialised. 'And how are are *you*?'

'Not a fucking clue.'

'Good. That means you're normal. If you were fine already, I'd be worried.' She kissed me on the forehead and turned back to her bacon. 'Eggs? I'll put some more bacon on as well, this is for me. Didn't think you two would be up this early. Scramble?'

She'd always called scrambled eggs *scramble*. Ever since I was a clumsy toddler with the world's most hideous lisp. She pronounced it with a lisp now. I mimed clipping her round the ear. '*Scramble* would be brillo.'

'Give me fifteen minutes.'

I made two cups of tea with honey and took them back to the spare room. Mark had got dressed and was standing at the window. He accepted his tea with a nod, then went back to looking pensive. 'What-a-gwan?' I asked.

'Eh?'

'What's going on.'

'Oh. Just . . . thinking.'

'You? Never.'

'I mean, practically.'

'*You? Never.*'

That got a smile. 'Money,' he said.

'What about it?'

'I haven't got any. Well. I've got about eight quid in loose change in my wallet. I'm assuming my bank account is closed. And I've only got my school uniform to wear.'

'I can lend you some money. It's OK.' I tried not to think about the fact that I'd quit my job. I wasn't in a brilliant financial state as it was – I owed Stuart quite a bit and it had occurred to me that I might have to throw myself on Pauline's mercy. I knew she wouldn't mind, even if I did. Absolutely no way was I going to ask my mother. 'I'll pick you up some stuff from the charity shop. If you don't mind looking a bit . . .'

'Like a charity case?'

'Yeah. And to be fair, at least you never wore school shoes. You've got your Vans. If you only had school shoes to wear, that'd be *rrrubbish*.'

He nodded. 'Well, I could come and pick some—'

'No.' It came out firmer than I'd intended. He looked surprised, maybe even hurt. 'Sorry,' I said, 'but think, Mark. *Really* think. You're so good at it. You disappeared. Completely. The weirdest mystery ever. And now you're just . . . back. The second weirdest mystery ever. Or . . . possibly the same mystery, actually. You can't just wander into town and go to the shop.'

'It's been seven years, Vanessa! People aren't going to—'

I rapped on his head with my knuckles. 'Hello? Anybody home? Think, McFly, think. You know what it's like around here. This town has been frozen in time for like fifty years. Everyone and everything are practically identical to how they were when we were sixteen . . . when I was sixteen . . . when you . . . you know what I mean. So people *are* going to recognise you.'

He was finding this really hard, I could see, and I felt bad. 'Sorry,' I said, again. 'I don't want to be harsh. But you understand. You're the same as you were because it's not been any time for you. Llangoroth is the same as it was because . . .'

'Because it's always the same.'

I nodded.

'OK. Fine. I'll stay here while you . . . what are you going to do?'

'I need to go and see my mother. Make up some excuse as to why I'm back.'

'You're not going to tell her about me?'

I raised one eyebrow. Mark nodded. 'OK. Stupid question.'

'I'll make something up. Then I'll go and get you some things from the shop. A toothbrush and clothes and stuff.'

'Can you get any weed?'

I was poised to say that I was never here anymore, I had no connections, I wouldn't know where to begin looking, but then I remembered what I'd just said about the town always being the same. 'To be honest,' I said, 'I can probably get some off the exact same people we used to.'

'Will you?'

'Are you sure it's a good plan?'

'I think it's a fantastic plan.'

I didn't think it was a terribly fantastic plan, but I said I'd see what I could do. 'You want bacon and eggs?'

'Yeah.'

'Come on then. To the kitchen with you.'

We sat at Pauline's little kitchen table while she cooked our breakfast. Mark noticed yesterday's paper on top of a pile of cookery books and grabbed it, his eyes lingering over the date for a long time. I didn't say anything. Pauline set down two plates of toast, bacon and scrambled eggs and we ate.

Halfway through the meal, Mark said, 'I'm not getting a lot of this news.'

'No,' I said, ineffectually.

'Can you fill me in?'

'On seven years' worth of news?' I kicked myself internally for that. I felt like I shouldn't keep rubbing it in.

Mark laughed, though. 'Fair enough. Can you give me the . . . I don't know. The highlights? The Cliff Notes?'

I swallowed a mouthful. 'Basically . . . imagine everything that could possibly have gone wrong or been fucked up, either through carelessness or deliberate malice, on a global scale. That's the news.'

Mark nodded. 'Fair enough.'

'Oh, and they have these things called animated gifs, which mean you don't ever have to describe your feelings or opinions in words, you can just show people a five-second clip from *My Little Pony* instead.'

'Cool.'

'Don't worry, Mark,' said Pauline. 'It's just as foreign and terrifying to me as it is to you.'

He laughed. 'Thanks.'

We finished breakfast and I had a shower and got dressed. 'I'm going to go and do some shopping, then pop in on Mum. Mark should stay here, obviously.'

'Of course,' said Pauline. 'I'm surprised nobody recognised him yesterday when he was out and about.'

'Yeah. Thank God for that.' I gave her a hug. 'See you later.'

'Are you not going to call Sheila before you go?'

'Nah. If I just turn up, there's a chance she might not be there. But she *always* answers the phone. It's like some quantum thing.'

Pauline seemed to consider reprimanding me, then decided against it. I smiled, gave Mark a quick hug which turned into a long hug, then exited pursued by a bear.

It was grey but warm and smelled like home. It had been a long time since it had smelled like that, a long time since I had felt genuinely fond of it, with no caveats. I walked down the street, smiling at a couple of people with whom I was on smiling terms, and headed for the middle of town, which was the usual very relaxed bustle of chatting and shopping.

I passed a friend of Pauline's, a smiley woman who worked at the bank. 'Oh hiya, Vanessa,' she said. 'All right? How's uni?'

'Hiya,' I said. 'Great, thanks. It's great. I mean, I'm not actually *there* anymore . . .'

'Oh! My, time flies doesn't it. How did you do?'

'Yeah not bad, thanks. How are you?'

'Oh, you know, struggling on!' She laughed. 'Well, best be off. Take care.'

'You too.'

I went into the charity shop, nodding and smiling at the little old lady behind the desk, who had always been there and would always be there. I scrutinised the clothes racks and eventually left with a dark blue suit jacket, a pair of jeans that might have been too long, a pair of cords that might have been too short, three T-shirts and a hoody. All that for fifteen of your English pounds. Even charity shops were cheaper in the country.

After picking up a toothbrush and a few other toiletries,

I took a deep breath and headed down to my old house. Past the first pub I'd ever frequented, aged fifteen, which was now a bed and breakfast with different owners – people 'from off', as suspicious locals put it. Past the train station and the tractor parts dealership, back to the old road, with the old hills looming. Past the same old cats, the same old dogs, just slightly more hoarse of bark and decrepit of leg, miaowing and panting from behind the same old gates. The same old people who smiled politely and said 'Good morning' as though I'd never been away. Maybe I hadn't. Maybe I'd dreamed it all.

And then there I was, outside my front door. I took another very, very deep breath, knocked three times and waited.

When my mother opened the door and saw me, she did a double-take so comical that I had to giggle, which defused the tension a little. 'Vanessa!' she said. 'I . . . this is a surprise.'

'Hi Mum.' I stepped forward and gave her a hug, which she returned more warmly than I'd been expecting. 'How are you?'

'I'm fine. When did you get here?'

'Last night,' I said. 'Really late, so I stayed at Pauline's.'

'You didn't ring.'

'It was a last-minute decision.' That was a plausible gambit, knowing me. 'Can I come in?'

'Of course, of course.' She turned and headed back inside and I followed, leaving the bag of bits and pieces by the door, hoping she wouldn't ask about it.

We went to the kitchen and I took a seat at the old table. 'Tea?' Mum asked.

'Could I have a coffee, actually?'

'Of course.' She put the kettle on and turned and looked at me. She looked quite good. She'd lost weight and she seemed less . . . *put-upon*, despite what Paulie had said. She didn't smile, but that wasn't much of a surprise. 'Your hair is purple.'

'It is.'

She didn't like it, I could tell, but she moved past it quickly. 'So what are you doing back?'

'Got a few days off. Thought I'd pop up.'

'Really? Well. It's nice to see you.' She sounded like she meant it.

'You too. How are things?'

'Oh, you know. No better, no worse.' Standard. She opened the mug cupboard and took out the same mug she always gave me, the one with the happy giraffe. 'New headmasters and headmistresses everywhere. Couldn't run a bath, even with instructions.'

'Shit,' I said, sympathetically.

'Vanessa, please.'

'Sorry.'

She made me a tiny cafetière in silence. Mum didn't do instant coffee, goodness no.

'Thanks,' I said, taking it and sipping. 'Phwoar. Rocket fuel. Have you heard from Izz at all?'

'I spoke to her at the weekend.'

'She OK?'

'Yes.'

The legacy of my having ruined Christmas hung in the air like a bad-smelling mist, and I scrambled for something to say. Luckily, Mum decided to break the awkward silence by bringing up something even more contentious. 'Have you heard from your father?'

'Not for a while.' Even if I had, I wouldn't have said anything. It was better to act like I had entirely severed contact with Dad, who I knew from his most recent email was happy and quiet up in Scotland with Mandy, a woman he'd worked with at the bank for years. A very nice woman who we'd had round for dinner several times. Dad swore to me that he hadn't done anything until he was absolutely sure that he and Mum were doomed, and I believed him, but if Mum had been a bit prickly before the divorce, she was razor-sharp now, so whenever she talked of 'that tart from the bank' – 'tart' was about as profane as she ever got – I just nodded. 'I think he's . . . he's all right.'

'Oh. Good.' Only my mother could pronounce the word 'good' in such a way that it sounded like 'I hope he gets prostate cancer'.

'Mum,' I said. 'Um . . . random question. Say somebody moved somewhere and didn't leave a forwarding address. How would you go about finding them?'

Mum frowned in confusion. 'What? Well . . . I wouldn't. Not if they didn't want to be found.'

'But say . . . *hypothetically*, if you needed to find them. Really needed to.'

'Well . . . whoever handled the sale of their house might have some information. I don't know how you'd go about getting it, I imagine it would be confidential. Or there's the internet, I suppose. You can find anything on the internet, can't you?'

'Mostly porn.'

That almost got a smile, which was more than I'd managed to get out of my mother for a long time. And with a reference to pornography as well. Maybe she was going soft. 'Why do you ask?' she said.

'It's . . . for a story.'

'Ah. Have you been writing much?'

'Not really. This is the first thing for a while. But it's . . . going quite well.'

I wondered if she knew I was lying.

She definitely did.

Sometimes I thought about how totally certain teenage me had been that I'd got things past her. Little white lies like that, or disgraceful whoppers, like stumbling in at nine in the morning with eyes the size of dinner plates, saying yeah I'd got some sleep at the party but not enough, and then going to bed for the rest of the day. And most of the following day. I'd always been so sure I'd got away with it, that she was blissfully ignorant of the truth.

To be fair to her, she'd never directly called me on any of it. It all just went down in her mental grudge book in case she needed material for a passive-aggressive dig at a later date.

Classy bird.

We talked for a little while longer, about some things in the news, a bit about work. I decided not to tell her I'd quit my job. She offered to make lunch but I said I had some things I needed to get on with, but that I'd pop back at some point. 'Well, ring first,' she said. 'In case I'm out.'

'OK.' Another pleasantly warmer-than-awkward hug, then I left. She didn't comment on my bag of stuff, which I now noticed had the sleeve of the jacket and the head of the tooth-brush poking out. She probably figured it was one of my 'whims'. That was what she used to put everything down to. Everything that wasn't my bad attitude, anyway. Vanessa's 'whims'. Vanessa and her 'whimsy'. 'Oh, Vanessa. You're so . . . whimsical'.

Hmm.

CHAPTER SIX

'**A** BLAZER.'

'Yeah.'

'Is this like *Doctor Who*? I'm regenerating as an indie bell-end?'

'Not everyone who wears a jacket with jeans is an indie bell-end.'

'No, you're right. Non-specific bell-end in a hoody and blazer combo.'

'Ha. Haha. Ha. Ha.'

Mark slipped the jacket on over the faded green T-shirt and cords, which had managed to be just the right size. *Skills me*, I thought. He looked at himself in the mirror and shrugged. 'Fine, I guess.' He turned to me. 'What do you reckon?'

I nodded. 'Fine.'

'Fine.' He took the jacket off and put it on the bed. 'Still not sure about that, though.'

'Don't be such a diva.'

'All right then. So what happens next?'

I held out the Bob the Builder toothbrush. 'Brush your teeth while I ask Pauline some stuff.'

'Cheers, Mum.'

'Don't ever call me that again.'

Pauline was at her computer, writing an email. I couldn't believe how quickly I'd adjusted to all this weirdness, but somehow, despite Pauline being the single coolest, most switched-on person I'd ever met, I was more surprised at how calm she was. I think it was because she was a proper grown-up and it didn't feel like grown-ups should take things like unexplained time displacement in their stride.

I'm nearly a grown-up though, aren't I? I thought.

No. I was not. And neither was Pauline. She was an adult, but definitely not a grown-up. 'Pauline?'

'What do you want?' She shot me a sly look over her glasses.

'What do you mean?'

'I know that voice. It's never changed, not since you were little. "I want something and I'm going to be just as sweet as it's possible to be in order to get it".'

I gave her a hug. 'I'm absolutely, *entirely* certain I don't know what you mean.'

'Get to it.'

'Well, I *do* have a bit of a favour to ask. You know how you know basically everyone around here . . .'

'Mm?'

'Well . . . do you have any friends at the estate agents?'

'I might do.'

'Might you be able to persuade them to part with private information?'

Pauline raised her eyebrows. 'Unlikely.'

'Really?'

She sat back in her chair and took off her glasses. 'You want to know where Mark's dad went.'

'Even if he didn't leave a forwarding address, surely he'd have left them some way of getting in contact with him?'

'I would imagine so.'

'The bank as well. Do you know anyone who works at the bank?'

'I know most of the people who work at the bank. Gloria and I have a curry night once a month.'

'Pauline, it's *so*, so important that we find him.'

'I know, Vanessa.' She took my hand. 'But . . . it's not like in films and books, when something strange happens and suddenly normal rules cease to apply . . .'

'I *know*. But we have to try. He's on his own.'

'He isn't. He's got you. And me.'

'But . . . his dad.'

She nodded sadly. 'I'll see what I can do. Maybe this is a silly question, but have you tried looking him up on the internet?'

'Not yet.'

She got up and gestured towards her computer. 'You do that. I'll make a few calls, but I can't promise anything.'

I opened every search engine I knew and typed in first Gary Matthews, then Gareth Matthews, then Gareth Luke Matthews. By this time Mark had come in and pulled up a chair next to me. He'd spiked his fringe up, just as he used to. Back in secondary school I'd thought it looked cool. Now it looked a bit, well, secondary school.

'Anything?' he asked.

'An investment banker auf Deutschland.'

'Probably not him.'

'No. Some random Facebook pages. Also not him.'

We also found an antique dealership in a nearby town, which was fairly bizarre, as well as an IMDB entry for a guy who'd appeared in more shitty direct-to-video sci-fi action movies than I'd had hot dinners, a picture of an extremely fat man eating baked beans out of a bathtub, and some porn. Of course. Once the laughter had subsided, I sat back and sighed, deflated.

'It makes sense,' said Mark. 'Dad never really had time for new technology. He doesn't use the internet . . . at least, he didn't. He wouldn't have a Facebook or anything.'

'You'd think there'd be *something*, though.'

'Do I come up?'

'Yes. A few times.'

'Really?'

'Well, there's your MySpace.'

'Which you made.'

'And your Facebook.'

'Which you made.'

'And . . . um. Newspaper articles. From when you . . . you know.'

'Oh.' Mark was quiet for a moment. 'Can I have a look?'

'Do you really want to?'

Quiet again. 'No. Not really.'

Pauline came in. 'Well. Good news and bad news. Good news is, Sal at the estate agents did have a number and an address for Mr Matthews. Bad news is, she's not sure if he's still there, the details are old.'

'OK. Have you tried the bank?'

'I'm really not sure about that . . .'

'You said you knew everyone! *Curry*!'

'Yes, but Sal is so indiscreet about everything, I'm surprised she still *works* at the bloody estate agents. Gloria et al are not going to be so free and easy with private information. It's *illegal*.'

'But—'

Pauline looked momentarily exasperated. 'Vanessa, I'm sorry, but I can't just tell them that Mark – excuse me talking about you like you're not here, Mark – has inexplicably re-materialised, can I? Which doesn't leave them with much of an incentive to risk their jobs, does it?'

She was being Aunt Pauline now, rather than Paulie. It still made me feel embarrassed and sulky, like the child who hadn't got her own way. 'No,' I said. 'Sorry.'

Mark spectacularly failed to suppress a snort of laughter.

'What are *you* snorting at?'

'Nothing.'

I gave him my best *look*. 'OK,' he said. 'Not nothing. Just . . . you're twenty-three. And when she talks to you in that voice, you still look like a grumpy kid.'

'You don't even know what I looked like as a grumpy kid.'

'Something like that,' said Pauline, ruffling my hair.

I growled at her, but couldn't not smile. 'Well, where was the address and the phone number that Sal gave you?'

'Up north,' said Pauline, in her best Northern accent. 'A small town called Corford. About three hours by train.'

'OK . . . well . . .' I started to think again, but my phone interrupted me. I took it out without looking at the screen. 'Hello?'

'Hi.' Stuart. Shit. I looked guiltily from Mark to Pauline – *well done Vanessa's face, very sly there* – then left the room without saying anything.

'Hi,' I said.

'How are you?' He sounded uncomfortable.

'Um . . . OK. You?'

'Yeah. I was just thinking . . . how long are you going to be away?'

'I . . . I'm not sure.'

'OK. Well . . . I was wondering if maybe we could have a chat. About stuff.'

'Stuff?'

'Yeah.'

'I . . . I kind of thought that everything . . . that I said everything.'

'I don't know if I said everything.'

That was a fair enough statement. 'All right,' I said. 'Well. OK. I'll let you know when I'm coming back? Now's not . . . sorry. It's just not a great time.'

'Oh. OK, then.'

'Sorry. Are you—'

'It's fine. I'll see you soon.'

'Sorry—'

'Bye.'

'OK. Bye.'

I hung up, put my phone on silent and took a moment to compose myself before returning to the living room. They were both looking at me quizzically but I painted on a smile. 'Terribly sorry about that. So, where were we? Oh yeah. Can I have the phone number?'

Pauline held out a piece of paper on which she'd written the address and number. I was about to dial when Mark put a hand over mine. 'No.'

'What?'

'Don't dial it. Not yet.'

'Why?'

He shook his head.

'No,' I said. 'Tell me what's wrong.'

'I . . . it doesn't matter. 'Scuse me.' He got up and left the room. I frowned at Pauline, then followed him.

He was standing in the spare room, staring out of the window, fiddling with the zip on his hoody, a familiar gesture of confusion. I stood a little way away from him, unsure of what to say. He spoke for me, eyes still fixed on the world outside. 'What if he doesn't want to see me?'

'What do you mean?'

'It's been . . . *fuck*.' I'd never heard his voice crack like that, like the rug had been completely pulled from under him. 'Seven years. Seven years, I've been dead. As far as he knows. And imagine, imagine, I just turn up at the door, and not only am I alive, but . . . I haven't aged. Not a day. He might . . . I still can't believe how well you and Pauline are taking it. Well, you . . . I mean. You're different. But my dad . . . I was so keen to find him, but now I don't know if it's a good idea.'

'Of course it is! He'll be overjoyed to know you're alive!'

'What if I disappear again? What if he's happy to see me and then I just vanish? I don't know what's going on.' He closed his eyes and dragged his fingers through his hair. 'I don't know what to do.' He started to shake and one of his fiercely closed eyes squeezed out a tear. I walked gingerly over to him, put my arms around him and hugged him to me for a long time, letting him cry, making myself not cry.

A little while later, while Mark was having a quiet sit outside, I went to the phone, entered the prefix that would withhold the number and dialled.

After four rings, Mark's dad answered. 'Hello?'

I hung up.

CHAPTER SEVEN

'**M**AN, VANESSA.' LUKE grinned that familiar lop-sided grin, like one half of his face was too wasted so the other half was gamely picking up more than its fair share of slack. 'S'good to see you again.' His voice was a little deeper, a little huskier, his dreadlocks a little more matted, but he still had that twinkle in his eye, in his smile. He even had the same phone number, which had been handy.

'Yeah,' I said. 'You too.' I was leaning against his desk in his cramped bedroom, which was as perfectly preserved as the rest of Llangoroth; I was practically getting holodeck-quality flashbacks just from standing here, of stoned hang-outs, binging on films, preparing for or recovering from parties. He still lived with his mum, his oblivious, happy little mum, who bustled around downstairs running after his younger brothers and sisters while Luke sat on his bed and weighed out an eighth of crumbly weed. I still wasn't convinced this was a good idea. I hadn't smoked the stuff for years. But I had to keep reminding myself that from Mark's point of view it had only been two days since he'd last had a smoke. And that was a long time for him. Would have been a long time for me too, back then.

'What are you up to these days?' I asked. 'You working?'

'Bits and pieces,' said Luke. 'Bit of mechanic-ing. Bit of electrician-ing. Bit of DJ-ing.'

'Still DJ-ing. Nice.'

'Until I die, man.'

'I'd like to see you play again. Was always the best raving when you got on the decks.' No word of a lie. Luke had always been my favourite of the many, *many* amateur DJs our area seemed to spawn. His own particular selections of joyful, bouncy reggae and jungle always filled the dancefloor, without fail. Not that the serious DJ heads cared – it was kind of hilarious seeing them standing sour-faced behind the decks, twitching, desperate for Luke to finish so they could whack on the floor-clearing hard techno that sustained them. Funny times.

'Ah cheers, man,' said Luke. 'Nice one. Yeah I'm playing at the Cattlegrid next Friday if you're going to be about still?'

'I don't know. Maybe. I've got some things to be doing.' I looked out of the window. The sun had started to peek through the grey and the town looked lovely. 'To be honest, I was surprised you were in at this time on a Saturday afternoon. I would have expected you to be at the aftermath of Friday's party, taking your own body weight in some mystery powder you identify with a random series of letters and numbers.'

Luke laughed. 'Good guess. But it's basically impossible to get LB490PQ_56 these days. Goddamn war on drugs.'

'Shame.'

'Innit. Plus I'm trying to have just the one hardcore night per week these days. And there's a Deep Forest rave tonight, so . . .'

Ah. Deep Forest raves. I'd attended a few of those and I'd never quite been the same. 'Sorry,' I said, making a show of cleaning out my ears. 'Did I hear that correctly? Is that the legendary Luke Morgan, the fabled DJ Luke Skywanker, being a bit sensible?'

'Haha. Luke Skywanker. Forgot about that. It's Will Feral now.'

I laughed. 'Nice. William's your middle name, isn't it?'

'Man, your memory *is* good. Even I forget that sometimes.' Luke chuckled. 'And yeah, I guess I'm trying to be a bit sensible. S'all relative. I'll turn up at the forest at about eleven and then we probably won't leave until Monday, if the weather holds out. Actually, even if the weather doesn't hold out. So yeah. Relative.'

'*Monday?* Don't you people have jobs?'

'Bank holiday, bruv.'

'Oh, so you'd only crack on until Monday on a bank holiday?'

Luke thought for a moment, then laughed and shook his head. 'Nah.' He carried on with his methodical measurings. 'You in touch with Laura?'

My stomach lurched a little. 'Not really.'

'Still? That's a shame.'

'Yeah. You?'

'Seen her a bit, try to go for a drink whenever she's back. She's good.'

'Good.'

There was a miaowing at the window and I turned to look, glad of the distraction. A fat, fluffy white cat was standing on the outside windowsill, pawing at the glass. I dimly remembered that Luke's cats all had swear words instead of names. 'Which one's that?' I asked. 'Twat? Bastard?'

'Jess.'

'Oh.' Maybe not.

'Don't let her in. She'll be all over this shit.'

'Of course your cat would love weed.'

'She doesn't love weed. She just loves to interrupt me in the middle of important operations.' Luke tipped the green into a bag, sealed it up and handed it over. I gave him twenty quid and he grimaced, as if embarrassed. 'Um,' he said. 'It's . . . I'm kind of having to do it for thirty these days.'

'*Thirty?* On the eighth? Are you havin' a *giraffe*, sunshine?'

'Sorry. But . . . actually, nah, forget it. You're an old mate. Twenty's fine.'

'No, I can give you another tenner if you—'

'No, no, no. Twenty's fine.' He took some tobacco and a long Rizla from his bedside table and started to skin up. 'To be honest, I don't like selling it for thirty. Try not to. It depends who it comes from, you know? Some of the guys I get it off . . . they're not nice guys. Not in it to be social and have fun. They just want money.'

'Mm.' I was trying not to laugh, his little face looked so serious. 'Everywhere you look, capitalism's fucking shit up.'

'Yeah. And the thing is, people don't really complain, either. Everyone around here's so desperate to get stoned that they'll pay anything. So I forget sometimes.' He smiled. 'Sorry.'

'You don't have to apologise, numpty. Are you sure?'

'Yeah, yeah. For you, my friend, twenty.'

'Cheers.' I wondered whether he'd have given it to me for free if he'd known who it was actually for. Then I tucked the thought away at the bottom of my brain, tucked the baggie away at the bottom of my bag and put my hand on his shoulder. 'Well, cheers, Luke, my lad. I've got to head off now. Sorry to buy and run.'

'Whatever, man. I know I'm not even a person to you. Just a supplier.'

'Yeah. Actually, to be honest, you're not even that. You're pretty much just a vending machine, except with weed instead of sweets. Do you even have feelings?'

'Nope.'

'Just the way I like it.' I leaned over and gave him a half-hug, trying not to spill the joint he was making.

'You sure you won't stay for one?' he asked.

'Nah, I'm fine, cheers.'

'I'm hopefully going to spin some records at the forest tonight, if I can get Teddy and the rest of his hardtek posse off the decks for long enough.' He licked and stuck his joint. 'You should come up if you can.'

My insides scrunched a bit. I knew I'd probably really enjoy it. Catching up with all those reprobates, who I knew from Facebook would definitely be there. I also knew that Mark would enjoy it . . . until people started screaming. It most likely wasn't a great plan to turn up in a dark wood full of people off their heads on various nuclear-strength hallucinogens, arm-in-arm with a ghost.

'I will if I can,' I said. 'If not, pint next time I'm back?'

'Fo shizzle, Vanizzle.'

That stopped me where I was. He'd always used to say that to me, back in the day, and I hadn't heard it for so long. It made me want to cry. I gave him a proper hug, which seemed to surprise him, but he smiled and this time the other half of his face joined in, like it knew it was important. 'Take it easy, you,' I said.

'Always do, sister. Good to see you.'

'You too.'

I picked up some tobacco and Rizlas on the way back to Pauline's. I couldn't bring myself to buy long Rizlas. I'd always felt embarrassed buying them back when I was a proper little teenage stoner. Now I was effectively a grown-up, it was even worse.

Mark was playing the piano when I got back. He stopped as soon as he saw me, but I shook my head and waved my hand. 'No, carry on.'

'Nah, I was just fiddling.'

I handed him his stuff and he smiled. 'Sweet. Thanks. I will pay you back when I can.'

'Mark?'

'What?'

'Shut up.' I ruffled his hair. 'You don't have to pay me back.'

'I will. And don't do that to my hair.'

'Because I'll mess up your fringe?'

He gave me a brief but effectively withering look and started skinning up.

'I probably won't have any,' I said. 'So if you just want to make a little one . . .'

'You won't have any?' Genuine surprise. I'd go so far as to say he was shocked.

'No. I only really smoke it at parties these days.' Lies. I hadn't been to a party in ages. And I hadn't smoked any when I had. Strictly gin, which as far as Mark was concerned was for old ladies.

'Oh.' He looked disappointed, but carried on making a full-size joint anyway.

'Are you going to smoke that all to yourself?'

'Yep. Unless Paulie wants some.'

'Doubt it. She doesn't smoke tobacco anymore.'

'Smokes the *reefa* though, still?'

'Think so.'

'Good girl. Not like *you*. You square.'

'Hmm, yeah. Actually, the main reason I don't really smoke it anymore is that as soon as you disappeared, one toke on a spliff made me miserable and paranoid and anxious, rather than warm and giggly and relaxed. So maybe just shut up and don't judge me.' I didn't say all that. I just said the last three words and watched him meticulously roll, stick and light his joint, the same motions I remembered from the dim and distant past. Then he sat back and chugged it, smiling, the same deeply contented reclining motion, the same smile. The room quickly filled with heavy, sweet fog. I was almost tempted to have some, it smelled so nice. Like festivals and sunshine and barbecues and beers by the river. Like being young. But I declined, even though Mark kept offering it to me. Eventually he started to annoy me a bit, so I went to the kitchen and made a cup of tea and tried to think about real things.

Bloody druggies.

I heard the front door open and close and felt momentarily panicky, but then Paulie spoke, because obviously it was her. 'Crikey Mikey! Smells like Woodstock in here.'

'Sorry, Paulie,' said Mark. 'Just really needed a smoke.'

'Where did you get it?'

'Vanessa got it for me.'

'Smells nice. Roll me up a little one, would you? With no tobacco? Just to keep for later. I haven't bought any for ages. All the stuff my friends get these days is crap.'

I had to laugh. And then, staring at the steam as it began to emerge from the kettle spout, half expecting some nightmarish face to appear in the hot gaseous folds, I started to think.

About the things I was seeing.

About Mark.

About whether or not they were a coincidence.

About how unlikely it suddenly seemed that they were a coincidence.

Slow on the uptake? *Moi?*

I walked to the doorway and peeked out. Mark and Pauline were laughing as Mark rolled her a little pure joint of her own. He was Mark. He had to be Mark. My friend, back from the dead, or wherever he'd been. A wonderful thing. *Miraculous.*

I shook my head and made tea, thinking *we'll see.*

'We can get there on a train,' I said. 'Well. Two. There's one connecting train from here a day. If we get that one, we can be up there in three hours.'

Mark had reacted quite well when I'd told him it was definitely his dad's address. Now he looked troubled again. He shook his head. 'Not today. It'll be really expensive on a Saturday.'

That wasn't the reason, but I left it. 'Doesn't matter, we've missed the connection anyway. We could get a later one, but that would involve *three* connections and take about five hours, allowing for changeovers.' I checked tomorrow. 'We could go tomorrow. That wouldn't be too bad.'

Mark looked at it. 'Have economics changed in the last seven years?'

'Probably. I don't understand them, so I wouldn't know. What's your point?'

'What I mean is, that amount of money *there* . . .' Mark pointed at the screen. 'Seven years ago, that was expensive. Is it still expensive?'

'Well. Yeah.'

'Try Monday.'

We tried Monday. It was a bit cheaper. 'We'll go Monday,' said Mark.

'Mark, you don't have to worry about money, seriously.'

'And you never know,' said Pauline. 'Mr Matthews might reimburse you for the fare.'

Tactful.

'It's not the money,' said Mark. 'Well. It is the money, a bit. But also, I think I need a bit more time to adjust. It's going to floor him. When he sees me. And it would be good if I'm slightly more . . . I don't know. Together? It'll make it easier.'

'OK,' I said. 'But are you sure you don't want to phone him and speak to him first?'

'No,' said Mark. 'To be honest, I don't think he'd believe it. He'd think it was someone playing a prank. He needs to see me. Face to face.' He still didn't sound convinced that seeing his father was a good idea. I sort of didn't blame him. I'd never known Mr Matthews very well. At all, even. But I knew he was at best difficult and at worst . . . was this whole thing just really stupid?

Who knows.

'So . . . shall I book for Monday, then?'

'Yeah,' said Mark. 'Monday.'

'Are you—'

'Yeah.' Conversation closed.

The phone was ringing and Pauline got up to answer it. 'Hello?' Her eyes shot to me. 'Sheila! Hi sweetie, how are you? Oh . . . yes, yes. She just turned up last night, out of the blue. I . . . tonight? Well, that would be . . . yes she's just popped in. I'll ask her.' She put her hand over the receiver. 'Ness, your mother says she'd like to make dinner for us tonight.'

My eyes widened. That didn't sound like Mum. And it also didn't sound like something I terribly wanted to do. I looked at Mark and shook my head. 'I don't want to leave—'

'I'll be fine,' said Mark. 'I'll just stay here, hang around, listen to tunes. It'll be fine.'

'Mark, I don't want to leave you alone . . .'

'And I don't want to stop you doing stuff.'

'Hold on a minute, sorry, Sheila,' said Pauline. 'She's just faffing around with something, as usual.'

'I don't *want* to have dinner with my Mum,' I whispered. 'I told you about the last time we had dinner together. It was fucking *appalling*. It was the *worst*.'

Also partly my fault, to be fair.

'You should go,' said Mark. He was looking at me and I suddenly felt the way I'd used to feel when we were the same age, like he could see through the bullshit that was clogging up my brain, like he really *knew* things.

It was confusing. But I nodded reluctantly. 'OK. But—'

'*Don't* ask me if I'll be all right. Because I will. I'll just chill by myself.'

I nodded at Pauline. She took her hand off the receiver. 'Yes, that'd be lovely, Sheila. What time shall we come by? About seven. Great. Do you want me to bring anything? All right. OK, see you later. Love you. Bye.' She hung up and looked at me quizzically. 'She sounded quite bright and chirpy.'

'Wow. I think that just surpassed Mark as the week's weirdest occurrence.'

'Vanessa.' Pauline gave me a reproachful frown, but her face wasn't really built for such expressions and it morphed almost instantly into a smile. She sat down and picked up the newspaper and I booked two train tickets for Monday.

'I'm going to go and sit in the garden,' I said. 'Do you want to?'

'In a bit,' said Mark. 'I'm going to play the piano. If that's OK?'

'That'd be lovely,' said Pauline.

'Cool,' I said. 'See you in a bit.'

'Vanessa,' says Isobel, touching my shoulder awkwardly. 'Wherever he is—'

'Don't say it.' I knew it would be something like this. I just want to be left alone to cry, to wallow, to let the black hole in my stomach grow and grow until it fills me from end to end, until it's bigger than me, and I'm the one filling it, until there's nothing to feel.

'I'm just—'

'Don't!' I sit up, pulling away from her. She looks affronted and her nose does that thing it does when she knows she's right yet you insist on arguing with her, that little scrunch, that little screw, that little wrinkle that makes me want to fucking punch it right back into her face. 'Just because you've clasped God to your fucking bosom doesn't mean you know shit about grief, all right?'

'I'm just saying that maybe I've got some perspective that you—'

'I don't care if you think he's having a better time in

Heaven!' I yell, even though that's not what she said. I can feel anger overtaking misery now and it actually feels good, it feels good to be furious when all I've been feeling is despair. I want to make the most of it. 'I don't care if you think it was God's plan for him to disappear!'

'Everything happens—'

'Everything doesn't happen for a fucking reason! What kind of crazy horrible plan is that? What reason? And what makes you so special that you can fucking understand it?'

Isobel's gone red. I can see that she's trying not to lose her temper with me, because even though she is being insufferable, she does know I'm hurting. She's trying to use her faith for good. But I don't care. And I'm not ashamed of not caring. 'I don't understand it,' she says. 'Not completely. No-one does.'

'Then what's the fucking point?' I scream, louder than I even want to. Neither of us speaks for a minute after that, Isobel shocked and unsure of what to say, me panting because I screamed so loud. I recover first. 'Apart from giving you the satisfaction of thinking you're better than me because I get wasted and have fun and you'll only open your legs for fucking Jesus—'

She gets up to leave but I follow her. In a horrific, painful way I'm enjoying this, and I'm not even ashamed. 'Apart from you lording the moral high ground over me all the fucking time, what use is it?'

She's not looking. She's going downstairs. I'm following. By now our parents will have heard, but I don't care. I don't give a shit. 'My best friend is gone!' I yell. I'm crying again now, and screaming through it. 'And you're trying to tell me he's better off? That he's happier now? Fuck you! Go fuck yourself, you pious little bitch!'

76

Mum comes out of the kitchen. 'Vanessa!' she cries. 'How dare you use such language! How dare you speak to your sister that way? Control yourself!' I can see Dad behind her, unsure of whose side to take, as usual. Staying out of it, as usual. Wanting a quiet life, to sit and hide behind the paper. As usual.

'Well tell her to keep her bullshit to herself!'

'I was just trying to help!' Isobel is shouting now. And crying. I've crossed a line. This will not repair itself in a hurry.

'Calm down, both of you!' says Mum.

'Mark didn't even believe in your fucking God! Nor do I!'

'Vanessa,' says Mum, audibly trying to control her own anger, 'I will not have this in my house. This shouting, this language—'

'It doesn't matter!' I turn to my dad. 'Fucking say something!' He doesn't. Mum is shouting again, how dare I speak to my father like that, although I know she wishes he'd get off the fence for once in his life, but I just turn and pull on my shoes and go to the front door. 'Mark's gone,' I say, voice dead, all screamed out. 'Nothing matters.' I slam it behind me.

Nothing matters—

'Hi.'

I jumped. Mark smiled. 'Sorry.'

'S'all right. Just havin' a think.'

'You?' He sat down next to me. 'Implausible.'

'Shut it.' We laughed. 'Are you *sure* you're all right being on your own tonight?'

He rolled his eyes. 'Of course I am. I've been on my own at least three times before in my life.'

'You know what I mean.'

He put an arm around my shoulders. 'It's scary. Really

77

scary. And weird. All this. But having you, even if you are much older and wrinklier—'

'*Watch it.*'

'Joke. You make it not so bad.'

CHAPTER EIGHT

'HOW ARE THINGS at the cinema?' Mum asked.
I froze mid-way through a mouthful of chicken casserole and tried not to look guilty or worried. I swallowed, smiled a hideously fake smile and said, 'Fine. You know. Pays the rent.'

She nodded. 'Nice to have a bit of time off.'

'Yes. Needed to come back and see a few people.'

'Well, it has been a while.'

Now to most people, that would have sounded like an innocuous comment, even friendly. But Mum had a superb talent for subtext and the slightly barbed edge made it abundantly clear that I still had at least one foot in the doghouse for my behaviour at Christmas. Pauline picked up on it too, I knew she did, because she glanced at me momentarily, obviously worried that I was going to say something everybody would regret.

But I just nodded. 'Yeah. Been really busy. It's nice to be back, though.'

We ate for a little while longer. Mum had thoughtfully cooked my favourite of her vast repertoire of dishes, and after months of my irregular diet of microwave meals, fish finger curry and croissants – neither Stuart nor I were anything resembling cooks – I was happy to just eat something nourishing in silence.

Until, that is, my mouth decided to say 'I'm sorry' without consulting me.

Mum looked up. 'What?'

'I'm sorry,' I said. 'For Christmas.' Oh God. Why was I bringing this up?

Mum looked surprised. I didn't often apologise. Mostly because I'm not often in the wrong. And to be honest, I'd only been slightly in the wrong at Christmas. 'Well,' she said. 'Thank you. That's . . . gracious of you.'

'It's just . . . you know how Isobel winds me up.' Of course, I had to qualify it. Couldn't just apologise and leave it at that. Oh no. That would never do.

Mum nodded magnanimously. 'I do.' She took a sip of white wine. 'I also know how you wind *her* up.'

Fair point. 'Yeah.' I had another mouthful, but my mouth suddenly seemed more interested in seeing how far it could push the conversation into the danger zone than it was in eating, and as soon as I swallowed I said, 'It's just the religious thing infuriates me *so* much.'

Pauline actually gave me a very gentle kick under the table at that point. Her face maintained the sweetest, calmest smile you could imagine, but I knew she was thinking *oh for God's sake. Here we go again.*

Mum raised an eyebrow, like a snake considering whether or not to strike. 'Don't forget,' she said, in that quiet, warning tone that I remembered so well from childhood. And adolescence. And adulthood. 'The "religious thing" is my "thing", too.'

'I know,' I said. 'I do. And it's not that I don't respect it. But you keep it to yourself. It's *your* thing. You don't shove it down my throat. You don't use it as a stick to beat me with.'

I was on seriously dodgy ground here. But once again,

Mum just nodded. 'I understand. But you need to control your temper, Vanessa. You respect that your sister and I believe what we believe, and we respect that you don't believe—'

'Maybe *you* do.' *Oh God*, I thought. *Shut up Vanessa. Shut up. Shut up.* 'I really don't think she does.'

'She does.' A slight edge was creeping back into Mum's voice. An edge of *I don't want to continue this conversation and if you persist I'm going to lose my temper.* 'So just try not to make it an issue.'

'Anyway,' said Pauline. 'This casserole is delicious, Sheila. Even more than usual. Have you changed your recipe?'

Nice one, Pauline. Mum smiled. It was a shame she smiled so rarely, because it really made her face look nice. 'Thank you. More sage. And a few other herbs.'

'It's really lovely.'

I managed to leave religion, Isobel and any other remotely controversial subjects alone for the rest of the main course, and pudding, and coffee, and suddenly it was time to go and I realised, to my surprise, that I'd had a really nice meal with my mother. It made me feel good.

'Thanks,' I said, as Pauline and I left. 'That was lovely.'

'Are you staying at Pauline's again?'

'I'm meeting some friends,' I said. 'Then I probably will stay at Pauline's, yes. Might be late, so . . .' I wondered if she minded. If she did, she didn't show it. I said I wasn't sure how much longer I'd be around but I'd make sure to pop in again, and I hugged her and we went.

The first thing Pauline did was pretend to clip me round the ear. 'I *know*,' I said. 'I know.'

'You're just lucky she was in a good mood.'

'She was, wasn't she? It was nice.'

'Could have turned nasty though.'

'I wasn't saying anything *bad*.'

'I know that. I shouldn't say this as you're both my nieces, but Isobel's holier-than-thou attitude absolutely drives me around the bend as well. When she does that *face* of hers, I want to give it a good slap.' Ah. Auntie Paulie after a few glasses of wine. 'But you shouldn't bad mouth her to your mother. It's not on. It's not *sisterly*.'

'I just wanted to explain that I didn't mean to ruin Christmas . . .'

'I'm sure she knows you didn't *mean* to.'

'Oh thanks. "Of course you didn't *mean* to ruin Christmas, Vanessa, but you ruined it anyway, well done, good show, happy New Year".'

'Shut up, you silly girl.'

We got back to Pauline's and I immediately called for Mark. 'Oi! We're back.'

There was no answer. He wasn't in the kitchen or the living room. Maybe he'd got so stoned he'd fallen asleep. I checked the bedroom. No sign. The bathroom was empty. The garden was empty. That only left Pauline's room. Somehow I wasn't panicking. I knew he wouldn't be in Pauline's room, but I went anyway, still calling his name. He wasn't in there. I stood in the hallway, looking around, feeling strangely cold. Pauline was standing at the other end of the hallway looking at me.

'He's not here,' someone said. Someone with a tiny, cracked voice, like a chipped doll's teacup.

'Vanessa . . .'

'Where is he?'

She came over and put her hands on my shoulders and looked into my eyes and spoke as calmly as she could.

'Vanessa,' she said. 'Don't panic, all right? Take a deep breath. OK? Breathe. *Breathe.*'

I tried to take a deep breath but it was hard. They were starting to come in short gasps. I felt as though the floor was cracking beneath my feet, that any second it would crumble away and leave me tumbling through nothingness. My arms were going numb.

'*No,*' said Pauline, forcefully. 'Don't do that. Breathe *deeply.* You mustn't—' She staggered as I collapsed into her arms, unprepared for my weight, or for the force of the collapse, or both. I hadn't really said her name properly, it had come out as a splurge of noise, and now I was hyperventilating fountains of tears into her chest, shaking, trying not to think it, couldn't think it, couldn't think it . . .

Think that Mark was . . .

Mark was . . .

I managed to take one very long breath. I exhaled it as a dozen little choppy ones, but then I tried again, and again, managing to slow the breathing, cool the heat that was rising in my chest, count *one two three four five ten fifteen twenty.* I felt as though I'd gone back in time. Back to the moment that I'd first realised, the first time the knowledge had truly hit me, the knowledge that Mark was . . .

'Pauline,' I said. 'What if he's gone again?'

'Vanessa, you're overreacting. All right? You're overreacting. I understand why, but you have to calm down. He's probably just gone out.'

'Gone *out?* Gone *where?*' My voice rose, but I reined it in. 'Gone to see his friends who've spent the last seven years thinking he's dead?'

'I don't *know.* But panicking isn't going to help, is it?'

Stern, loving authority. That definitely did help. 'Does he have a phone?'

'He does, but it doesn't work anymore. We tried it.'

'All right. Well, where might he have gone? Maybe he fancied a walk. Maybe he went to the shops . . .'

'It's eleven. Shops shut at ten.'

'He wouldn't have been silly enough to go to a pub . . .' Pauline frowned. 'Might he have come to find us?'

'He knows where my house is. He would have found us.'

He's disappeared again, I thought.

'I'm going to go out and look,' I said. 'You stay here in case he comes back.'

'No, I'll drive you—'

'If he comes back, someone needs to be here.' I turned and ran out of the house.

As I ran, I forced my brain to work as fast as it could. The shock of Mark not being there had already blasted away the wine cloud. I was in logic mode. Cold adrenaline. If I didn't find him, I could have a breakdown later. In the meantime, I needed to think properly. I started to list all the places of significance from when we were younger. If he had just gone for a walk, then he would blatantly have gone to one of them. I composed a shortlist, worked out an order in which to visit them, kept running.

First stop nearest to Pauline's was a little wooded area by the river, where we'd smoked our first spliff together. We'd always gone there to smoke and chat. No Mark, although there were some other kids who heckled me as I ran on, and I resisted the urge to go back and twat them as hard as I could and tell them they had no business being here, that they had no *clue* how to conduct themselves. Pathetic excuses for young

84

people.

All right Grandma, I thought, *calm down.*

There were more potential areas along the river and I scoured them one by one. The stony beach where we'd once made a campfire and fallen asleep, only to be woken at seven in the morning by a policeman because my Mum had freaked out when I'd not gone home. Mark wasn't there. And he wasn't at the graveyard, where we'd occasionally hung around just for the sake of being weird, or at the periphery of the field at the edge of town, the site of many merrily spangled camping trips.

I checked his old house, whose new occupants I'd never met, but he wasn't anywhere, not in the street, not hanging around in the garden. I even entertained the thought that he'd gone a bit loopy and tried to break in, but there was no sign of that. Plus, it was ridiculous.

That only left one place I could think of.

I sit on the swing, not really swinging, sucking at my lollipop, nodding my head to the Now *album on my CD walkman. It's a cool day, and brown leaves skitter and scatter in the wind.*

Someone has appeared at the gate at the bottom of the park. I squint to see. It's a boy. The new boy in my class, the one who appeared for the first time today and didn't speak to anyone. He's pretty but a bit weird.

He's seen me. He's walking towards me.

He's coming to speak to me.

I wait until he's standing in front of me, then take out one earphone, like it's a massive effort. I try to look . . . what's the word? Nonchalant.

'Hi,' *he says.*

'Hi.'

'I just started at your school. I'm in your class.'

'I know.'

He nods at my earphones. He doesn't seem at all nervous. 'What are you listening to?'

'It's African. You probably wouldn't have heard of it.' It's not African. It's Britney.

'Oh. No, I don't know any African music.' He holds out his hand, which seems proper weird for a twelve-year-old. 'My name's Mark.'

'I know.' I had actually forgotten. I shake his hand. 'I'm Vanessa.'

'Nice to meet you.'

What. A. Weirdo.

I was so out of breath by the time I got to the community centre car park that I had to walk to the playground, clutching my side. A few boy racers were parked in front of the community centre, revving the engines of their souped-up dickmobiles, hideous commercial dance crap screeching from their stereos, underage girls in tiny tops draped over the bonnets, swapping fags. It would have made me feel sick if I'd cared in the slightest about anything except finding Mark.

There were a couple of people in the playground. I squinted as hard as I could and my heart fluttered and bounced. It was Mark. It was definitely Mark. A small cloud of smoke rose above his head.

Then my heart did something else, a strange flop, because he was talking to someone.

A girl.

I got to the gate and stood there. The girl was sitting at the bottom of the slide, Mark leaning against the climbing frame. He passed her the joint he was smoking. She was so young. Barely sixteen.

What the hell was he doing smoking weed with a sixteen-year-old?

Vanessa, I thought. *Come on.*

Oh yeah.

I didn't know what to do. I stood there, hands on the gate, which I noticed they'd painted bright red since I'd last been here, feeling first a little stupid, then really stupid, then close to lobotomised.

I'd nearly had a panic attack.

And he was just here, chatting to some girl.

I recognised her, too. She was the younger sister of a girl who'd been in our year. What had her name been . . . Jenny. I couldn't remember much about her, we hadn't hung out. All I could recall was that she put it about a bit, to say the least. And that wasn't me being uncharitable. She'd seemed perfectly content to do so.

This girl, her sister, had been nine years old when I was sixteen.

When *we* were sixteen.

She was seven years younger than Mark.

Except she wasn't.

Mark looked towards the gate and saw me. I couldn't see his expression, but he said something to the girl and started walking in my direction. I saw her head droop slightly, disappointed. I stood, wondering what I was going to say.

'Hi,' he said.

'Hi?'

'What?'

'Is that it?'

He looked uncomfortable. 'I . . . sorry.'

'You didn't even leave a note.'

'I needed to have a walk. Clear my head.'

'You could have left a note.'

'Sorry.'

I nodded towards the girl. 'Who's yer mate?'

'Oh . . . no-one. I was just in here having a smoke and she came over and started speaking to me.'

'What's her name?'

'Um . . . Leah, I think?'

'Yes.' *Leah Morgan.* Memory is funny.

'I thought you didn't—'

'She's Jenny Morgan's little sister.'

His eyes widened. 'You're *joking.*'

'Nope.' I felt quiet and awkward. Deflated. Ridiculous. 'I'm going back to Pauline's.' I turned and walked away.

'Hold on . . .'

'You don't have to come.' He came after me, not bothering to say anything to what's-her-face, which I enjoyed for a petty, shameful second. He tried to put his hand on my shoulder but I kept walking.

'I'm *sorry!*' he said. 'I was just chatting to her.'

'It's fine. It's none of my business.'

'Oh for God's sake, you don't think—'

'I don't *think* anything. It's fine. You can do what you like.'

'Vanessa, I'm sorry. I should have left you a note. But I was going nuts just pacing around.'

'It's *fine.*'

'It's obviously not fine.'

I didn't want to have this conversation in such close proximity to the boy racers and their stupid wenches. I didn't answer, just walked, not looking to my left or to my right. Mark took the hint and didn't speak until we were nearly at Pauline's. Then he grabbed me, physically stopping me from walking, and made me look at him. 'I'm really sorry.'

'I was really scared,' I said. So lame and pathetic. I felt like I might cry and I didn't want to. If there was one thing I absolutely was *not* going to do right now, it was cry. Lame. Lame. Lame. I turned and kept walking.

We got back and Pauline yanked the door open. 'Mark!' She breathed deeply in relief. 'Where the hell were you?'

'He went for a walk,' I said. 'I'm going to bed.'

I walked through to the living room and Mark started to follow me, but Pauline stopped him, saying 'Hold on a second, would you, Mark?' in a voice that sounded almost deceptively gentle.

I went and changed and got into bed and lay in the dark for a while. I didn't hear any raised voices, but Mark came in a little while later and whispered that he was sorry again. This time it sounded like he understood. Part of me didn't want to say anything. Fuck him, he could lie there and feel bad, thinking I was still pissed off when I was mostly feeling relieved.

But I whispered 'OK', because I am a wimp. Then I made myself go to sleep.

I jerked awake suddenly. Pauline's. Spare room, the barest suggestion of light at the window.

And . . .

Oh . . .

Oh.

I rolled over in super slow motion, a movement taking hours, a movement full of years, of tearful nights, of raging against . . . whatever. And when I completed the turn, there he was. Sleeping peacefully on the floor, tangled in blankets, all small and . . . and . . . *present*. Here.

I'd been pretty good up until now. Apart from my meltdown over his walkabout last night, of course. But mostly . . . yeah. Fine.

Now, though . . .

I scrambled out of bed, feeling it coming, geysering up inside me, skin breaking out in crawling, hands shaking. I stumbled through to the living room, fell face down on the sofa, buried my face in a cushion and *cried*. It felt like the only thing my body knew how to do. It wasn't the unexplained sadness, it wasn't sadness at all, really. It was just . . . everything. Utter overwhelmingness.

He was really here.

How many times had I wished for this? How many variations had I played with in my head, practically acted out, in so many different bedrooms? The knock at the door. The knock I'd just *know*. The explanations. How he'd been kidnapped, kept for years, and had finally managed to put his escape plan into operation, kill the bastards who took him from us, from *me*, come back to us. To me. Or how he'd freaked out or something. Run away and joined the Army, like John Cusack in *Grosse Pointe Blank*, a film that had wallpapered countless stoning sessions in Luke's room. Of all the possible stories, that last one had obviously been the most far-fetched . . . but also not. Far-fetched because why would Mark be so cruel, take that film that we'd enjoyed together so many times, take that story and turn it into something to wreck me? But maybe *not* far-fetched because, in some of my darkest moments, I'd wondered if he'd done it on purpose. To wreck me. To punish me for something. Maybe not even consciously. Maybe I just deserved it.

And then, of course, the inevitable *God it's not all about you, you self-centred cow* spiral.

So much tangle.

And now he was here.

How was he here?

Maybe it *was* punishment? Maybe this whole thing, the messed-up stuff I'd been seeing, the sadness, Mark being his young self, a symbol of everything I wasn't anymore . . . or had forgotten how to be . . . maybe I did deserve it. I'd had the nerve, the fucking *audacity* to do something that resembled getting on with my life, despite losing him. Maybe this was the universe's way of scolding me. Shouldn't have forgotten him.

Like I'd ever forgotten him, really.

Fuck you, universe.

And, y'know, it's not all about *you*, Vanessa, you self-centred cow.

A sob became a laugh. And some time later I went back to bed and fell asleep pretty much instantly.

I didn't even look at him.

CHAPTER NINE

S OMEONE SHOOK ME and I growled, keeping my eyes screwed shut.

'Come on,' said Pauline. 'It's midday.'

'Don't care.'

'Don't make me get the cold water out.'

'You wouldn't.'

'Try me.' She shook me again and I growled again, pulling the duvet over my head. My ears started to get used to being awake and I heard the buzz of the shower, then Pauline tidying up Mark's bedclothes. Then her voice, confused. 'Ness?'

'What?'

'Do you know what these are?'

I poked my head out from under the duvet. 'What what are?'

She held up four feathers that she'd clearly extricated from the bedding on the floor. They were big and pure white and covered in delicate blue lines, like veins.

'No,' I said. 'Maybe he went birdwatching yesterday.' I grunted and retreated back into soft, warm darkness.

'Oh well.' I heard the window open as she threw them out. 'Come on. You missed breakfast but I'm going to make Sunday lunch. Sheila's in the kitchen.'

I popped out again. 'You're joking.'

Pauline smiled sweetly. 'Yes, I am. But I *am* going to make Sunday lunch. Come and chop some vegetables.'

'Yes ma'am.' I sat up and rubbed my eyes. 'Maybe . . . maybe we *should* invite Mum, though?'

'I thought about it.' Pauline looked sad. 'I'm sure she'd like it. But it's either her or Mark, isn't it? We can't just shut Mark away while the three of us eat. And we can't have them both sitting down together. I'm pretty sure Sheila would have a coronary of some kind. I'm surprised I haven't, to be honest.'

'You're an ex-hippie though, aren't you. I'm sure you saw weirder shit on acid in the Sixties.'

'Oh yes, because literally everyone was on acid in the Sixties,' said Pauline, shooting me a sarky look. 'We had it in our tea instead of sugar.'

'Yum.'

'And anyway, I wasn't even a teenager at the time.'

'OK, OK. I'll come and be chopping buddy. Just need to get dressed.'

'There's a good girl.' She smiled and left the room, just as I heard the shower switch off. I got dressed hurriedly and went after her, wanting to put off speaking to Mark for as long as possible. I couldn't work out whether I was still annoyed with him, or if I had realised that I was a wise and mature person who could rise above a silly mistake. I estimated that it would take a little while longer before I reached a decision.

All the chopping was done by the time he came in. 'Morning,' he said.

'Afternoon,' said Pauline.

'Hi,' I smiled, immediately realising that I had risen above the silly mistake, seemingly against my will. He smiled as well, immediately realising that he'd been let off the hook complete-ly, and I kicked myself inside my head. Couldn't be letting him get away with everything. Just because he was a miracle . . .

Sunday passed quietly. We had dinner and listened to Pauline play some piano, and she and Mark smoked and I didn't, although their fumes were enough to get me giggly. It felt normal, which was what I needed, and more importantly what Mark needed. I wasn't sure if he was aware that I was constantly observing him, analysing his expressions and what he said, trying to fathom whether he was actually coping as well as he seemed to be, or if it was just a really convincing act. It was a bizarre deja-vu, trying to read this mostly unreadable person. I wondered whether, had he just lived normally for the intervening years, I'd have been able to make sense of him by now. I wondered what might have happened in those years. And it spiked me hard in the belly so I stopped thinking about it and laughed as Pauline tried to tell us a story about her adventures in a Spanish commune in the Seventies. She was having difficulty because she'd smoked another one by now and was giggling more than she was speaking.

Evening fell and I remembered that I needed to phone my mother. I tried to compose myself, quickly gave up and made the call. I managed to hold it together quite well, explaining that I was off again for a few days but that I'd be back here before I went home. She didn't ask what I was going to be doing, just said it would be nice to see me when I popped back and that it had been nice to see me yesterday. I agreed and hung up, feeling good about myself and my mother, which was a lovely change.

Back in the living room, Mark and Pauline were laughing about something. 'What did I miss?' I said. 'Are you laughing about me? What are you saying about me? What's so funny about me? What did I do?'

'We're not laughing about you, you goose,' giggled Pauline.

'I know. I was . . . it was a thing. Never mind. What's the chuckling?'

'Talking about how I don't have a clue what's going on with music now,' said Mark, 'and neither does Pauline, and how we're both like old people—'

'That is *not* how the conversation went!' said Pauline. '*Old?* Bloody cheek. I was just *saying* that a lot of modern music sounds dreadful to me, which I know is the biggest cliché that can ever come out of a . . . a *mature* person's mouth . . . but the fact is—'

'So we're both *mature* people, then.' The two of them disintegrated into giggles again.

'Yeah,' I said, watching stony-faced. 'Real mature there, guys.' I couldn't maintain the face for more than a few seconds, though. And why would I want to, when I could be laughing with these two?

'I like *some* new music,' said Pauline, when we eventually calmed down. 'A lot of new music, in fact. But some of it my ears just don't understand.'

'Just be thankful you've never listened to gabber,' I said. 'Maintain your innocence.'

'Oh God, is that still around?' said Mark.

'It will outlive us all.'

He shuddered.

'Should I just not ask?' said Pauline.

'Best not,' I said. 'Let us talk more of the new.'

'So what *is* new music?' said Mark.

'Please,' I said, in my best alien voice. 'Tell me more of this Earth custom called . . . *newmusic.*'

'But seriously, bro.'

'Plenty's new. Like literally fifty thousand new genres, new artists . . .'

'But what's *good*, bro?'

Did he used to call me bro? I made a show of thinking hard. I *was* thinking hard, so it wasn't . . . haha . . . hard. 'Urmm . . .'

'Go on, show me some stuff.'

'Me too,' said Pauline. 'Educate us, most hip of young things.'

'You're weird, Pauline,' I said. 'It's like you get *older* when you get stoned.'

Pauline blinked owlishly at me. Then she said, in a very prim voice, 'Piss off.' And we all crumbled again.

When that latest bout of giggling had passed, I nodded as though I was acquiescing to the most enormous favour in the history of favours. 'OK, *fine*.' I grabbed Pauline's computer, brought it through and, amazingly, managed to hook it up to her hi-fi. 'How in God's name have you got the right leads for me to do this?'

'No idea, hen,' said Pauline. 'Things just . . . materialise.'

I felt as though I should have glanced meaningfully at Mark, but it was a bit cringe so I didn't. Instead I started playing songs off YouTube. Songs I'd fallen in love with since he'd been gone. Songs we hadn't shared, from before and since. Songs that had kept me company when I'd been on my own wandering around London, or figuratively on my own at the flat while Stuart cracked on with his own stuff. Songs by Radiohead, Massive Attack, Bon Iver, This Is The Kit, Syd Matters, Placebo, Regina Spektor, Neutral Milk Hotel, Elliott Smith. And it was only when I had to turn off 'Waltz #2' less than a minute in because it was making me feel funny that I realised what I was doing: I was basically playing my wallowing playlist. My *on the Tube to nowhere in particular, feeling poetically lost and alone* playlist, which also doubled as my *lying on the bed staring at the ceiling, oh well at least I'm not listening to* Metal Machine Music *again* playlist. And everyone was far too stoned for it, but too polite to request that I try for a cheerier vibe, or suggest that maybe I wasn't quite fulfilling the brief. I even started to feel like Mark *knew* what it was, what the songs signified, what I was not-quite-subconsciously doing, maybe Pauline too, like my emotions were in the air, as thick as the spliff smoke, thicker, a melancholy silver-black fog, so I cut gracelessly through it with a big stupid grin and a too-loud 'Anyway' and played something silly instead. Then I went to the bathroom, locked the door, turned the light on and saw two reflections in the mirror.

One was definitely me. I put my hand up and touched my face, and she touched her face. Me. The other one was also me, but her hair was black and she was *behind* me, too far behind to really be there, because the bathroom door was right behind me and she was standing further behind me, but the bathroom door was behind *her*, although the bathroom didn't seem any bigger, except it was . . .

I blinked. She was just standing there, pale, so pale, her lips moving as though she was trying to tell me something, but with the volume turned off. She looked like she was forcing herself to be calm, although I could see ripples of panic round the edges, and I tried to ask her what she was saying but found that I couldn't make a sound either, so I strained my ears trying to hear what she was saying and thought I could make out whispering, but it was *just* too faint. I reached out towards the mirror, trying to touch her reflection, but when I did it made her recoil with such force that she *shot* back and hit the bathroom door hard, so hard that I *felt* it, and she coughed up a spray of dark blood as black as her hair and I jumped and screamed and the naked bathroom lightbulb exploded, showering me with little pieces of hot glass.

I fell against the door and heard several more glassy pops outside in the hall and other rooms. I heard Mark yell 'Woah!' and Pauline cry out. Then banging on the door. Pauline's voice: 'Vanessa! Are you all right? Let us in! Vanessa!'

'I'm OK . . .'

'Loads of the lights just exploded!' said Mark.

'The bathroom light did too.' I fumbled for the lock and opened the door. The hall was in darkness, outlines of things barely suggested by the faraway orange of street lamps. I was glad they couldn't see how pale I was.

'Are you sure you're all right?' asked Pauline.

'You screamed,' said Mark.

'Shock. The lights . . .'

'You screamed *before* the lights went out. I heard you.'

I could feel their suspicious eyes in the dark. 'Oh,' I said. 'Yeah. Just . . . saw a spider. Biiiiig spider.' I didn't sound like I'd just seen a spider. But what else was I going to say?

We set about fixing the lights. Luckily only the bulbs were damaged, the actual fittings were OK. Pauline didn't have enough spares, but at least we weren't in complete darkness. It wasn't every light in the house, either, just those in the hall, living room and spare bedroom. The whole time we changed bulbs Mark kept glancing at me, all suspicious. He obviously knew there was something else up, but I was too busy thinking. This was the first time the awful things I'd seen had been accompanied by something so violently *physical*. And Mark and Pauline had both experienced it.

I didn't know what that meant, but at least I wasn't alone. And that made me feel a *tiny* bit better.

'So how old are you?'

'Eighteen.' This is a lie, although not by much. The guy, Dean, or Dave, or whatever, nods and smiles. 'How old are you?' I ask, exhaling smoke like some kinda badass.

'Twenty-two.'

'Cool.' It's not cool. It's just an age. I've never particularly been into older boys. 'Are you at uni then?'

'Just finished.'

'What were you doing?'

'Building surveying.'

Wow. I picked an exciting one. 'That sounds interesting.'

'It was all right. I'm pretty much guaranteed a job when I start looking. Just, you know. Having a bit of fun at the moment.'

By now we've walked from the club to a car park round the corner and I'm sitting on the bonnet of a car. He's standing over me. I don't really know what I'm doing. Well, I do. But I'm not entirely in charge. Dan or Dave smiles. 'Know what I mean?'

'Yeah.' No. Who cares.

He leans in to kiss me and I let him, dropping my cigarette. It's quite nice, I suppose. I sort of kiss him back, let him carry on kissing me, let him put his hands on me, let him move them over me. They move to certain places far too quickly though and I half protest, although maybe not enough for him to notice, or maybe he doesn't care, I'm not sure. All I know is I'm starting to feel something in my stomach, like I've swallowed broken glass and it's being churned around, and I suddenly can't think of anything worse than having this ape eating away at my face, his big clumsy hands on my body.

I push him off. I'm crying. And ashamed of that. 'No. Stop, please.'

He looks confused and angry, stands there red-faced. 'What?'

'No. Not . . . I'm not.' I get up and walk off. He doesn't walk after me, which is good. I don't know what the men are like here. Back home, they wouldn't have walked after me, although the story would have been all over town by the next morning and I certainly wouldn't have been the heroine. But I don't know this city. I'm sure there are plenty of men who would have chased after me and—

'Fucking cocktease!' he yells.

That gives me a laugh. I'm glad. Laughing isn't crying.

Part of me is laughing at my stupid self. Like I'm outside, looking in, shaking my head, laughing. Not that I should be laughing. Should be scolding. Here I am, wandering a strange city, looking for . . . for whatever. But not really looking for it. And more of the girls I know have suffered the consequences of unwanted attention than haven't . . . and when is it not in the news . . . and here I am . . .

But I just want to feel stuff.

Feel stuff that isn't . . . that stuff.

And why the fuck shouldn't I.

I can't always be owing everyone my most perfect behaviour.

But I want to go home.

Except I really don't want to go home.

I cross the road, feeling even younger than I am, and hurry down some random, glistening street, keeping my head down. Don't want to make eye contact. Ghosts everywhere. Well, just the one ghost. But everywhere, still. I end up walking along the river, multicoloured city light glinting off the choppy waves, and up onto the bridge. I stand there and look into the water and light another cigarette, remembering how much my sister hates water, especially deep dark water where you can't see below the surface. Which is all the water in Britain basically. I don't mind it. I even like it a little. I watch it for ages, smoking, feeling like a character in a film. When I toss the orange butt away it flickers downwards, leaving a brief trail of tiny embers behind it.

Then it's gone.

CHAPTER TEN

PAULINE GENTLY NUDGED me awake at ten o'clock, wafting a cup of coffee under my nose. I sat up, ready to do my pissed-off owl routine, but decided against it. I looked down at Mark, still asleep, as peaceful as he'd ever looked, and it made me smile briefly, before the memories of last night clawed their way to the surface of my brain. Then I just felt tired and uncertain again.

'Thanks,' I said, taking the coffee.

Pauline sat on the edge of the bed. 'I'll drive you to the station.'

'It's OK—'

'Oh I know you're perfectly capable of walking.' She smiled. 'Don't flatter yourself that I'm your personal taxi service. I just think it would be better if Mark didn't walk through town in broad daylight.'

'Tell *him* that.'

'It was night-time . . .'

'Doesn't matter.' I glugged down some coffee. 'Still could have been seen. He *was* seen.'

'Well.' Pauline looked down at him. 'He's . . .'

'Never mind.' I necked the rest of the coffee. 'I'm going to have a shower. We'll have breakfast then go.'

When I came back from my shower, Mark was just getting up. 'Morning,' he said, smiling.

'Morning.'

He took his towel and went to the bathroom while I sat, struggling to pull socks over my still-wet feet. I glanced at his bed.

There were more feathers in it.

I reached down and scooped them up. There were six, big and white, criss-crossed by those peculiar blue veins, like tiny rivers. I sniffed experimentally. They didn't smell like Mark. And they didn't smell . . . bird-y. They smelled slightly hot. Slightly old. Slightly . . . something. I went to the window to throw them out, but something compelled me to keep one. I put in on the bedside table before going to the kitchen.

'Don't you have work today?' I asked, putting some bread in the toaster.

'This afternoon,' said Pauline.

I leaned against the counter, fiddling with my hands. Pauline looked up from the paper. 'What are *you* going to do about a job?'

'Dunno.'

'How are you off for money?'

'I'll be all right.'

'Will you?'

Truthfully, I wasn't sure. I knew I would have enough for this month's rent. I'd done quite a lot of overtime before quitting and abstained from going out, except for the odd drink here and there. I'd have to do some calculations when I got back to the flat . . . whenever that was. At least Stuart would be flexible with me. He could afford to be . . . but also he just would, because he was good.

I couldn't rely on that, though, for numerous reasons. I needed to find something new. I hated the idea of going on the dole. I knew how hard they made it for people.

'I'll be OK,' I said.

'Maybe it wasn't such a clever idea to quit.'

'Mike wasn't going to let me come back here.'

'You could have found another way around it.'

'Was kind of reeling from the Mark revelation.' I buttered and Marmited my toast. 'Anyway, don't worry about it. It was a bollocks job anyway. I'll find something else. Once all this is straightened out.' Cos you literally couldn't move in London for decently paid jobs that didn't make you want to drink yourself into an early grave.

Pauline listened for a second, to make sure that the shower was still running. 'Finding Mark's father isn't the end,' she said. 'You know that.'

I didn't answer. Just munched my toast.

'The best case scenario is that his father is overjoyed and takes him back in.'

'You don't think that's going to happen?'

'I'm not sure. It could go either way.'

'I have no idea what else to do,' I said. It came out much more matter-of-fact than I'd been expecting it to. 'Literally not a clue. I'm just doing . . . I dunno. Whatever feels right.'

'Which is what you always do.' Pauline smiled fondly. 'Even if it ends up completely ruining Christmas.'

'No-one's going to let me forget that, are they.'

'Well, *you're* not going to let yourself forget it.' She looked back down at her newspaper. 'Why should we?'

I managed a brief laugh at that. Very brief. 'Um, Pauline?'

'Mm?'

'You know those feathers you found in Mark's bed?'

'Mm.'

'There were more this morning.'

She looked up. 'More?'

'Yeah. Six.'

Pauline frowned. 'They're strange, aren't they? The colours? Have you asked him about them?'

'No.' I heard the shower switch off. 'Should I?'

'Might be an idea. It is a bit peculiar.'

I finished my toast and returned to the spare room. Mark came in a few minutes later, his hair a wet mess, and I held up the feather I'd kept. 'Where'd ya get this?' I asked, jauntily.

Mark raised an eyebrow. 'Dunno. I've not seen it before.'

'Really? It was in your bed.'

'In my bed? No clue. Maybe it's from the pillow.'

It wasn't from the pillow.

'What time's the train?' he asked.

'Soon,' I said, putting the feather down. One more thing to put on the back burner. 'Pauline's going to give us a lift to the station *so nobody sees you*.'

Mark looked abashed. 'Yeah. Sorry again. About going out. Really. I just . . . I didn't think. Nobody saw me except that girl. And she didn't have a clue who I was.'

'What did you tell her?'

'That my name was Dante and I was passing through on my way to Vegas.'

'Whatever.'

He smiled. 'No, really.'

'Dante.'

'Yep.'

'Vegas.'

'Uh-huh.'

I shook my head. 'Weirdo.'

Twenty minutes later we were ready. Mark had re-iterated

that he didn't want to call his father, he just wanted to turn up, which I thought was probably a bad idea. Well. It definitely wasn't a *good* idea, at any rate. Pauline checked that there was no-one in the street before we got in her car and we made Mark put his hood up, just in case. 'Just pretend you're a celebrity,' I said.

'Vomit,' he replied, sulkily.

We pulled up by the little station and Pauline and I checked that there was nobody on the platform that we knew. Against all the odds, it was empty. I promised I'd keep her posted and the train chuntered in and we boarded.

We sat at a table facing one another, because we both liked to be close to the window. We had one hour on this train, a ten-minute stopover, then two hours on another train. There weren't many people, just a few old folks and one sullen teenager absorbed in her phone.

The train pulled out. It was one of those days when the sun can't make up its mind whether to perform or not, so the light kept on shifting from grey and shadowy to summery incandescence. Mark was watching the countryside ripple by, hidden behind his thought mask, and I wanted to tell him what I'd been seeing, so much so that I actually opened my mouth. It was enough for him to turn and look at me expectantly, but I turned it into a yawn and smiled. He smiled back like none of this was anything remotely resembling a thing, then turned back to the window. He looked so at ease. I couldn't burden him with more weirdness now.

'Do you remember that time at the beach?' he asked, still looking out of the window.

The sea unrolls like the sky's living reflection, greedily licking at the shore.

'Yes.'

Mark leans back, twirling our only cigarette around his middle and index fingers.

He leaned back. He still wasn't looking at me. His brow and cheeks were knitting and knotting, as if he couldn't quite remember something, or at least couldn't remember the significance of something. 'The sea,' he said.

Sometimes I feel as though I could just walk straight in. Not swim, not straight away. Walk into the sea until it's over me, completely over me. Until I'm part of it. And then I swim, I swim straight down, and there's a new world down there. A luminous forest. Soft bubble mountains.

'The way it . . .' He stopped. All the sounds were filtering away, the vibration and rattle and thud of the train, the muffled croon of the old folks at the other end of our compartment. I could almost hear the sea beneath Mark's breathing.

'I was thinking about humans.'

'I dreamed about it last night,' he said. 'That time. Every minute of it, exactly reproduced. To the tiniest detail. Everything we said. Everything we felt. Getting out of the last car.'

We climb out of the little red Polo and wave to the friendly lady as she drives away.

'The red Polo. And then walking down to the sea. And there was nobody there for miles. The whole beach, deserted.'

The length and breadth of the beach is just sand and shells and seaweed. Not another soul to be seen. Not even a trespassing footprint. I look at Mark and we smile. 'Best idea ever,' I say.

'And we sat for hours.'

'I was thinking about humans.'

My feet were suddenly cold, so cold, and when I looked

down at the floor of the train I saw why: they were bare, submerged to the ankles in salt water. Of course they were cold.

Mark shook his head a little and sand cascaded from his hair. 'There was one point,' he said. 'One point when . . . I thought I was losing myself.'

We sit and watch the sea endlessly devouring itself. I don't look at Mark for a while, embarrassed and annoyed that I somehow trivialised whatever he was thinking. As if it didn't matter to me. And when I do look at him, I almost jump. He's still sitting there, but he's staring so intently at the sea that I'm not sure he's actually there. Really there. I feel completely alone.

I slipped my feet out of the sea and brought my knees up to my chest, listening to the drops fall from my white toes, off the edge of the seat, tinkling as they return to the water.

'Like we were both gone for a while,' Mark said. 'Forever.'

I don't want to say anything. I feel like I shouldn't, like I shouldn't jolt him from this waking dream. Like you shouldn't wake a sleepwalker.

'I felt like I could just walk straight in,' he said. 'Not swim, not straight away. Walk into the sea until it was over me, completely over me. Until I was a part of it. And then swim, swim straight down, and there would be a new world down there. A luminous forest. Soft bubble mountains.'

I turn away and just stare at the sea and tell myself to stop being silly.

'I'm not sure if there were people there. There might have been. Or maybe they just weren't people. They were more like . . . light. Light and laughter. And they played with colour all day, colours that made tunes. I swam down and then I was walking, walking among them, and the water was the most comfortable thing in the world.' He smiled. 'And I just stayed there forever.'

He finally made eye contact with me and it hit me like waking up. My feet were safe and dry in my shoes and socks. The train thumped. The two old people chattered away. And I wasn't quite sure what had happened.

'It was a good dream,' said Mark. 'But . . . scary. And . . . I don't know. It was the first lucid dream I ever remember having. Cos I knew that I was dreaming, cos everything was so perfect. So perfectly identical to the memory. Like the memory was a film I kept in my head and I was just running it for a second time.' He didn't seem to be talking to me now. He was just thinking out loud. It was a good thing, really, because I didn't know what to say. 'I don't even really remember where it finished,' he said. 'I don't remember waking up. I was just awake. And it seemed like forever had passed. Really quickly.' He turned back to the window. Just for a second, he looked a hundred years old. Just for a second.

I looked out of the window too. I could no longer hear or see the sea, just the gradual unravelling of fields and hills. That was good. Solid ground I could deal with.

Solid ground was good.

We had a longer wait for the next train than we'd expected, so I bought some overpriced coffee and sausage rolls and we ate and drank sitting in our standard places that we always assumed on any bench, anywhere: me sitting on it like you're supposed to, Mark sitting on the back with his feet on the seat. A little way up the platform a pinched, stressed mother was shrilly interrogating a guard about a late train, while her daughter played obliviously with a red ball. It slipped out of her grasp and rolled towards us and Mark hopped off the bench, bending to pick it up. As he moved, I saw his tobacco and Rizlas poking out of his pocket.

'You didn't bring your stuff with you?' I said.

'What stuff?' He rolled the ball back to the little girl with a smile.

'*You* know.'

'Oh. Yeah. There's only a couple left.'

'Mark!'

'What?'

'It's . . . dodgy. Carrying it around like that.'

'Since when?'

'What do you mean, "since when"?' Mark looked genuinely mystified. I knew how he felt. 'If you got, I don't know, sniffed or searched or something . . .'

'I won't.' He looked certain, and confused with it, as though the very possibility that he might be wrong was ridiculous. Cos things like that just didn't happen to Mark. 'It'll be fine. Chill out. You never . . .' He stopped.

'What?'

'Nothing.'

You never used to be such a moaning, paranoid killjoy, I thought. *Something like that?*

The train finally pulled in and we boarded. I sat down and immediately felt tired and Mark went back to staring out of the window, so I just closed my eyes and tried to think thoughts.

The air conditioning hums like it has a frog in its throat. The quilts are a deep pool beneath me. I slide off the bed and look from photograph to photograph: black and white, sepia, old

*tractors and older farmers, long-dead dogs with their tongues
extended in sloppy glee, smiling faces, stern faces. I pick up the
china cow from the dresser, like it's a priceless heirloom, an
antique treasure. It is cold and has no udders. I can hear the
sounds of America outside. City sounds, although this is the
deepest countryside.*

*I walk out onto the landing, down the stairs, to the hallway
. . . but these boards are bare . . .*

*This is Mark's hallway. I keep walking, through to his
kitchen, where someone sits at the table, still, hunched over.
For a moment I think it is Mark. Then something or someone,
something or someone that isn't me, tells me that it's not Mark.*

*Mark's father stirs. He mutters something but I can't hear
it. I want to walk away. I'm not sure. I'm in complete control,
but not.*

*He stands and turns and his face is red-eyed, distorted with
crying. He hurls a handful of feathers at me and they drift
accusingly to the floor. He screams something about her, then
he comes towards me and I know he's going to—*

I opened my eyes. Mark was looking out of the window. 'Was
I asleep?' I said.

'What?'

'Was I asleep?'

'Maybe for a second. You only just shut your eyes.'

I frowned. Mark cocked his head. 'You all right, bro?'

'I . . .' *I don't know.* I looked at him, right at him. He looked
worried. 'I think I . . . had a dream.'

'You think you had a dream?'

'I don't know. I wasn't asleep for long?'

'Hardly. The train literally just left the station.'

It wasn't a dream, though. 'It was more . . . kind of like a memory? It started off as mine, but . . .'

Eyes red with crying.

He hurls a handful of feathers at me.

And now there was another echo, as if part of the dream had come back, but a part that was underneath, buried. A voice, strangled with pain, fury. *'You're like her.'*

I knew whose voice it was.

'I don't know if this is a good idea,' I said, before fully realising that I was saying it.

'What do you mean?'

'This trip. This . . . mission. I don't think it's . . .' I felt so disorientated. My head was thick.

Mark leaned forwards and took my hands. 'Vanessa,' he said. 'What did you dream about?'

'You.'

'Me?'

'Yes. And . . . your dad.' Should I be saying this? It could just have been a dream. Dreams usually were.

But then again, with everything that had been happening lately, I was pretty sure that I could attach a little more significance . . .

Or maybe I just felt that I could?

'My dad,' said Mark.

'He . . . I don't know if . . .'

'If he's going to be pleased to see me.'

Our eyes locked and I could see the pain that the thought inspired in him. Bright and piercing. 'It was just a dream,' I said, so unconvincingly that it was embarrassing.

'But I've been thinking this from the beginning.'

'Mark—'

'How much is it going to mess up his life, having me back?'

'It's not going to mess up his life! I don't know . . . he might be . . . he *should* be over the moon . . .'

'But to be honest, I don't know if I can handle it,' said Mark. 'I don't know if I can handle *either*. If he wasn't pleased, that would be hard. But if he *was*, if he was over the moon, that would be hard too. Maybe . . . harder. I don't know if I can hack it. Not yet, at least.'

The grown-up in me wanted to tell him, and myself, to put this silly dream business aside. This was reality. The real world, where a parent who lost their child years ago would obviously want them back, couldn't possibly want anything more . . .

'Let's get off at the next station,' he said. 'Just get off and go somewhere. Explore. Adventure.'

Instead of saying *no*, I said, 'Really?'

'Why not? It's what we always do.'

Always *used* to do.

But . . .

Something rose inside me. *Why* not? Literally, why the hell not? Why shouldn't I just take back what I'd lost? Why should I treat what had happened like a normal person? A real person? A grown-up? The Vanessa that Mark knew wouldn't have. So why should I? Just because grown-ups built the world for grown-ups . . .

Fuck grown-ups.

I hadn't felt like smiling before, not at all. But now I did. 'I think that's a *capital* idea.' I took out my phone, lingered guiltily over an ignored text from Stuart, then switched it off and put it at the bottom of my bag. The smile wasn't going anywhere. And when Mark smiled as well it was a smile I *knew*, the smile we used to share, the gleeful, devious smile of plans to be made. In a flash, I felt like the last seven years hadn't happened. *Poof.*

Gone.

CHAPTER ELEVEN

WE DISEMBARKED AT the next station. It wasn't a main one, luckily, as our tickets wouldn't have worked. Except, of course, that I didn't care about that.

We walked down the steps and Mark sniffed the air. 'Which way, do you reckon?'

'Hmm. Town or countryside . . .' I took out my purse. 'Let's try the old method.' I fished out a two pence piece. 'Heads town, tails countryside.' I tossed it and Mark caught it, smacking it down on the back of his other hand with relish. 'Countryside it is,' I said.

We bypassed the crooked bridge that led into town and headed in the opposite direction. There were two paths to choose from, a main road and a narrower country lane. No discussion there. We wandered down the country road, bordered by thick bushes buzzing with bees. Mark rolled a cigarette and we shared it, even though these days I was, at best, an annoying 'oh can I have one of yours' drunk smoker. The sun had finally made up its mind and the world had erupted into that gorgeous cascade of luminous greens and ripe yellows that I'd almost forgotten, having been hiding out in the city for several decades. I felt it filling my head with clean light, my lungs with new air. I felt it brushing the dust from memories I'd forced myself to bury: Mark and me climbing half-rotten trees, giddy with danger, Luke and Twig having a competition to see who could successfully throw a dead slug into the other's mouth as the rest of us watched, appalled and hysterical with laughter, six of us tripping balls at eleven in the morning and roly-polying down Pregnant Hill – not its real name – near Laura's house.

Laura . . .

'Hi.'

Laura looks up, surprised. 'Oh. Hiya.'

'How's it going?' I sit down. I can already feel that this isn't going to go well.

'Um, yeah. OK. You?'

'Yeah. Fine.' I stare into my lemonade. Laura sips her whisky nervously. 'What have you been up to?' I ask, not looking up.

'For the last two years?'

That makes me look up. The expression on her face hurts. Seeing that expression on the face of a friend, once a best friend, directed at me. It's not angry, really. Just . . . like she can't be bothered. 'Never mind,' I say. 'Sorry.' I get up.

'Vanessa,' says Laura. 'I . . . I tried. I really tried, really hard. I came to see you so many times . . .'

She had.

'I was devastated too,' she says. 'We all were. But we grieved together. You wouldn't let us help.'

I hadn't.

But I couldn't. I couldn't grieve with them.

I just couldn't.

'I didn't stop coming round because I didn't care about you,' says Laura.

'I know.'

'I just . . .'

'I know.' I stand up. 'I know. It's fine.' It's not fine. If I tried

116

right now, I know I could start the process, start repairing. If I sat back down and laid myself bare, threw myself on her mercy, said I missed her, that I wanted to make it all up, she would respond. We might even cry over some old memories.

But I don't sit down. I leave my drink and I walk away and I don't look back.

For a second, the brightness dimmed. Then it blazed again and my heart leapt and I looked over at Mark and he was just looking around at things, marvelling at the way the trees shone, delighting in the glow of the grass.

'Track!' he said, running past me to a dirt track that led right up through the woods to our left. I followed him and we scrambled up the steep bank, using broken trunks for handholds. Every now and then we'd pass a tree and there'd be an explosion of startled birds above, bursting pockets of life; everywhere was *so* alive, it was bringing me out in goosebumps. Mark had more energy than me, which made sense. I rarely got any kind of exercise. He'd been doing this less than a week ago. The years of smoking and drink and drugs had not yet taken a toll.

We got to the top of the wood, flipped another coin and headed left along another dirt track. Within minutes we reached a clearing where we stopped, the breath torn from our chests by the view.

You could see the whole country for miles. Higgledy-piggledy splatters of fields, brown, green and bright yellow, plastic farmhouses that fitted between thumb and forefinger, sprinklings of sheep, and every now and then a little village or town. And so many hills, looming benevolently like sleepy giants. Mark sat down and started to roll a joint and I stood at the edge of the clearing and breathed it in.

'Not bad, eh?' said Mark.

'Not bad.'

I sat by him and we smoked for a while and didn't say much. There wasn't much that needed to be said right now. The weed went straight to my head, joining forces with the lazy heat to drive all the remaining energy from my legs, and I went floppy, wishing we'd brought some water. Mark lay on his back and hummed and I stared fixedly at the furthest hill I could see, trying to find it within myself to stand up.

As I sat there I started to think. And there it was, rising beneath the warm gold thickness, like a monster burrowing its way up from under sand. Anxiety. Things I should be doing. Things I should be feeling.

Stuart had been trying to get hold of me.

Stuart who I'd chucked pretty unceremoniously.

Stuart who deserved more from me.

Stuart who'd only ever been decent.

I look up from my book and see the guy entering the library. I move my hand as surreptiously as I can to hide my face. He doesn't see me. He greets a couple of people in a vague way, like he can't be bothered to really remember them properly, then he disappears upstairs.

First one night stand of my university career.

Some third year who'd lasted about ninety seconds, then sneaked off while I was in the toilet.

Although naturally he'd stopped off to steal some yoghurts and a new jar of peanut butter from the kitchen as he'd made his escape.

Yoghurt and peanut butter.

And I let him put his penis inside me.

First one night stand of my university career. Fingers crossed it's uphill from here, because this feels like a low, low place.

'All right?'

I jump. Stuart holds up his hands. 'Woah! Sorry. Doing some deep thinking, were you?'

'Deep. Unfathomable.' I move my bag from the other chair so he can sit down. He has a coffee and a fat textbook. Journalism ethics.

'How's it going?' he says.

'Dandy. You?'

'Yeah, I'm good ta.' He sips his coffee. 'I . . . this is probably none of my business . . .'

'If you're prefacing it with "this is probably none of my business", then it's definitely none of your business. But go on.'

'I . . . someone said they saw you getting in a cab with Colin Cooper last night?'

Oh Jesus fucking eternally humiliated Christ.

'Really?' I ask, trying to sound noncommital. 'Name doesn't ring a bell.' *Well. The Cooper bit doesn't. Colin certainly does. A whole lotta bells that should have remained un-rung.*

Stuart doesn't believe me but he does a good job of not showing it, which is nice of him. 'Well, anyway. Just . . . it isn't any of my business, but I'm just . . . I guess I'm warning you? To watch out for him? If that doesn't sound weird. Or . . . overbearing. Or . . . patriarchal?' *Bless this stumbling feminism.* 'I've got a couple of mates in his year. He's got a reputation.'

'Really?' *Now I sound positively bored.*

'Yeah. Player. And skanky too, apparently. I heard—'

'I don't really want to know. But thanks.' *Fucking hell, I'm glad I made him put on a condom. And he actually whinged*

119

about it. Guy's probably riddled. Note to self – go to the clinic just in case, because I deserve a fun day out this week.

'No problem.' He glances at my notepad. 'Journalism ethics?'

'I haven't even started that yet, to be honest. I'm super behind.'

'What are you scribbling then?'

'Just a play.'

'A play?'

'Yeah.'

Stuart smiles. He has a nice smile. 'Well, I'll leave you to your play. See you in class?'

'Maybe.' Probably not, to be honest.

'See ya.'

'Bye. Thanks for the advice.'

'No problem.' He walks away and I feel a little bit sick.

But also not sick.

That had been the first time. The first glimmer of anything. Two years and a number of significantly more successful one night stands had passed before the second glimmer. I could remember our first date vividly. It had started off awkwardly – he'd chosen a new restaurant-bar-combo place that turned out to be pretty bad. But then we'd clocked that all they'd been playing since we'd got there was Randy Newman, and realised that they were planning to play Randy Newman for the duration, and we got all giggly and bonded over how endearingly un-cool Randy Newman was.

You'd be forgiven for wondering if Randy Newman had become 'our guy' after that. Our ironic living room dancing music. He didn't, though. We didn't do much ironic living room dancing.

I was suddenly aware of time again. Horribly aware. And looking at Mark, still so young . . .

How had so much changed for me in seven years? Seven years wasn't even that long, was it?

Mark sat up suddenly, eyes flashing. 'Let's go.' He jumped to his feet and walked off and I managed to find the energy I'd been looking for and scrambled after him. As we negotiated our way back down towards a main road, he asked, 'How's Laura?'

'Fine, I think. Don't really see her anymore.'

'Really? That's . . . how come?'

'Just . . . you know. Time and stuff.'

'Fair enough. Tom?'

'Him and Erin had a baby.'

'You're *joking* me.'

'Not at all. They called him Phoenix and he's three years old.'

'*Phoenix*? You *are* joking me.'

'Cross my heart and hope to die.'

'Christ. Luke?'

'Literally the same guy.'

'Glad to hear it. What about Wes?'

'He's good. He's engaged. To a man, actually.'

'Huh. I did always kind of wonder.'

'They're literally so cute together it makes me want to kill myself.'

We rejoined the main road and walked for about half an hour before we came to a village. It was small and quiet and seemed like a relic of fifty or more years ago, which I supposed was appropriate. We bypassed the main street and headed around the outskirts.

Mark suddenly came to a halt, grabbing my arm to stop me. 'What?' I said.

'Look.'

A little way ahead I could see a tall white war memorial with a wreath on it. Three young guys, not older than fifteen, were hanging around by it, smoking. One of them was in the process of very purposefully stubbing his cigarette out on the memorial. Mark shook his head and strode towards them. I stood still momentarily, confused, before hurrying after him.

'Oi!' he called.

The three lads got up, zeroed in on him, sized him up. It was almost animalistic.

'Shouldn't you be in school?' said Mark.

'You fuckin' what?' said the boy who'd just stubbed his fag out.

'I *said* you should be in school.'

'It's half term,' the first boy sneered, even though I was pretty sure it definitely wasn't. 'And who the fuck are you?'

'Yeah, who the fuck are you?' said one of the others.

Mark rolled up his sleeves. 'I'm the guy who's going to administer you young scallywags a sound thrashing for desecrating a monument to our fallen comrades.'

What the hell are you doing? I thought.

What the fuck *are you doing?*

What the actual literal fuck *are you DOING?*

'Who's that?' said the third boy in a seriously nasal whine, nodding towards me. 'Bring your big sister along, did ya? Fuckin' pussyole.'

Little *shit*.

Although I suppose it could have been worse. He could have said 'your mum'.

I'd also never heard a word as defiantly urban as 'pussyole' spoken with a pronounced rural twang.

It didn't really work.

The three lads ran towards us. Mark got the first punch in, sending one of them to the ground moaning. The other two jumped on him.

Bollocks.

There was nothing for it.

I dived in.

Ten minutes later Mark was leaning against the war memorial while I cleaned him up with a bottle of spring water and some tissues. I hadn't got off too badly, as the three lads hadn't really wanted to fight me properly – the last vestige of chivalry, perhaps – and had made a run for it when I'd taken out my phone and made a show of dialling 999. Mark had some rather nice bruises and a bloody nose, although he was still smiling.

'What the *hell* did you do that for?' I said.

'Thought it would be fun.'

'Fun? *Fun*? Since when do you fight for fun? Since when do you even know how to throw a punch? Mr Most-Philosophical-Pragmatic-Pacifist who ever walked the Earth? Hold that there.' He held a thick clump of blood-soaked tissue to his nose. 'Keep your head back.'

'Dunno what came over me, really.' His voice was comically nasal, although barely more so than that of the kid who'd made the sister comment.

'It wasn't that you were being honourable then? All that stuff about desecrating the memorial?'

'Well, that *was* a bad thing they did.'

I had to laugh. 'Mark . . . just tell me. Is this something

123

you're going to be doing often? Just so I know. We were lucky, they were country lads. Fairly harmless. City lads carry knives. The sort of knives that make Crocodile Dundee do a little bit of wee. Some of them have Uzis. Grenades. Bazookas.'

'I don't think I'll do it again. I got *owned*, bro.' He chuckled.

'That you did.'

'You weren't much help, either.'

'Hey! If I hadn't taken my phone out . . .'

'Oh yeah, I forgot about that. Thanks. You big girl.'

'I didn't just get demolished by three children. *You're* a big girl.' Wow. Well done, Vanessa. Impeccable feminism there.

'You're right, I am.' His grin subsided slightly. 'Weird. I really don't know what came over me.'

'Well, just try to keep it in check, please. Has the bleeding stopped?'

'Yeah.'

For a second we held each other's eyes, our heads just a bit too close together, but I snapped out of it quickly and stood up. 'You don't look too bad. Won't attract too much attention. Come on. I need a drink.'

We sat in the grotty village pub's tiny beer garden, me with a Drambuie and Mark with a pint of lager. I'd been expecting strange looks from people, but apparently we didn't look as conspicuous as I thought we did.

Mark stared at me as he sipped his pint. 'What?' I asked.

'Were you happy?'

'When?'

'Before.'

'What, when I had to deal with the fact that my best friend

had vanished into thin air? Not really.' *Tactful,* I thought. *Excellent diplomatic skills. I'm sure the U.N will be on the blower any day now.*

Mark took it well though, laughing wryly. 'No . . . that's not what I meant. I'm sure it was hard. For a long time. But . . . there was a point when you were OK. When you had a new life.'

'Yes.'

'And were you happy?'

I slugged back the last of my drink. 'I don't really want to have this conversation.'

'OK. Sorry.' He downed his pint. 'Let's go to the sea.'

'The sea?'

'Yeah. You know where.'

'I don't know if that's a good idea.'

'So? When did we ever care if something was a good idea?'

'Also, from a purely practical point of view, it's really far away.'

'OK. That's a fair point. Maybe we shouldn't go now. But soon?'

'Maybe.'

He stood up. 'Shall we carry on?'

'Mark . . . where are we going?'

'I don't know. I thought that was the point. We're just *going.*'

I nodded and made myself smile. Made myself feel what I'd been feeling earlier. It wasn't as hard as part of me wanted it to be.

We stood outside the pub and Mark tossed a coin, which I caught, slapping it down on my palm with the appropriate enthusiasm. 'Right.'

So we went right. We walked through unfolding miles of luminous countryside, the smells of blossom, cut grass and pure *warmth* taking me rushing back once again to old summers, some that I had shared with Mark and some from many years before, back when I was a clumsy child in dungarees, the immortal summer holidays of childhood, day after day of playing in the sun. It made me feel so *light*, so light that my grown-up thoughts of getting a train back, of how I shouldn't have switched off my phone because of Pauline and Stuart, of money, of jobs, of how irresponsible, if delicious, this whole thing was, all just floated free. They stayed tethered, still orbiting, but lighter and far away, like a bunch of balloons I had tied to my belt. Every now and then I heard them bumping together, but I could no longer feel their weight.

We cut across fields and walked along the banks of rivers, skimming stones, and sat on low boughs and smoked cigarettes, talking in the old nonsensical blurts, consciousnesses streaming. Whenever we'd done this as teenagers, even when we'd hitch-hiked to the middle of nowhere and wandered from there, I'd never once felt lost, although I'd rarely had a clue where we were. I felt the same today.

It made me wonder why we choose to move to unfamiliar places and do things we don't like.

'Weird about those lightbulbs last night,' said Mark.

We were leaning against a gate by the side of the road, watching a field of lazy, meandering cattle. I've always found cattle quite interesting to watch. The fact that they're so big but do so little. It always seems like there's more going on in their heads than they let on. I knew that was most likely bollocks and that they were probably completely vacant, but it gave me a giggle to think about them having secret intellectual lives.

Those lightbulbs . . .

Now I could just hear the lightbulbs popping.

See the terrified face of the other Vanessa in the mirror.

'Mm,' I said. 'Weird.'

Mark looked at me slyly. He had his way-ahead-of-you eyes in. 'What did you scream at?'

'A spider. I told you.'

'Oh yeah, of course. But you lied about that.'

I didn't look at him. I wanted to tell him, but I knew what he'd do. He'd blame it all on himself. He'd feel even guiltier for reappearing than I knew he already did, no matter how well he hid it. 'Mm,' I said again.

'So what was it?'

'You're not the only weird thing to happen lately.'

'I know. Didn't you say the other one was your mum being bright and chirpy?'

I laughed. 'Other things too.'

'Weirder than me?'

'You're definitely the weirdest. But not the only thing.'

'You're not going to tell me, are you?'

'Probably not.'

Mark shrugged. 'Fair enough. I know you'd tell me if I needed to know. So I guess I don't need to.'

'Reverse psychology and emotional blackmail in one. Impressive.'

'Am I to glean from that that you think maybe I *do* need to know, but you're worried about telling me?'

Once again I found it hard to believe how young he was. When he spoke like that, it was like he was older. Older than he'd felt when we were the same age. Older even than I was now.

'I will tell you,' I said. 'Just not yet. I need to sort it out in my head first.'

'OK. That's acceptable.'

'Very magnanimous of you. Let's get going, shall we?'

We kept walking and I ventured something. 'On the train, when you were saying about your dream. The sea dream.'

'Yeah?'

'Did . . . did anything funny happen while you were speaking? Like, funny in your brain?'

'That's not a very strange question at all.'

'It's the sort of question you would ask. Just more clumsily phrased.'

'Fair point.' He stroked his chin. 'Not . . . not exactly. I just felt like I wasn't there for a bit. Deep thought, that's all. Why? Did something funny happen in *your* brain?'

'It was like I wasn't there for a *long* bit.'

'Must be my masterful talking skills.'

'I don't remember you being this glib.'

'Must be a side effect of time travel.'

'Don't remember your comebacks being so snappy either.'

'Must be how snappy my comebacks are.'

'Eh?'

'You heard me.'

'OK, whatever.' I laughed. 'So is that your number one theory? Time travel?'

He shrugged. 'It's not really an explanation, is it? I think it's fairly obvious that I did travel through time.'

'Oh yes. Abundantly.'

'So "travelling through time" is the event. Any theory I have would be explaining *how* I travelled through time.'

'Alright, Captain Pedantic.'

We walked quietly for a minute. 'Magic, maybe?' said Mark.

'Eh?'

'The cause. Magic? Or a science experiment gone wrong?'

'Yeah, maybe someone in town was testing a time machine and they accidentally used it on you.'

Mark nodded. 'Very possibly. Who in our town do you think could have constructed such a machine?'

'There's like *soooo* many candidates.'

'Mr Barber?'

'Likely. What better way to unwind from standing behind the bar boring people to death than going all Doc Brown in one's shed?'

'Except I can't imagine Mr Barber being able to summon up 1.21 gigawatts of anything.'

'Agreed. So . . . time machine accident. What was the other thing you said? Magic? Possible suspects?'

'Mad Dog Woman always had a whiff of witch about her.' Mark started rolling another cigarette.

'I can't imagine her having time for witchcraft, what with cooing over all those malnourished canines.'

'Hmm. Yeah. Well, alternatively, there's a couple of teachers who'd fit in pretty well at Hogwarts.'

'You couldn't possibly be talking about Mr Davidson?'

Mark popped his freshly rolled fag into his mouth and snapped his fingers. 'I could possibly. Why?'

'Dumbledore beard. Gandalf voice. Eight feet tall, at a conservative estimate. Fond of riddles.'

'Four excellent reasons. But you missed out the fact that he always smelled of herbs of some kind.'

'I figured he got stoned before school.'

'Makes sense. How else would a remotely civilised person get through a day at that hell dump?'

'And the other one . . .' I racked my brains. There were a good few warty old battleaxes at our school who I could imagine turning someone into frogspawn if they misbehaved. 'Hillington?'

'Whyever would you pick her?'

'Well, I can't think of a better model for an evil old witch.'

'Maybe it was a *good* witch, though.'

'Well if *good* witches are in the running, you need to be more specific with your fucking *criteria*, mate.'

'OK, OK, OK. Mrs Hillington as an evil witch. Fifty points to Gryffindor.'

'Um, I ain't no Gryffindor, fool. The do-gooding jocks of the wizarding world. Fuck Gryffindor.'

'Fine. Ravenclaw.'

'*Ravenclaw?* Do I really look like I walk around with a Nimbus Two Thousand rammed up my arse 24/7? I am mortally offended that you would put me in with that shower. Sort it out, mate.'

'Good one, I see what you did there. So . . . what? Hufflepuff?'

'All the way.'

'Seriously?'

'Serious Black, mate. They've had a bit of a critical reappraisal since you've been gone. Basically the other three houses can get knotted, Hufflepuff 'til I die.'

'Man. The world got weird.'

I patted him on the shoulder. 'Sorry to be the bearer of bad news. So, we've covered magic and time machine explosions as possible explanations. Anything else?'

'Aliens? Not to point fingers, but this has Tralfamadore written all over it.'

I looked at him blankly.

'Tralfamadore?' he said again, over-enunciating every syllable.

'Saying a word I don't understand again but slower doesn't help me understand it.'

'Did you not read *Slaughterhouse Five*?'

'Nope. Sorry.'

He sighed and shook his head. 'Philistine.'

'Phyllis who?'

'Shut up.'

'Sorry. Seems that even with an extra seven years' preparation time, I'm still your intellectual inferior.'

'So it goes.'

We'd reached a long stretch of road with thick expanses of trees on either side. I nudged him in the ribs. 'Phyllis who?'

'Shut *up*,' he said, pretending to lose his temper and quickening his pace so he was a couple of feet ahead of me.

'Suit yourself.' I slowed down so he was more than a couple of feet ahead of me and walked by myself for a minute, smiling, full up with deliciously stupid banter. And peace. All I could feel was peace, all I could hear was ambient rustling, the occasional soft whirr of bird . . .

Mark seemed to be more ahead of me than I'd thought. It felt like he was getting further away, but the distance between us wasn't really increasing. I cocked my head curiously, but didn't bother to hurry. Too peaceful.

It must have been getting near autumn, because the trees that lined the road were starting to rust. Their leaves shimmered from light and dark greens to golds, delicate yellows, coppers and scarlets, finally wrinkling into dead browns. One by one, with a collective sigh that I felt ripple through my whole being, they detached themselves from their branches and became a dry, gentle rain, fluttering down to the road, whispering to one another. I tried to call to Mark. I didn't want him to miss this sight.

I didn't . . .

I didn't want to see it alone?

Wait . . . autumn?

It's May . . .

I tried to call but my voice wouldn't come.

I blinked.

He was a foot away, with his back to me, frozen to the spot.

I blinked.

We were knee-deep in dead leaves. The trees were bending, creaking, becoming dull and grey. Frosting over.

I blinked.

The water was coming. The sea, the whole sea, silent, miles away but rushing faster than I could think, rushing towards us, filling the road, filling the horizon. The trees began to fall, as weak and lightweight as papier maché.

Someone tapped me on the shoulder and I turned around, quite calmly.

It was me.

Me, all pale.

Black hair.

'Green jacket,' she said.

Then the sea hit me.

I opened my eyes. Jumped up. Looked around. The trees were green. Alive. There was no water. No extra me. I' d been on my hands and knees . . .

'Mark?'

Coughing. I turned and saw Mark doubled over in the middle of the road, coughing his guts up, coughing so hard I felt it burn.

'Mark!' I ran to him. His whole body was convulsing with the violence of the coughs. I stood helplessly and watched his mouth expel one, two, three, four feathers and a spray of saliva. The feathers floated to the ground, as gracefully as the dead leaves, and Mark fell to his knees, not so gracefully. He was shaking. I knelt and put an arm around his shoulders and he looked up at me, his eyes wet with pain and fright.

'What's wrong with me?' he whispered. I'd never heard him sound more like a child. He fell into my arms and I held him, just us, in the middle of the road. Luckily no cars came. I looked at the feathers on the ground. Pure white, with intricate, spidery blue patterns. They were beautiful, but they made me sad. A strange sadness. Deep and old, like I'd not felt since . . .

Since the dream I couldn't remember.

Since the writing that I couldn't understand.

Since I'd starting crying at the cinema, for no reason.

Since a life that felt like someone else's.

Since before Mark . . .

At that moment I decided. I needed to take him to his father. He was my friend, but he was a child. And I was a grown-up. I had to look after him. I had to stop paying attention to stupid dreams and weird feelings. I had to be a real person. I had no business on this flight of fancy.

This wasn't me anymore.

'Come on,' I said, helping him to his feet. 'We're getting a train.'

He didn't answer, just nodded dully, and I took his hand and we started to walk again. No coin. All I could think was *train*.

And *green jacket*.

CHAPTER TWELVE

WE HAD TO wait an hour for the first train and there were two more after that. It was going to cost a lot. The first was cramped and rattling and smelled like old sandwich, and Mark just stared silently out of the window while I fidgeted, not knowing what to say. My head was full, bursting, but there was a weird calmness there as as well, like a frenzied battle taking place on the surface of a still, tranquil sea. The two things didn't seem as though they should have been able to co-exist.

It was because I had someone to look after. As difficult as it was to see Mark like this, it's always easier to deal with other people's problems than your own. I'd kept the feathers in my bag and resisted the urge to take them out and study them.

At least now we knew where they'd come from.

Was it something to do with his journey? A consequence of moving from the past to now? If that was even what had happened?

There was no reason to expect that his father would know anything. But I couldn't indulge my whims any longer. Mark was not right. And Mr Matthews needed to see that he was alive. I switched my phone on, feeling ashamed for getting so caught up in childish adventuring, to find two missed calls, a text from Alice and a text from Stuart. Alice was checking that I was OK and asking when I'd be back. Stuart was also checking whether I was all right. Then he'd called a few hours later. I sent them brief replies with no real information, filling the rest of the available space with apologies. I didn't feel capable of addressing even the simplest of my old life's concerns.

We should have arrived at our destination already so I texted Pauline too, a pretty nonchalant text about delays and signal failures. Pretty far behind schedule but everything's OK, nothing to worry about, the journey continues. Easy. Much better than calling. That must be why text messaging was invented. To lie more convincingly.

I'd never been a very good liar.

'Are you ever gonna tell Mark?'

'What?' I say, absently. *I'm concentrating on threading various ribbons and other bits of shiny crap into Laura's grubby dreadlocks. It's fiddly.*

'You know what.'

'Don't think I do.'

'You're such a shit liar.'

'Honestly, I have no idea what you're talking about.'

'Vans, come on. You are in love with Mark.'

'I'm what.'

'You're in love with him! Properly. Proper job love. Hard love.'

I stop threading. 'I really don't think I am.'

'He's in love with you too, to be fair.'

'How the fuck can you tell? He ain't exactly Mr Emotional.'

'Yeah, fair play. But how could he not be in love with you? You're . . . I dunno, you're just made for each other.'

'We're best friends. We have been for years. I love him. I'm not in love with him.'

'You're such a fucking liar.'

'Shut it.' I go back to wrapping purple and red ribbons around a particularly thick, greasy dread in a double helix. 'Your hair is disgusting.'

'You and Mark are disgusting. Sometimes I catch you looking at each other. Not at the same time. But glancing. The passion! Seriously, it makes me horny just looking at you.'

'You're filth.'

'Tell me something I don't know, mate.'

'OK. We all know that you and Twig did a sex at the last Deep Forest rave.'

Laura pauses for quite a long time. 'OK. Fair dos. I didn't know that you knew that. I thought we were pretty sly about it.'

'Sly until you started gasping. I'd know that gasp anywhere. I've slept in far too many tents that were adjacent to yours. Or adjacent sleeping bags in the same tent . . .'

'Hey, that was just the once and I have said sorry like fifty thousand times. Anyway, stop changing the subject from your in-loveness to my boring sex life. We always talk about my boring sex life. Never your in-loveness.'

'Is that supposed to be a pun?'

'What? No.' Then the penny drops and she starts giggling. Laura's giggle really is the cutest giggle that ever there was.

'I'm not in love with Mark,' I say.

'You can lie to yourself,' she says, still giggling, 'but not to me.'

Mark started coughing again, loud and harsh, his eyes screwed shut, and I tried to reassure him while simultaneously looking around to make sure nobody was paying too much attention to us. Nobody was, luckily, because another feather burst from Mark's mouth and floated to the floor. The coughing abruptly subsided.

Mark looked at me, face red, eyes streaming. 'Do you think it's the . . . it's a side-effect? Of me being here?'

'I don't know. I . . . I feel like I should take you to a hospital, but that would mean them knowing who you are. And maybe finding out what's happened. And that means police and all sorts . . . so I'm taking you to your dad. He needs to be the first to know.'

Mark nodded slowly.

'I'm sorry,' I said. 'We should have gone already . . .'

'No.' He turned back to the window. 'I liked our little adventure.'

I sat back in my seat and watched him. There was something about his face, something different.

Impossible . . .

It had only been a few hours since the fight at the war memorial, but the cuts and bruises on his face were already much less pronounced, like days had passed, softening them into indistinct sketches.

I made myself not stare at him and looked around the compartment instead, hoping maybe some people-watching would take my mind off real things. Old ladies. Young man. Girls. Old man. Adults. Normal people. And . . .

Me.

Staring back at me from the other end of the train.

I jumped.

Blinked.

It wasn't me. It was a different girl, a stranger, much younger, leaning against the baggage rack, chewing gum, fiddling with her purplish-blonde hair.

Pull yourself together, Vanessa.

I looked at Mark again. He looked so appallingly vulnerable.

'Dan is nothing. He's nothing. You're so, so far above him.'

I can't answer.

I want him to kiss me.

But I know he won't.

So I'm not worried about looking sexy or cool. I just turn around and sob into his chest, sob for being so easily led, for being made an idiot of, for sleeping with the only absolute honest-to-god dickhead in our group. Sob for Hannah's look when she realised I knew.

Sob because now everyone will be talking about it.

Because I'm the one this will stick to.

Because even though Mark should have lost all respect for me, I know he hasn't.

After a while, I don't want to cry anymore. The fact that the booze has worn off a bit helps. And the cuddle, of course. Mark doesn't speak, doesn't offer platitudes, he just lets the hug do the talking. Lets me start to feel better in my own time.

I look up at him and smile. 'Ugh. Bet you think I'm a wet rag.'

He smiles. 'Well. I can't imagine why you're getting so worked up over a cast-iron dong like Dan. But, you know. Each to their own.'

I laugh and he takes my hand. 'Let's go for a walk.'

We walk. Erin's house is about a mile out of town, a gnarly little wizard's cottage halfway up a hill, and it doesn't take long to get to the top. There are fields of silent, sleeping sheep on either side of the narrow lane, and above us a Disney sky, with a billion stars fresh from a merchant's pocket. Some of them seem to tremble. Most of them are dead. That thought boggles my mind at the best of times so I don't think about it. We just stand there, in the middle of the road, staring up.

'Makes you feel tiny, doesn't it?' says Mark.

'Don't start.'

'What do you mean?'

'The "we're actually so insignificant" thing. I'm still way too drunk for that.'

'I don't know why people find it so off-putting. It always makes me feel better.'

'How?'

'Well, imagine. All the awful things there are on Earth, global warming and famine and war and disease and bandits burning down villages and raping and killing everybody who lives there . . .'

'This makes you feel better?'

'I'm not finished.'

'Sorry.'

'And corruption in politics, and everything else that makes you miserable or furious, and then the smaller things, like injustice at school and all the dickhead Dans in the world and what you're feeling now. All of that stuff, from the biggest to the smallest, what is it to that star up there?' He pointed at one particularly bright one. 'It's nothing. It's just little things happening. I'm not saying our stuff doesn't matter. I'm just saying that, in the scheme of things, if you compare it to that star up there, or a black hole billions of miles away, or the orbit of an asteroid, or . . . I don't know, the biological processes that make up a plant, or a forest, or the way the moon's gravity affects the tides, or the frequency of whale song, or the rings of Saturn, or the fact that Jupiter has one storm, just one storm, that's

bigger than about five Earths and has been raging for hundreds of years . . . all that . . . it doesn't make me feel insignificant. It just kind of puts things in perspective. The universe just gets on with it. So we should try to, as well.'

I don't know if it's the wisdom or the poetry that makes me feel better. Probably the poetry, because sometimes Mark's wisdom only sounds like wisdom. But it doesn't matter, because I do feel better. And I take his hand.

'Think about the human eye,' he continues, still staring fixedly at the sky. 'How complex it is. The human brain. How ridiculously complex that is. The Earth, the moon and the sun, their orbits. How cosmically insane all that is. The fact that it all just happened by chance, because of little accidents of biology and physics and chemistry, the fact that it's all here, it all found its own way, without even knowing it needed to. Think about all that. How absolutely mind-pummellingly beautifully fucked up that is. And tell me that Dan is still an eighth, an eightieth, an eight hundred billionth as important to you as he was a few minutes ago.'

It probably won't last, but right now, at this precise second, I feel better. I smile. 'I can't.'

'There you go. The universe doesn't give two shits about Dan. Why should you?'

I almost tell him I love him there and then.

But luckily I'm not quite drunk enough.

We got off the second train on another empty, godforsaken platform in the middle of nowhere. It was still sunny but I felt cold. And hungry. Unfortunately there wasn't even a vending machine, so we sat and stared dumbly at the screen that showed the departures. Our train was due in fifteen minutes, or in train station time, eight hours.

Mark seemed to be staring through the screen, rather than at it, so I gave him a prod. 'Penny for 'em?'

'Sorry?'

'Your thoughts.'

'What about them?'

'I just . . . never mind.'

He held my gaze for a second, then looked at the ground. We waited in silence, and the train arrived and we boarded in silence, and the forty-minute journey passed, again in silence. Finally we stepped off the train at Corford and headed through the tiny, picturesque station into the street.

I called up the directions I'd saved on my phone. Mark's dad lived about ten minutes from here. We walked, still not speaking, and I marvelled at how normal everything looked, people just doing things, the same things they did every day, errands and routines and appointments. The fact that every person I looked at so briefly, before instantly forgetting them, had a whole life stretching back through time, a whole life that had got them to this point, and then a whole life stretching forward, taking them wherever else they were going. And everyone they saw and forgot did as well. The thought of all those intersecting lines made me feel dizzy and a little sick and I forgot about what was happening for a bit, mechanically following directions, thinking cosmic thoughts.

It didn't feel like ten minutes had passed, but suddenly we were standing about fifty feet from the house. I looked at Mark. 'Are you ready for this?'

He nodded. He looked ill. I took his hand. 'I'll be with you the whole time.'

What might have been a smile passed beneath the surface

of his face for a fraction of a second.

We walked again.

We reached the end of Mr Matthews' garden.

Mark was gripping my hand so tightly that it hurt.

I felt like my heart was going to just launch itself out of my chest. Surely it couldn't be healthy for your heart to beat that hard.

The garden was small and plain. Tidy but not loved. There was a light on inside the house.

'Do you want to knock or shall I?' I asked.

Mark didn't answer.

I knocked, thinking about all the dramatic door-openings that had been happening recently.

It was all getting a bit silly.

Mr Matthews opened the door and blinked. 'Vanessa? What . . .'

His eyes moved past me.

They fell on Mark.

They got bigger.

'Hi Dad,' said Mark.

'*Mark?*' The ghost of a whisper. 'It . . . can't . . .'

'It is,' I said.

The silence that followed, in which Mark and his father just stared at each other, dark matter flying between them, was interminable. The expression on Mr Matthews' face was uncomprehending. Mark just looked lost. Eventually, because somebody had to do something, I asked if we could come in.

'What?' Mr Matthews asked. He seemed to have diminished in size since he'd opened the door.

'Please?' I said again.

He nodded and stepped aside so we could come past him.

I kept hold of Mark's hand. There was no hug. Mr Matthews made no motion towards his son. He closed the door behind us and led us into the kitchen and Mark and I sat down. Mr Matthews hovered by the door.

'Do you want to sit down?' I asked. It seemed silly inviting someone to sit down in their own house, but he nodded. He almost seemed grateful as he took a seat opposite Mark, like having somebody else suggesting things made this all easier.

He stared at his son. Stared and stared. Tears started to come. He stood up again and went to the window, keeping his back to us. We waited. He turned and sat down again. More tears. I looked at Mark and didn't think his face had ever been this opaque. I reached under the table to find his hand but couldn't, and he didn't offer it.

So I did the only thing I could think of. 'Tea?'

Nobody said yes, but nobody said no, either, so I put the kettle on. The whistling slowly filled the room and just as the kettle clicked off, Mark spoke.

'Please say something.'

Mr Matthews nodded as though he was trying out nodding for the first time. 'When . . . where . . .'

'I don't know,' said Mark. 'The day I . . . vanished . . . I'd been with Vanessa. I was on my way home. I passed out. And I woke up in the same place . . . but it was last week. Last Friday. It was like I just went to sleep and woke up seven years later.'

Mr Matthews looked pained, like it was too much for his brain. I knew how he felt. 'How?' he said.

'I don't know,' said Mark. 'I . . .' Words failed him and he looked down at the table. Mr Matthews was staring intently at his son, but . . . not. He was almost looking *through* him.

And there was no sign of happiness on his face. It had been so warm outside, but it was freezing in here.

I made three cups of tea. Mr Matthews took his, said thank you and put it down, clearly with no intention of drinking it. Mark sipped his. I just held mine, glad of something hot. Mr Matthews stood up and looked out of the window again and I looked at Mark, who just shook his head. I knew what the movement meant. It meant *we shouldn't have come.* I tried to communicate comfort, but only managed a simpering smile. I tried to say *just give him time, he's in shock,* but think I just made my eyes a bit wonky.

Mark stood up. 'We should go.'

Mr Matthews turned so abruptly that we both jumped. 'No. Don't.'

I frowned. The words sounded good on paper, but the way he said them . . . it wasn't a plea. It wasn't that he was upset that we might go. It wasn't that he wanted us to stay.

Something was starting to feel very wrong.

I couldn't help but recall the dream I'd had on the train. Or the memory. Or whatever it was. Suddenly I was glad that we hadn't shown Mr Matthews the feathers as I'd planned.

Suddenly I was scared.

'I need to . . . I need a minute,' he said. 'Please. Wait here.'

He left the kitchen and disappeared down a hall. Mark was shaking his head. 'This is wrong,' he said.

'I know. Shall we just—'

'Hold on.' Mark got up and followed his father down the hall, moving swiftly and silently. I craned my neck to see. He waited at the end of the hallway with his ear to a closed door, listening for perhaps twenty seconds. Then he ran back and straight past me. 'Come on. *Now.*'

I followed him out of the house, down the path to the road, adrenaline rising. He didn't stop, didn't look behind, not even to see if I was there. As soon as he reached the road he broke into a proper run, back the way we'd come.

Oh God, I thought. *What did he hear?*

I ran after him, chancing a look back through the kitchen window. Mr Matthews was there, looking out, and we made eye contact. Something burned inside me. He was shouting, gesturing for us to come back.

Nope.

I looked away and ran after Mark, catching up with some difficulty. So damn unfit. I could hear his father's voice now, agitated, angry, yelling for us to stop, stop now, we had to stop . . .

Mark ducked down a side road and I followed. Was this the way we'd come? I was too freaked out to remember. I just hoped that his sense of direction was working. We ran and ran, ran until I thought my chest was going to cave in, and finally, when I physically couldn't run anymore, I chanced another look back. I wasn't sure if Mr Matthews had given chase, but if he had, it looked like we'd lost him.

'Don't stop!' called Mark.

'I have to,' I gasped. 'I can't . . . why are we . . .'

'We need to get on a train,' said Mark. 'Any train. It doesn't matter. We need to be *gone* from here. Come *on.*' He grabbed my hand and dragged me and somehow I managed to run, despite every molecule of my body howling that I was going to pass out.

Back to the train station, up the steps. The barriers were open, thank fuck, and there was a train that was going vaguely in the right direction, thank *fucking* fuck. We jumped on and collapsed into seats and moments later the train pulled away. I felt like I was going to die, I was gasping so hard, and it was weirdly gratifying to see that Mark wasn't doing much better. Didn't seem fair for a heavy smoker to be fitter than me.

It was a good minute or two before either of us was able to speak, and we were immediately interrupted by a busybody ticket lady. I told her where we were going and she told me what we needed to do and quoted me a price that would have made me have a fit of some kind, had I not been absolutely terrified already. I bought our tickets and she buggered off. Mark was staring out of the window.

'What did you hear?' I asked.

'He was on the phone.' He sounded so calm again. 'He was asking for someone. Mr . . . something beginning with T. Turner, maybe?'

'Yes?'

'Then this Mr Turner, or whatever, must have come on the line. My dad said something like, "you said to call if my son ever came back". Then there was a pause. And Dad said I was there at his house, with a girl called Vanessa, an old friend. He paused again. Then he said "no . . . I know it's not my son". Then he said "when are you coming". Then I ran.'

I felt cold again. My hand found Mark's and this time he took it gladly. We both squeezed until I thought our fingers might break, but we didn't stop. 'What do we do now?' I said, not really to Mark, not really to anyone. Which was just as well, really, because nobody answered.

We were on the second train when Mark said, 'Maybe we shouldn't go back to Pauline's.'

'You think?'

'If he's sent someone after us, it's not going to be too hard to work out where we'll go. And we don't want to put her in danger.'

'Danger.' I shook my head. 'Danger from what? What's *happening*? Why would—'

'He doesn't think it's me,' said Mark. 'That's all. You can't really blame him, can you? Maybe he went nuts when I disappeared. He lost my mum. Losing me as well . . . maybe it was too much.'

Mark never spoke about his mum. All I knew was that she had left when he was still very young. His dad had never told him anything more than that.

'But who would he have sent after us?' I said. 'This Mr Turner, or whatever he's called. Police, maybe?'

'No,' said Mark. '"You said to call if he ever came back". "I know it's not my son". That wasn't the police.'

It's not my son.

The feathers.

It all had to connect, surely?

I took out my phone. 'What are you doing?' asked Mark.

'I need to phone Pauline. Tell her. Warn her. Ask her what to do.'

'What if this Turner person can track phones? Listen in?'

'I don't think that's likely, but it won't make any difference anyway. If he's going to find Pauline he's going to find her. The least I can do is warn her.' I dialled and waited.

She answered after two rings. 'Vanessa?'

'Hi.'

'What's wrong?' She knew immediately.

'We found Mark's dad. He . . . he freaked out. He phoned somebody. I can't explain much now, I don't *know* much. But he phoned somebody and said "it's not my son". He's sending someone after us. We don't know who. But whoever they are, they might track me down to Llangoroth. They probably *definitely* will. To Mum. Probably to you. So I'm warning you.'

'Where are you now?'

'On a train. We're thinking . . . maybe we shouldn't come back?'

'You absolutely *should* come back here. We can look after the two of you. Work something out.'

'But—'

'I know you thought you'd call and say *we're putting you in danger, hide while we sort it out ourselves.* That's not what's going to happen. You're going to come back here and I'*m* going to sort it out. I don't care what terrifying bastard shows up at my door. You come back here right now, young lady.'

I almost burst into tears with relief. I can't describe how glad I was to hear something like that. 'OK. I think we get in at about ten.'

'I'll be waiting. How is Mark doing?'

'I don't know. See you later. Love you.'

'I love you too.'

I hung up. 'We're going home again.'

'Where's home?' asked Mark.

'Llangoroth, of course.'

He nodded.

But he didn't look like he believed it.

CHAPTER THIRTEEN

WE WERE ON the last train, forty-five minutes from home, and I was sick of the sight, smell and sound of the bastard things. It was getting dark and Mark and I hadn't spoken for what felt like hours, so I popped to the toilet and washed my face, just to have something to do. I stared down the plughole, watching the bubbles blink, trying not to think.

When I looked up, she was there. The other me, pale and black-haired and hollow-eyed, standing there in some impossible extended space behind me. I didn't jump. It wasn't the terrifying sight that it had been the last few times.

I wondered if that was a good thing or a bad thing.

'Hello,' I said.

She looked pained.

'What do you want?'

She tried to speak, but no sound came.

'Are you me?'

She managed a nod.

'Are you trying to warn me?'

Another nod.

'You were trying before, weren't you?'

Another nod.

'What's happening? Is it connected? You? Mark?'

She slumped back against the door, looking exhausted, like just being there took more effort than she could manage. She closed her eyes.

'Please,' I said. 'Tell me what's happening.'

She opened her eyes again and I gasped. They were bleeding. And not just her eyes: her nose too, and her ears, thick streams of dark blood nearly as black as her hair, such an intense contrast with her deathly white skin that it made me feel sick, even though I wasn't usually squeamish about blood. Her legs gave out from under her and she collapsed to the floor. I turned slowly around.

She was gone.

I looked down at my hands. They were shaking. But it wasn't the sight of her, of the blood trickling from her eyes . . . *my* eyes. Those details were like a bad dream, initially terrifying but quickly dulled by reality.

No, I was worried about the warning.

That she'd been warning me all along.

That somehow she knew what was going to happen.

Pauline was waiting for us on the dark platform and I ran to her and let her hug me, allowing myself to feel momentarily better. Mark hung back. I didn't go so far as to let myself cry, but I breathed deeply from within the safety of the hug, drinking in her familiarity, her homeliness. When we broke apart she beckoned Mark and hugged him too. He hugged her back and I was glad.

She drove us home, where there was cold curry waiting for us. We blasted it in the microwave and took it to the living room and Pauline insisted on putting blankets over us, like we were recovering from flu.

'Mark,' I said, between greedy, coconut-sweet mouthfuls. 'I'm going to tell Paulie what happened. You're OK with that?'

He nodded and I explained. I stitched a few white lies over

our adventure – a train delay had necessitated a little wander around, which had then led to Mark's coughing fit. Then we'd gone and seen his dad. And although I wanted to recount this awful meeting in minute detail, every word and expression, every loom of furniture somehow made sentient and threatening by the poisonous atmosphere, I didn't, for Mark's sake. I kept glancing at him as I told the story, wondering how he was, how he *really* was, whether the event, the memory and the re-telling – sanitised as it was – cut as much as I thought they did. He didn't let anything slip. Just ate his curry slowly, evenly-spaced mouthfuls to avoid indigestion, a habit that had annoyed me when we were younger because I'd always eaten like someone was about to swoop in and steal my food, and I hated watching somebody else eat when I'd finished.

'Are you sure the name was Turner?' asked Pauline.

'Pretty sure,' said Mark. 'Eighty per cent.'

'And you're sure it wasn't the police?'

'Didn't sound like it. The things he said . . . he wouldn't have said that to the police.'

'What do we do?' I asked. 'If he's sent someone after us . . .'

'After *me*,' said Mark, quietly.

'After *us*. I was right there with you. He said my name on the phone.'

'We should never have gone.'

'Well, we did,' I said, unnecessarily harshly. 'So we have to decide what to do about it. It's not going to take this Turner person long to track us down here.'

'You don't remember anyone called Turner?' said Pauline. 'Anybody from before you vanished? A friend of your father's, maybe?'

'No,' said Mark. 'Nobody.'

'Well,' said Pauline. 'I'm just theorising. But . . . when you disappeared, and the police weren't able to find anything, maybe somebody else heard about it. Somebody working alone, or in a group, who has knowledge of bizarre mysteries. They may have approached your father, told him about similar events, or possible explanations that the police wouldn't have considered. Told him to contact them if he heard anything, or if you re-appeared.'

'Makes sense,' said Mark.

'I don't get it,' I said. 'If your dad was so worried when you disappeared, so upset, that he would talk to these kinds of people . . . I mean, I *imagine* that these kinds of people would be on the weird side of life . . . surely, once you re-appeared, he'd just be overjoyed that you'd come back? He wouldn't—'

'I look exactly the same,' said Mark. '*Exactly* the same. As if I never left. That's . . . that's got to be it. They must have told him something, or he saw something . . .'

For a second I had a flash. The memory of Mark's dad, a memory I couldn't place, that couldn't possibly be mine. Sitting with his back to me, or whoever I was inhabiting. Rising, eyes so full of fury and pain that it hurt to look into them. A handful of feathers in my face.

'Mark,' I said. 'The feathers.'

'I don't want to talk about them.'

'We *need* to talk about them. I'm sorry, but they must be connected somehow.'

'That had occurred to me.' His voice had taken on an unfamiliar sharpness. 'I've been thinking about it the whole time. But at the moment, I think whoever's chasing me is the priority.'

Us, I thought, although I didn't say it. 'Fine. So we have

two choices. We wait for them to find us and hope they're coming for a good reason. Or we run and try to find out who they are *before* they find us.'

'You're not running,' said Pauline. 'You're staying with me. I'm going to look after you.'

'Pauline,' said Mark, 'you can't.'

'What do you mean I—'

'I mean, if this person wants to hurt me, then whoever's standing between me and them is going to get hurt too. I'm not letting that happen.'

'We don't even *know* if they want to hurt you!' said Pauline. 'We know *nothing*!'

'I heard enough,' said Mark. 'Not risking it.'

'So we run,' I said. 'We can go to my flat in London.' Which wouldn't be awkward at all . . .

'They'll find us there,' said Mark. 'If they can find us here, they'll find us there.'

'We could go to the police,' said Pauline.

I shook my head. 'That'll just draw more attention to us.'

'But if we explain exactly what's happened—'

'They'll take Mark away,' I said. 'Or send him back to his father.'

'I'm sixteen,' said Mark. 'I can leave home and live with who I want. They can't legally send me back to Dad. But it's still going to throw up loads more complications. And for now there's just the one complication, which is . . . which . . . ugh . . .' He started to cough. It was gentle at first, but quickly deteriorated into a hideous, painful fit of retching. He slid off the sofa onto his knees.

'Get him some water!' I yelled, dropping down to the floor next to him. I held his shoulders, watching him expel feather after feather into a damp pile on the carpet. They were smaller than they had been . . . but now there was something else as well. On top of the coughing, he was moaning in pain, shuddering violently, and I could see something on his back, through his T-shirt. A rippling, irregular bulge, rising one minute, falling to nothing the next.

Pauline handed me the glass of water but I didn't take it. I just stared at Mark's back as the bulge re-appeared, shifting disgustingly, creating a damp patch on his T-shirt.

'My God,' Pauline whispered.

Mark was on his hands and knees now. He had stopped coughing but he was still moaning, quivering with the pain. 'Mark,' I said. 'Mark. I need you to take off your shirt.'

'My *back*,' he said, his voice a strangled gasp.

'I know, I know. Please, Mark, we need to take your shirt off.'

He nodded and raised his arms, wincing. I eased the shirt off as gently as I could . . .

Dropped it.

Jesus Christ . . .

The flesh around his shoulder blades was warping and twisting, the skin shiny with sweat. The blades themselves kept on extending outwards, far further than was natural, then receding, and there was a bubbling, asymmetrical lump between them that followed the same pattern, although when the shoulder blades went in it came out and when it went in the blades came out.

I looked at Pauline, who was aghast and helpless. All I could do was hold Mark around his waist, whispering that it was OK, although it wasn't OK and I didn't know what the hell to do, although . . . although . . .

Although the movements seemed to be slowing now. Yes, they were definitely slowing down. And Mark's moans were quieter, less desperate . . . until suddenly all the movement in his back stopped. The shoulder blades were where they were supposed to be, although the bulge between them was still there, a swelling about as broad as a handspan and about half as thick as a knuckle, sweaty and slightly purple around the edges, a clammy, awful bruise. I reached out and touched it gently. It felt just like normal flesh, not yielding to my touch, although Mark gasped as if it stung.

'Sorry!' I said. 'I'm sorry.' I helped him on with his shirt and sat him back on the sofa. He was panting with the aftermath of the pain, the exertion, the emotion.

'We need to take him to a hospital,' said Pauline.

'No,' he whispered. 'Please. Please . . .'

'Mark, there could be something seriously wrong with you. You need to see a doctor.'

'Do you know any doctors?' I asked. 'Anybody who would come?'

'I know nurses . . . but . . . Vanessa . . .'

'Please, Pauline,' said Mark. 'No nurses, no hospital. Not yet. I just need to sleep. I need to sleep and I'll be OK tomorrow. And we'll . . . we'll work something out. But I need to sleep. If it's worse tomorrow . . . then we'll go. I'll go to the hospital. But please. Let me sleep.' He could barely keep his eyes open and he was slurring his words.

I looked desperately at Pauline. She nodded reluctantly. 'All right. But—'

'Shit,' I said. 'What about . . . what if the guy comes in the night? This Turner person? Should we take Mark somewhere else?'

'He's too weak to go anywhere now,' said Pauline. 'We can hide him here. And if he does turn up . . . well, we'll see. If he knows what's good for him he'd better hop it.'

'And if he tries to break in?'

'Then I've got plenty of blunt, heavy objects whose acquaintance he can make.'

Thank fuck for Pauline.

We made a nest for Mark in the attic, hidden behind boxes of junk and piles of old jigsaw puzzles. He was asleep before we'd even finished tucking him in and I knelt for a minute, stroking his hair, my chest tight. It wasn't the most brilliant hiding place ever, but I was relying on Pauline being able to keep this Turner person out of the house. If she could do that, then we wouldn't have a problem. For the moment.

And if he tried to break in . . .

Then I will fucking kill him, I thought.

Pauline and I were far too stressed to sleep so we sat in the kitchen and drank herbal tea and smoked cigarettes and teased each other about not being smokers. We talked about Stuart, about Pauline's work, about what else I could maybe do now I'd quit the cinema, this and that. Like nothing had happened.

'You look exhausted,' said Pauline, after about an hour. 'You should go to bed.'

I shook my head.

'You won't be of any use to Mark if you can't keep your eyes open tomorrow.'

'I couldn't sleep. I'll just . . . I'll dream. I don't want to dream.'

'We *need* to dream. It keeps us sane.'

'Hmm.'

'There's something you're not telling me.' She came out with it so casually that I barely had time to raise my defences. I almost told her about the visions, there and then. The other me, frantic and bleeding. The memories that weren't mine. Everything. I felt like I *should* have told her . . .

But even though they weren't mine, they were *mine*.

Something I needed to work out alone.

And there was already too much to work out.

'Just stressing about money,' I said, which wasn't exactly a lie. 'I spent over a hundred quid on trains today.'

'Oh don't be silly,' said Pauline. '*I'll* help you out with that.'

I was halfway through a boilerplate 'you don't have to do that' deflection when someone knocked on the front door. Pauline and I both jumped and I started to get up, but she raised her hand and shook her head. She checked that the kitchen curtains were drawn, then went to the front door. I stood by the doorway, craning my neck so I could hear, using one hand to seek out the rolling pin I knew was in the drawer closest to me.

'Do you have any idea what time it is?' said Pauline. She had her formidable voice on. 'Who are you?'

'Pauline Cox?' A man's voice, English, soft.

'Who wants to know?'

'I'm looking for Mark Matthews. Would you please send him out?'

'I beg your pardon?'

'I know you're harbouring Mark Matthews. Please send him out.' Considering how quiet and measured the voice was, the implied threat made the hairs on my neck prickle.

'Mark Matthews disappeared seven years ago. Now if you don't mind—'

'I know that he has re-appeared. I know that he and your niece Vanessa visited Gareth Matthews this afternoon and that they returned here afterwards. So please don't waste my time.'

At this point I stepped into the hall and strode up to the front door, standing shoulder to shoulder with Pauline, trying to give it the big one. The man before us wasn't large, barely taller than me in fact, and had cropped blonde hair and small shark-like eyes. He was just standing there, nonchalant as you like, his hands hidden in the pockets of a green velvet jacket.

Green jacket . . .

'Mark's not here,' I said. 'And you'd better leave.'

The man, Turner or whatever, pursed his lips. My neck prickled again. 'I don't believe you,' he said. 'Send him out.'

'Who *are* you?' said Pauline

'My name is Lee Tourneaux.'

Tourneaux. Not Turner.

'And,' he said, 'the "boy" is my responsibility.'

'I heard those inverted commas,' I said. 'He *is* a boy.' I should have been shutting myself up and shutting the door. But if he knew anything . . .

'He isn't a boy,' said Tourneaux, matter-of-factly. 'He is an abomination, like his mother, and dangerous. And it would be in your best interests—'

'Are you *threatening* us?' said Pauline. Her voice was hard, but there was a tremble there. 'Who the hell do you think you are? I'm on first-name terms with every police officer in this town. Some of them live nearby. I could have them here in minutes.'

'But you won't.' Tourneaux smiled. It was a bad smile. A smile with murder behind it. Like he wouldn't think twice about treading on a little girl's face on his way to carry out his mission. 'Because you don't want them to know about Mark Matthews any more than I do.'

'*Abomination*,' I said. 'That's what you said.'

'Yes.'

'He's my *friend*. And if you call him anything like that again, I'm going to twat you with this rolling pin.'

Pauline drew breath sharply. Tourneaux just laughed. 'That's definitely the most amusing threat I've heard this year. Now please, either bring Matthews to me, or I'm going to—'

'He's not *here*, fucko,' I said. 'He overheard his dad talking to you and we ran. I suppose you know that.'

He nodded.

'Well we got to the station and he said he didn't want to put me in danger, and he ran away. I tried to chase him but he disappeared. He doesn't have a phone. I have no idea where he is.' I looked him straight in the eyes as I lied, trying not to think that every word might signify a number of years off my life. My voice shook a little and Pauline put a fiercely protective arm around me. 'So,' I said. 'I *don't* know where he is. If you want him, you'll have to chase him, although I don't hold out much hope for you. Boy's pretty good at disappearing. And if you ever come here again, if you *ever* threaten me or my aunt again, or if the time ever comes when I genuinely am standing between you and Mark, you will be beyond sorry. Now get lost, *motherfucker*.'

Tourneaux's lip curled but he overruled it, turning it back into a smile that had all the warmth of a severed head in a winter puddle. 'Fine. Have it your way. But you *will* be seeing me again.'

'Fuck you.' I slammed the door. Pauline watched through

the peephole until she was sure Tourneaux was gone and I slid slowly down the wall to the floor, a cold, hollow feeling in my stomach. I looked up at her. 'What are we going to do?'

'I don't know,' she said.

'What's going to happen now?'

'I don't know.'

She didn't know.

I didn't know.

But somebody did.

We didn't do much more talking. Pauline poured us each a whisky, which we slugged back quickly, gave me a hug and told me I was very brave and very stupid. Then she put me to bed, saying that we would discuss things in the morning.

The whisky had made me feel momentarily better, but as I lay there in the dark I started to feel scared again. And stupid. Tourneaux terrified me. I didn't want to know what he was capable of.

And I'd lied to him and threatened him and called him a motherfucker.

Which, to be fair, wasn't something I would willingly have taken back.

I had to do something. I went to the bathroom, locked the door and stared into the mirror, concentrating on my own face, imagining it duplicated, misting into view behind me. 'Please,' I whispered. 'Please come. Please tell me. Tell me what's happening. Tell me what's going to happen. I have to know. I have to save Mark.'

Nothing. No second reflection. No ghostly me staring back. I concentrated harder, tensing until I felt that my body might shatter. 'Please. Come. Come. Come!'

Again, nothing. I relaxed, let the hurt roll away, shook my

head. This was stupid. She told me nothing useful when she came of her own accord. I doubted she was going to tell me anything useful if I somehow managed to summon her.

And I couldn't rule out the possibility that she was just a figment of my on-the-edge-of-cracking-up imagination.

I moved sideways, reached for my toothbrush . . . and there she was. Vanessa with the black hair, standing behind me, pale and solemn. I looked her in the eye and smiled. She didn't return the smile. I turned around, hoping she wouldn't disappear. She didn't. She was standing right in front of me. Speaking words of wisdom. Hopefully.

I held out a hand, but she recoiled. 'Sorry,' I said. 'But . . . can you tell me?'

She started to move her lips, but no sound came out. Every now and then I could hear a whispered syllable, but nothing to latch onto, so I waved my hands and shook my head. 'No, no. Sorry. I can't hear you.'

She rolled her eyes in frustration, clenching her fists. Blood was starting to trickle from one of her nostrils. 'No!' I cried. 'No! Don't disappear! Don't—'

She flew backwards against the door as if blasted with a gun, spitting blood . . .

A red flash . . .

And I was in the corridor of a house. Mark's old house. I knew it instantly. The smell, the pictures, the décor. This was the old house, in Llangoroth. Years ago.

The front door opened and Mark came in. His movements were jerky, as though they were dropping frames, like everything was running on a computer that wasn't powerful enough. He walked right through me and somehow, even though it was impossible, even though this had never happened, I knew when this was. It was the day he'd vanished. I watched him walk down the hall to the kitchen. Saw him stop in the doorway, his school bag sliding off his shoulder. In the kitchen sat his father, hunched over the table. I couldn't hear anything, although I was sure Mark was speaking.

I saw his father rise.

Turn.

Face contorted with pain.

I saw him lunge and knock Mark down. An avalanche of furious fists.

I tried to scream but nothing came out. I tried to shut my eyes because I couldn't bear it, but I had no eyes. I watched Mr Matthews beat the life out of his son, bellowing silently, tears and spit and blood flying.

I fell to my knees in Pauline's bathroom. The other me was gone.

I curled up into a ball and tried to make my mind blank.

CHAPTER FOURTEEN

KNOCKING. KNOCKING. UNCOMFY hard floor face. Knocking? Voice? 'Vanessa? Are you in there?'

Mark. I dragged myself groggily into a sort of half-kneel and unlocked the door. Mark frowned down at me. He looked ill. 'Are you . . . have you been in here all night?'

'Fell asleep. What time is it?'

'Eight. I just woke up.'

'How's your back?'

He ignored that. 'Did anything happen last night?'

I nodded.

'He came? Turner?'

'It's Tourneaux. And yeah. He came.'

We went through to the kitchen and made tea while I described what had happened.

'Do you think he believed you?' asked Mark. 'That I wasn't here?'

'Don't know. He left.'

'Might be a trick. Might just be biding his time.'

'Yeah.' I put my head in my hands. Mark patted my shoulder awkwardly. 'I don't know what to do,' I whispered.

'No suggestion of a motive?' Mark asked.

I managed to chuckle at that. 'All right, police procedural man.'

'I just mean . . . anything? Like, who's he working for?'

'Nothing. Just that . . . he really doesn't like you. Or

whatever he thinks you are. He . . .' I sat bolt upright in my chair, because something had come whirling back into my head. Something Tourneaux had said that I'd missed in my fear and anger.

'Your mother,' I said. 'He mentioned your mother.'

Mark frowned. 'What? Why? What did he say?'

'Just . . . he said that . . .' I didn't really want to repeat it. 'It's not very nice.'

Mark's eyes widened. 'Oh shit! Something not very *nice*? Yeah best spare me that, not sure I could handle something not nice, would really spoil this delightful week.'

'OK Sarky McGee, I get the point. He . . . he said you're an abomination.'

'Right . . .'

' "Just like his mother". That's what he said.'

'An abomination just like my mother.'

'Yeah.'

Mark leaned back in his chair. 'Well. That's . . . interesting.'

Another jolt. The memory . . . the memory on the train. Of Mark's father. The first version, before the jerky, brutal run-through I'd endured this morning.

Something about *her*.

You're just like her. That's what he said.

Just like her.

'Mark?' I said. 'Your mum. Did . . .'

'I know her? No. You know I didn't. She vanished before I was a year old. That's all my dad ever told me.'

'But might anybody else know what happened?'

'I don't know. I've never had any contact with her side of the family. I don't even know if there are any. I don't know her maiden name . . . God. What am I talking about, I don't even know what her *first* name was.' Tears were lining up in his eyes, ready to jump. 'It was one of those things that my dad never, *ever* talked about. And I just . . . I don't know, I just sensed that I couldn't ask him. It was too painful for him. I wondered, obviously. I wanted to know. But . . . I was terrified to ask. And there was nobody else.'

'What about his family?'

'He has a brother in France, I think, but I've never met him. As far as I know they haven't spoken all the time I've been alive. I don't know his name either.' The tears were falling now, quiet, dignified tears that he barely seemed to notice. His voice didn't even waver. 'Jesus. Pretty hopeless case, eh? The lonely abomination.' He smiled bitterly.

'Shut up,' I said. 'You're not hopeless. You're not alone. And you are *not* an abomination.'

'How do you explain the feathers then? The convulsions? My brand new bulge? I had to sleep on my side the whole time last night, lying on my back was excruciating.'

'How is it this morning?'

'Still hurts.'

I nodded. 'Well . . . I can't explain them. Yet. But someone might be able to.'

'Who?'

'I dunno. The internet's a big place.' I got up and made another cup of tea and took it through to Pauline's room. 'We're going to do some research in the attic,' I whispered.

'You're up before me,' she mumbled. 'Did the world end?'

'Yes.' I gave her a kiss and ran to grab her laptop. Mark was hovering in the kitchen. I beckoned. 'Come on, you. We need to keep you upstairs, just in case that arsehole comes back.'

'What are we going to do?'

'We're going to do investigating.'

I set us up in the attic with the laptop and some toast and compiled a list of things to research. Mark's symptoms, time travel, the name Lee Tourneaux, any occult or supernatural groups. I made myself a comfy-ish seat and set to work.

This is going to be a long day, I thought.

It turned out to be a long three and a half hours, because that was as long as I could stomach futile internet research. Searching for the feathers yielded pages about recurring visual themes in anime-inspired videogames, films about owls and some bollocks about angels. Researching the bulge led to lots of unhelpful medical pages with eye-poppingly graphic pictures. There were about fifty thousand occult groups on the internet, each one weirder and less relevant than the last – and with increasingly terrible-looking websites. And of all the Lee Tourneauxs I found – there were several – the only vaguely interesting one was a guy in Devon who owned the world's biggest collection of sheep skulls.

'Sorry,' I said. 'The internet fails again. They might as well just unplug it.'

'I always said it would never catch on,' said Mark. 'Oh well. At least that guy with the sheep skulls was a laugh.'

'Are you ready for some lunch?' Pauline called up the stairs. She was making beef stew.

'Yes please!' I yelled.

'Good, it'll be ready in a few minutes!'

I closed the laptop and rubbed my square eyes. 'Can you think of *anybody* who might know something about your mum? That seems like the only vaguely useful lead we have.'

'If I'd known anyone,' said Mark, 'I would have asked them years ago.'

He said it mildly, matter-of-factly, without a hint of irritation, but I still felt like a dickhead. 'Of course,' I said. 'Sorry. Um . . .' I ran my fingers through my hair. 'Shit. Shitting *shit*. If only we'd known some of this stuff before we'd visited your dad.'

'He's not my dad,' said Mark. 'Not now.'

'Mark . . .'

'He said I wasn't his son. And he sent some psycho after me. After you and Pauline. He is not my dad anymore. If he ever was.'

'But he still knows something. He knows a lot more than us.'

'Well, we can't just turn up at his house again. For one thing, I don't think I could handle spending another whole day pissing about on trains.'

'Agreed.'

'And anyway.' Mark shook his head. 'You saw how he reacted.'

'We didn't have a chance to *explain* anything, though. Or ask anything. We just ran.'

'If you've got a method of getting information out of him that doesn't involve a random, horrible meeting at his house and bypasses that nutbag Tourneaux, I'd love to hear it.'

'Give him a ring?'

'*Give him a ring*.' Mark did his best sardonic eyes. 'That journalism degree was worth every penny, clearly.'

'It was worth it in other ways. I had a few pretty banging nights out. Let's get some lunch.'

Pauline had closed all the curtains in the living room and

kitchen so there was no possibility of any unwanted attention from outside, and we all sat down at the living-room table around a big pot of orgasmic-smelling stew. 'How are you today?' she smiled at Mark.

'Bit better. No coughing or feathers or weird spasms so far.'

'Well, that sounds like a good day to me.'

We sat and ate and I enjoyed the feeling of thick stew nourishing and strengthening me, suffocating the confusion and helplessness like wet sand on a fire. The feeling, and the smell of the food, reminded me of Pauline's old kitchen, back when she'd lived up a hill out of town with an ecological hip-pie-biker hybrid named Tammy. That kitchen had been like her living room turned up to eleven: the most comforting, hospitable space I'd ever been in, bar none, always smelling of herbs and tea and lovely food, with a warm fire burning in winter and cold fruit drinks on tap in the summer. I'd been eleven when she and Tammy had split and she'd had to sell up and move to Llangoroth. I'd cried for days. Mostly about that kitchen.

'So did you find anything?' asked Pauline.

'No,' I said. 'We're sort of stumped. There are only two people who know anything – Tourneaux, who I want to keep at least a fifty-foot pole's length away from, and Mark's dad.'

'Who I doubt is going to be very helpful,' said Mark. 'I don't really want to risk that mission again.'

Pauline turned her spoon over and over, moving some potatoes around in her bowl.

'I literally can't think of anything,' I said. 'Which is pretty pathetic.'

'Don't be so hard on yourself,' said Pauline. 'It's difficult to research something that nobody seems to know anything about. Mark . . . you moved here when you were twelve?'

'Yes.'

'From . . .'

'Near London. And before that, a little town down south.'

'Have you ever been back to either?'

He nodded. This was the first I'd heard of it.

'And you didn't find anything?'

'No,' he said. 'People remembered me and my dad, although they didn't really know us. They said we always kept ourselves to ourselves. No-one could tell me anything about my mother, nobody had met her.'

'It seems to me that your father is the key,' said Pauline. 'We need to go back to his house. All of us, this time.'

'Tourneaux, though,' I said. 'He's the problem.'

'Not the only problem,' muttered Mark. His contempt for his father came off him in waves.

'If we all went,' I said, 'and cornered him . . . he'd have to tell us something. And we have to face it, Mark, he's bound to know some of the answers. If not most of them. He's our best source.'

Mark glowered down at the table, although he didn't argue. He knew that it was true, that it was necessary, even if he didn't like it.

'I imagine that Tourneaux is still in town,' said Pauline. 'And he'll know if we leave.'

'If we sneak to the train station-' I said.

'No more trains,' said Pauline. 'We're all going this time. I'm going to drive us.'

'Pauline—'

'Don't even *contemplate* arguing with me, Vanessa.'

'OK,' I squeaked.

'So we need to get out of town without Tourneaux seeing, or following,' said Pauline. 'And we need to get to Mr Matthews' house and corner him before he can make any kind of call.'

'We don't even know where Tourneaux is,' said Mark.

'I agree that he's probably still in town,' I said. 'So I'll go out and look.' Pauline started to object, but I held up my hand. 'It's broad daylight. I will be *fine*. If I see him I'll keep walking and I'll make sure I stay near crowded areas. Not one street in this town is empty between the hours of eight am and eleven pm. I'll be absolutely fine. I need to get out of the house anyway. If I find him, we're one up. And if I don't, we're no worse off.'

'I don't like it,' said Mark.

'Tough. *You're* staying in the attic.'

He really didn't like that, but he accepted it. I went and got dressed properly and guiltily checked my phone. I had lots of missed calls and texts but I just couldn't right now. There were more important things.

'Be careful,' said Pauline, as I left. '*Please.*'

'Always am.'

Such a massive lie.

It was the kind of day that hazy memories are built around. Soft and golden, lightly breezy, fresh country smells wafting, a distant soundtrack of swaying trees and contented bleats and chugging tractors. The kind of day when I'd wake up on a Saturday morning (provided I wasn't still awake somewhere from Friday night) and leap out of bed and call Mark and the others and we'd run down to the river or head up to the woods with picnics and climb and build dens and piss about like we'd be young forever, drinking booze we'd pilfered from parents or persuaded older kids to buy for us.

As I walked, I thought. Tourneaux had arrived late at night. He had to have come in a car. He might have already booked into the Llangoroth Hotel, or one of the three or four local bed and breakfasts. Or maybe he'd slept in his car. It was afternoon by now, though, so he had to be out and about. I doubted someone like him did lie-ins.

I headed to the hotel first, but nobody of Tourneaux's description had checked in. Next I headed to a B&B by the river, owned by a family I knew, the Bowens. Mrs Bowen was outside hanging washing, and after the usual cheery back and forth I asked her about Tourneaux, spinning some guff about a friend with a missing phone. No joy. Already feeling discouraged, I started off in the direction of the next B&B.

Then I stopped.

What if . . .

I turned and hurried back in the other direction, towards Mark's old house. It was a long shot, but worth trying. I rounded the corner and looked down the street. My stomach turned over. A battered dark brown car was parked a few doors down from the house. Sitting on the bonnet with his back to me, watching the building, was a short figure in a green jacket.

Jackpot.

I made a note of his number plate on my phone, just in case. Then I crouched down behind a severely ripe-smelling bin and watched Tourneaux watch the house. He didn't stay for very long, eventually getting back in his car and pulling away from the kerb. What was he up to?

And what should I do?

It wasn't enough to know his face, name and vehicle. We

needed him out of the way so we could get out of town. Even if I ran now, I doubted I could get back to Pauline's in time.

The way he was going would take him up through town, though. And yours truly knew more than one short cut.

To the bushes!

I reached the bottom of the high street just in time to see the brown car swing into a parking space at the top. Result. I slowed down as I headed up the hill, uber-casual, my eyes flicking between the shops, the pub and the car. Tourneaux got out and strolled down the hill and I saw him see me, although he barely reacted.

I looked towards the pub. A couple of middle-aged men I remembered from my underage drinking days were having a lunch-time pint, sleeves rolled up, sweaty from their morning's exertions. They were on the opposite side of the road to Tourneaux, as was I, but definitely within seeing and hearing distance.

Was this a good plan?

Let's find out, I thought.

I crossed the road and met Tourneaux on the other side. He stopped and looked me up and down, one eyebrow raised. His jacket was zipped up to his chin, which seemed strange in this heat. 'Decided to come clean?' he said. 'Hand over your friend?'

'Lol, no.'

'Then what do you want?'

'I wanted to ask you some questions.'

'Right here? In broad daylight, on a crowded street?'

'Why do you want him?'

His eyes narrowed. 'It's not your concern. If you don't have any information for me—'

'You'd better stay away from me and my aunt,' I said. 'And my friend.'

'You *do* know where he is.'

'I have no idea where he is. But it doesn't matter. You'll never find him.'

'This will all unfold smoothly and painlessly if you just *tell me*.'

'Suck my dick,' I said, to my surprise as much as his.

Tourneaux's left eye twitched in anger. I knew he wanted to grab me, slam me against the wall and tell me what was what. But all he did was adjust his jacket in such a way that I saw a very definite bulge inside it.

A definite gun-shaped bulge.

'You'd better stay out of my way,' he whispered. Then he turned and went into the shop.

I stood for several very long seconds, breathing deeply, my chest thudding. Once again it felt like that should have been it for my heart, surely no human organ could take this much stress. It passed, though, and by the time Tourneaux emerged from the shop I was long gone.

I ran into Pauline's living room and she jumped up from the sofa. 'Well? Did you—'

'We need to get away ASAP,' I said. 'He's got a gun. He's a fucking nutcase.' And I'd told him to suck my dick. Optimal strategy.

'A *gun*? Well, we can tell the police . . .'

'The police? The local Llangoroth police? Are you actually being serious?'

Pauline thought for a moment, then nodded. 'You're right.'

'God,' I said, as what had just happened started to sink in. 'I thought I could goad him into attacking me, that those guys would step in and help . . . but he had a gun. I might have got them killed. *Shit . . .*'

'Calm down,' said Pauline. '*Calm down.* We—'

Banging at the door. We both jumped. Tourneaux's voice: 'You had better open up and give him to me *right now!*'

Shit. 'OK,' I whispered, my mind racing. 'We're out of time. I'm going to run out the back and lure him away.'

'Vanessa, *no*—'

'*Don't argue, Pauline.* I'm going to lure him away, make him think I'm Mark.' I grabbed Mark's hoody from the sofa and pulled it on. 'You wait here until the coast is clear, then get Mark and drive to the garage at the very edge of town. The red one, you know. Evans'. I'll meet you there. Please, Pauline, just do it. Get up in the attic *now.*'

Tourneaux was still banging on the door. 'Give him to me!'

'*Now*, Pauline!'

Pauline hugged me quickly, her eyes wet, then ran to the ladder that led up to the attic. I grabbed a bread knife from the kitchen, took a deep breath and ran myself, making sure I made a big noise slamming doors. He needed to hear me. I pulled the hood right up, unlocked the door that led to the garden and banged it hard as I ran out. I heard Tourneaux's voice from the other side of the house. 'Hey! *Hey!* Come back! You come back *right now* and I'll make this quick and easy!'

I sprinted the length of the back garden and vaulted the fence, trying not to think about the fact that I was not in any way fit. I could hear Tourneaux negotiating the wooden door that separated the garden from the alley at the side of the house. That catch had always been a pain in the arse. I had a head start.

Hopefully it would be enough.

Pauline's house backed onto a steep bank and I pelted down it, slipping and sliding on loose earth, reminding myself that I'd done this hundreds of times, I knew how to navigate it, I wasn't going to fall. Amazingly, I stayed upright. I scrambled across the river at the bottom without getting too wet and headed along the edge of the adjacent field. I risked a glance behind and saw Tourneaux stumbling down the bank after me, barely keeping his balance, and I *ran*, faster than I'd run yesterday, maybe faster than I'd ever run, down the field, towards the copse of trees, heart and blood thundering and bubbling, so certain I was going to die, but even more certain that I was going to get away, but even more certain that—

This unhelpful, circular thought process was gratifyingly broken by the sound of a tumble and a splash behind me, followed by a loud, angry 'SHIT', and against all odds I smiled. That was the chance I needed. I ripped off the hoody and hung it from a branch, hurriedly positioning it so that it - hopefully - looked like someone was trying to hide behind the tree. Then I sprinted to the other end of the copse, my chest burning. I climbed clumsily over another hedge, jumped the river again and ran back up the bank, blood drumming deafening rhythms in my ears. I felt like I was going to pass out now, but I couldn't, I *couldn't*, it wasn't allowed, it wasn't possible.

Somehow I struggled to the top of the bank and hopped over the fence into someone else's garden, one of Pauline's neighbours'. I hoped that nobody was about. Apart from anything, I didn't want them falling foul of a wet, angry psychopath. I ran past some toy dump trucks and a big trampoline, the kind whose owners I'd always been jealous of, and heaved myself up and over their wooden door with exactly zero grace.

Behind me, at the bottom of the hill, I heard a 'SHIT!' so strangled with fury that my boiling body went momentarily cold. He'd found the hoody.

I still had time.

I emerged on Pauline's road, looked to my right and saw Tourneaux's vehicle parked a little way away. The final part of my much-better-than-earlier plan fell into place and I grinned and ran over to the car. I made short work of the tyres, slashing two deep, satisfying gouges in each, then ran again, tucking the knife into my waistband. It wasn't very safe, but I didn't want people to see me scurrying around town brandishing a big knife. I had a reputation to uphold, after all.

At the very edge of the estate a couple of kids were messing around on bikes. Delightfully, I knew one of them, a lad named Stevie who lived near my mum. I stopped, fumbled in my wallet and produced a tenner, which I pressed into his hand. 'Stevie! Please can I borrow your bike?'

The stunned kid looked at the money as though Christmas had come early, which was sort of how I felt. 'Yeah!'

'I'll leave it at the red petrol station at the edge of town, you know where that is?'

'Yeah!'

'Thanks! You're a legend!' I threw my leg over the saddle and pedalled away as fast as I could. The bike was way too small and I must have looked totally ridiculous riding it, but it suited my purposes. I pedalled and pedalled, my chest in agony, oxygen hard if not impossible to come by, my legs feeling like someone had set to them with a meat tenderiser, but I was also energised with adrenaline and with my triumph over my pursuer, with the visceral satisfaction of messing up his day.

Best of all, there was a massive hill between me and the petrol station, and when I reached it and let myself fly down, I actually let out a 'Wooooooo-hooooooo', feeling like a kid again, the ecstatic rush of freefalling down a steep hill on two wheels.

I *got away*, I thought.

I AM AMAZING.

I got to the petrol station a few minutes later, discarded the bike and ran to Pauline's car. The engine was already running. I dived into the back seat, yelling '*Drive!*', and Pauline drove, and I sprawled on my back, panting and gasping for air.

Mark turned around in the front seat and raised one eyebrow. '"Drive"?'

'Oh . . . come on,' I managed to choke out. 'Don't tell me . . . you haven't always . . . wanted to . . . run away from a murderous . . . nutcase . . . then leap into a car . . . and shout *drive*.' There were several painful, spluttering gasps between each word, but Mark got the gist.

He smiled. 'Nice one, bro.'

But I couldn't speak anymore, so I just lay back and let my aunt drive.

CHAPTER FIFTEEN

TEN OR SO minutes into the journey, I sat up, cold with shock. 'Mum! What if—'

'I rang her,' said Pauline. 'While we were waiting for you.'

'You did? What did you say?'

'I said that I couldn't tell her much, but if there was ever a time for her to just trust me and listen, it was now. I said there was a man in town who might come to her house. A bad, profoundly un-Christian man. I said that he might go to her house because he wanted something from me that I didn't have.'

'You didn't mention me?'

'No. I knew she'd be worried enough about me without bringing you into it. As far as she's concerned, you're still out of town.'

I hoped nobody I'd bumped into would casually mention to her that they'd seen me. Llangoroth was that sort of place.

'I described Tourneaux, gave her his name and said that if he came to the door, under no circumstances was she to let him in, and she was to immediately call the police if he didn't leave when she told him to.'

I sat back, feeling a little better. 'Thank you.'

'She's my sister. Of course I was going to warn her.'

I wondered if I'd have thought to warn my own sister and then felt ashamed to the very core that I had to wonder.

'So what happened?' asked Mark.

I described my escape and my outwitting of Tourneaux. Pauline grinned. 'That's my girl.'

'Fair play,' said Mark. 'Didn't know you had it in you.'

'You serious?'

'Nah. I've always known you had it in you.'

'That's better.'

We drove for nearly an hour, half-heartedly playing I-Spy and Botticelli, until Mark suddenly said, 'I'm starting to wish we hadn't just run for it yesterday.'

'Hmm?' I said.

'If we'd just stuck around, we wouldn't have done all this faffing. Eight hours of trains and then four hours of driving today.'

'There's no plan,' I said. 'We're just . . . faffing our way along.'

'Yeah. But we'd have had time to ask him questions yesterday.'

'We needed time to think of the questions, though, didn't we? We needed Tourneaux to mention your mother. We needed to know how desperate he was.'

'I suppose.'

'And this is the last thing he'd expect us to do,' I said, hoping I sounded like some sort of strategic mastermind.

'We just need to make sure Mr Matthews doesn't tell him,' said Pauline.

'He won't,' said Mark.

I wasn't sure what to make of that. 'What's the plan when we get there, do you reckon?' I asked.

'We sit him down,' said Mark, 'and I give him a good talking to.' It should have been funny, but the way he said it was profoundly un-funny. I remembered his sudden departure from the script yesterday, when he'd launched into a fight with those boys, momentarily transforming from the Mark I knew so well into somebody completely *else*. God, that was only yesterday . . . and they were just some lads defacing a war memorial. This was his father, who had kept so much from him, who had sent this horrible guy after him, this . . . what? Assassin?

I thought of the Mr Matthews I'd seen in my vision, or whatever it had been. Half mad with emotions I couldn't understand. Beating Mark to the ground.

It wasn't something that was going to happen, though.

It was something that *had* happened . . .

Except it hadn't. It couldn't have.

The back seat of the car suddenly felt very big, and I felt very far away from the people in the front.

It couldn't have happened.

It *didn't* happen.

But it would have.

It would have, if Mark hadn't disappeared.

My head was starting to hurt. I wondered if this was the time to come clean about what I'd been seeing. I'd put it off so many times, worried that they'd laugh, or think I was mad.

'We need to be careful of your dad,' was all I said.

'I know,' said Mark.

'You don't, though. I . . . I've been having more dreams.' Dreams. That was the easiest way to put it. The hows and whys didn't matter now. 'I had one about him. I saw . . . I saw him lose it. Completely lose it. He beat you.'

'He has a temper,' said Mark. 'I already know that.'

Something else he'd never mentioned.

'Did he ever hit you?' I asked, so bluntly that I shocked myself.

'Vanessa,' began Pauline.

'No,' said Mark. 'Never. He's come close, once or twice, but he never actually did it.'

'He might have,' I said. 'If you hadn't vanished.'

'We can do "maybe" all the way,' said Mark. 'But we're going now, and it's going to be worth it. I'm going to get some answers.'

'OK.'

Mark coughed once, hard. When he took his hand from his mouth, there was a tiny feather in the palm. 'Fuck.' He opened the window and threw it out and I watched it disappear, absorbed into the world.

Between us, we managed to navigate a pretty good route to Corford. It took just over three hours and we listened to John Martyn and KT Tunstall, the only two CDs Pauline had in the car, twice each, which made this seem less like a tense, potentially dangerous mission and more like a family trip to the seaside. Mark didn't have any more coughing fits or spasms and he even cracked some jokes, which made me feel a hell of a lot better, even if rather too many of them were about how angry Tourneaux must be.

We finally pulled up on Mr Matthews' street, parking at the end so we could spy on his house. 'He might be at work,' I said. 'It's only just half three.'

'No,' said Pauline. 'I saw him at the window.'

'So . . . what now?' I said.

'Pauline,' said Mark, 'my dad wouldn't recognise you, would he?'

'I doubt it. You think I should go first?'

'Element of surprise? You could pretend to be . . . I don't know, doing a survey or something?'

Pauline laughed. 'I'll try and come up with something a bit better than that.'

'I don't know about this,' I said, thinking of the furious violence I'd seen in my mind. 'He might—'

'It's a bit late to start trying to coddle me,' said Pauline. 'Don't worry. I'll be fine.'

'So you distract him at the front door,' said Mark. 'We'll sneak in around the back and get inside. Somehow, you need to get inside with him.'

'Ask for water or something,' I said. It had got hotter and stickier as the day had progressed, so I imagined that gambit would probably fly.

'And we'll be waiting,' said Mark.

'OK,' said Pauline. 'Well. Let's go, shall we?' She sounded so completely unfazed by what we were doing. I think I loved her more than I'd ever loved her in my entire life right at that moment.

We got out of the car and Pauline headed for the house while Mark and I ducked down a side alley that connected this street to one running parallel. Midway down the alley it split off into another, thinner one which ran between the two sets of houses, allowing access to their back gardens. We ran along, counting.

'Here it is,' said Mark.

The wooden door was locked but we shimmied over the fence and crossed an empty patio to some French windows. These were unlocked and we snuck into the living room as quietly as possible. Bare walls, bare floorboards, a single candle flickering on the windowsill, an old TV, a worn armchair and one shelf with a few books on it. The place felt so terribly sad that I shuddered; it clung to the walls, like some kind of sucking mould. It was of a piece with what I'd felt after those dreams that I couldn't remember.

Mark opened the living room door a crack. We could hear Pauline and Mr Matthews' voices.

'I didn't realise anyone was moving out,' said Mr Matthews.

'Yes,' said Pauline. 'At the end of the road. I'll be moving in and I'm having a look around the neighbourhood, saying hello and all that. No harm in being friendly, eh?'

'Not at all.'

'Sorry to be cheeky,' said Pauline, 'but I couldn't trouble you for a glass of water, could I? It's boiling out here.'

'Um . . . all right.' He didn't sound happy, but he obliged, moving aside so that Pauline could come into the kitchen. She looked around nervously, her back to him. He shut the front door and came past her, filling a glass of water from the tap.

Pauline took it and smiled. 'Thank you very much. I'm sorry for intruding like this. I just wanted to get the measure of the place, you know? Always hard moving to a new area.'

'Of course.'

'May I sit down?'

'Um . . . all right . . .'

Pauline sat down and Mr Matthews joined her, looking about as awkward as it's possible to look.

That was our moment.

Mark ran in and Mr Matthews leapt to his feet, his chair tumbling to the floor with a clatter that hurt my ears. 'Mark!' he cried. What little colour there had been in his face drained away.

I ran past him to the window and yanked the blind down. Mr Matthews looked ready to flee, but Mark held up his hand.

'No.' There was a coldness in his voice, a steely anger more intense than anything I could remember hearing from him. It scared me, and it must have scared Mr Matthews too because he stayed completely still. 'Sit down,' said Mark. '*Gareth.*'

Mr Matthews sat. Pauline was standing by the kitchen door, barring the exit, and I leaned against the sink, keeping my eyes locked on Mark and his father. Mr Matthews looked at me, then at Pauline. 'All in it together, eh?' He looked back at me. 'I wasn't expecting to see you again.'

'After you sent a psychopath after us?' I said.

'Tourneaux? He's not—'

'He is,' said Mark.

Mr Matthews' eyes dropped to the table. 'Come for revenge, have you?'

'We've come for answers,' said Pauline.

Mr Matthews looked at her through narrowed eyes. 'You'd be the aunt, I suppose. I should have known something was up. Long days . . .' He said the last two words almost to himself.

Mark was standing about a foot from him. He made no move to sit down. 'Answers,' he said. 'I want to know what the hell's going on.'

'You tell me.' Mr Matthews' voice shook. 'My son vanishes from under my nose . . . and now you appear. Out of nowhere.'

'He *is* your son,' I said, feeling my shaky hold on my temper become much shakier. 'How can you—'

'Vanessa,' said Mark. 'Leave it.' He stared at his father, who couldn't seem to bear to make eye contact. 'What's my mother's name?'

Mr Matthews jerked like he'd been whipped. 'What?'

'My mother. What's her name.'

'Why—'

'Look,' said Mark, 'you can probably tell that I'm not very happy. And I can tell that, for some reason, you're afraid of me. And there are three of us. And we're not leaving until we're satisfied. I don't want to hurt you. But I need to know. I need to know what the hell is going on.'

His father shook his head. A tear trickled down his cheek. 'I'm not—'

'*Tell me her name!*' Mark brought his fist down on the table and the rest of us jumped.

After a moment, Mr Matthews spoke. 'Her name was Aisling.' His voice cracked as he said the name. I imagined it had been years since he'd said it aloud.

'And what was she?' said Mark. His voice was completely steady.

'I don't know. I never . . . I never knew, exactly. Just that she was . . . different.'

'Different *how?*'

'She hid it from me,' said Mr Matthews. 'For three years I looked after her, and she never told me. Hid what she was. Then one day she said she was pregnant. With you. And I . . . I told her we should get rid of it. We had no money. I . . . I wasn't ready.'

I kept an eye on Mark. There was barely a flicker, nothing to suggest he was even mildly perturbed by this revelation.

'She said she had to keep it,' Mr Matthews continued. 'She couldn't get rid of it, of you. Not even if she wanted to. Physically impossible. I asked her how that could be. She said . . . she said she'd show me.' He looked up now, looked Mark

186

straight in the eye, and for the first time Mark buckled slightly, knocked off-balance by the ferocity of his father's gaze, the emotions that crackled in the air between them.

'What do you mean?' he asked.

'She took off her shirt,' said Mr Matthews. 'Closed her eyes. And . . . wings. She grew wings. They unfolded from her back, spread out. Huge. White.'

With little blue veins, I added in my head. I could hardly breathe.

'Like angel wings,' said Mr Matthews. 'Exactly as you might imagine those to look. I couldn't speak. I was terrified. I wanted to run . . . but I couldn't. I asked her if that was what she was, an angel, although I'd never believed in such ridiculous ideas. She said no. She said she wasn't sure what she was, that she'd tried to research her family, what she was, and found nothing. She was a rarity. Maybe a one of a kind. She said she could . . . she could heal things. She showed me. Brought some dead flowers back to life.'

'Amazing,' whispered Pauline.

Mr Matthews shook his head. 'No. Not amazing. Profoundly disturbing. She was suddenly, at that moment, a different creature. A different species. Even the way she spoke was different, now she had admitted what she was. I said . . . I told her I couldn't be near her. I couldn't . . . but the baby . . . she said she had to carry it through. She wanted to, anyway, but . . . anyway. She begged me to stay.' He looked up at Mark and I felt like there should have been at least a hint of love in the look, but there was nothing like that, just a whirlwind I couldn't understand, a whirlwind that chilled me through and through. 'And I stayed.'

Mark nodded. 'And then?'

'She died,' said Mr Matthews. 'Shortly after you were born. All that power, whatever it was, and she couldn't . . .'

'And you kept me,' said Mark. 'Surprised you didn't just chuck me in the nearest bin.'

'I couldn't . . . I . . . I held you. I *named* you. I . . .'

'Spare me,' said Mark. 'So my mother was some kind of . . . creature. She died. You got stuck with me. Let's skip forward a bit. Who's this Tourneaux prick? Why did you send him after me?'

'I didn't *send* him, I—'

'Answer the question, *Gareth*.'

Mr Matthews took a deep, greedy breath, as though telling this story was sapping the life out of him. 'You never showed any signs of being like your mother. I was concerned that I might change, she made allusions to . . . other effects that her kind could have on those around them, on those they loved. On those who loved them . . .'

'Well clearly you *didn't* love her,' said Mark. 'So yeah. I wouldn't worry.'

His father's eyes fell again. 'I . . . kept a close eye on you. Of course. But there was nothing, and for that I was profoundly grateful. I could barely stand the idea of her . . . but you were normal. I was so glad.'

How can he just sit there and say this stuff? I thought. *What the hell is wrong with him?* I was crying quietly. So was Pauline.

'Then,' said Mr Matthews, 'on the day you vanished, I went up to make your bed and I found feathers in it. A pile of them. Just like your mother's. Just sitting there, on your bed. You must have shed them in the night, left without even noticing. I found them and . . . I went a little mad. I drank nearly a whole bottle of whisky. I was beside myself. You weren't my son. You were your mother's. You were going to be like her, and I would be powerless to do anything.'

And then he came home and you beat him to death, I thought.

'And then I didn't come home,' said Mark. 'Bit of good luck for you.'

'I . . . it wasn't like that . . .'

'I don't care,' said Mark. 'I don't care how you felt, not then, not in the meantime, not now. I want information. Facts. Who is Tourneaux?'

'A few months after you vanished,' said Mr Matthews, 'I received a call from him. Out of the blue. He said he had some information about my wife and possibly my son. He came to the house. Said he'd been researching your mother's . . . species. That it was some sort of mutation. A . . . "genetic anomaly".'

'Did he use the word "abomination"?' I asked, through gritted teeth.

Mr Matthews jumped as if he'd forgotten I was there. 'No . . . he just said that he'd been tasked with ensuring that such dangerous anomalies did not pose a threat to the public. He said he'd found a few more around the world. That steps had been taken to . . . imprison them.'

'I bet,' said Mark.

'He was very convincing,' said Mr Matthews. 'He knew things . . . more than anyone could have known. And eventually he got it out of me, about the feathers I'd found in your bed. He said that you were an anomaly, a mutation, like your mother. He said some . . . there was some biology, various things—'

'Like what?' asked Mark. 'Don't skimp. I want all the gory details.'

I wanted to say *Mark, stop*, but I couldn't.

Mr Matthews looked him in the eye again. 'Tourneaux said that your mother's species . . . to reproduce, a sperm is required, but only to ensure birth. To spark it off. Create the right reaction. Everything about the child, it all comes from the mother. The father's contribution just . . . expedites the process. The child shares nothing with him. No genes, no DNA.'

That sounds like a whole heap of bullshit, I thought.

'Hence me not being your son,' said Mark, lightly. Too lightly. *Far* too lightly. 'Neat. Handy for you.'

No, Mark. These are lies.

Anyone could see.

Anyone but a grieving, confused father.

Anything to make some sort of sense.

'Carry on,' said Mark.

'Tourneaux said you'd probably realised what you were and run away. But he said that I needed to contact him if I heard anything. That you were incredibly dangerous. I said I would. I meant it. And then I heard nothing for years . . . until yesterday, when you appeared at my door, identical, like no time had gone by at all.' He shook his head. 'What more proof did I need.'

'So you phoned your friend,' said Mark, 'who was only too happy to pop out on a little errand.'

'I can't have anything to do with it,' said Mr Matthews. 'With you. I just can't. I . . .'

'I suppose it must be a blessing,' said Mark. 'Having someone else appear to clean up the mess for you. And you can just get on with your . . . is this a life? Knowing you betrayed the mother of your child *and* your child? Must make for some sleepless nights. Rather you than me.' He cleared his throat. 'Who does Tourneaux work for?'

'I don't know. I honestly don't.'

'Give us the phone number you have for him.'

'I—'

'Give us the fucking number, now.' Still Mark didn't raise his voice.

Pauline grabbed a pen and paper from the sideboard and wrote down the number that Mr Matthews gave. 'Good,' said Mark. 'OK. So. Anything else? Anything else that might be useful?'

'No. That's everything. But I—'

'Then we're done.'

'What are you going to do?'

'That's none of your business,' said Mark. 'Nothing I ever do, from now on, is your business. Even if I bump into your friend again, even if I end up in some lab, or on some kind of altar. You're not my father. I'm not your son. I have everything I need from you. You won't see me again.' He turned away and left the room.

'Mark,' said Mr Matthews. 'Please.' His words became shouts and then sobs. 'Mark! Come back! *Mark!*'

Pauline and I followed Mark out of the house, leaving Mr Matthews to shout at nobody. Mark walked up the street to the car. A normal walking pace. Casual.

'Mark,' I said. 'What—'

'Can you guys just give me a minute?' His voice was still so level.

'OK,' said Pauline. 'We'll just . . . we'll be here.'

'Thanks.' He got into the car, closed the door and lay down on the back seat. Then he started to scream and pound the ceiling with his fists. The noises were muffled, but they were still awful, as awful as anything I'd ever heard. Strangled, anguished, desperate, like a hole had been ripped in him and everything was just pouring out, everything that he was. I turned to Pauline and collapsed into her chest and we held each other and sobbed, leaving Mark to his pain. Crying and crying, as if we could all just cry the sadness out of us, and be at peace.

CHAPTER SIXTEEN

AN HOUR LATER we were sitting in a dingy roadside café, drinking bitter, tepid coffee and eating what seemed to be freshly regurgitated chilli con carne, served to us on drooping paper plates by pale souls with thousand-yard stares. At least, Pauline and I were eating. Mark was just looking at his. I was trying to speak practically to Pauline, mostly to make myself feel better. 'What do you think we should do now?'

'I'm really not sure,' said Pauline. 'Do you think he'll call Tourneaux?'

'I actually don't,' I said. 'There was a look in his eye when we left. Like he knew he'd gone too far. I'm guessing he'll do nothing.' I forced down another mouthful. 'But it sounds like Tourneaux is even more of a nutcase than we thought he was, spouting that shite. So we need to be really careful.'.

'I'm wondering if now is the time to call the police,' said Pauline.

'That has to be our last resort,' I said. '*Has* to be. We don't know what chaos might come if we tell them.'

'Who's going to notice a bit more chaos?' muttered Mark.

'We can't go back to Llangoroth, either,' said Pauline. She gasped. 'Oh my God, which reminds me!' She took out her phone and turned the volume on. 'Five missed calls from your mother. Oh dear. I . . . I'm going to need to tell her something.'

'Let me talk to her,' I said.

'But she doesn't know you're involved—'

'I'll call her.' I took out my own phone and switched it on. The usual missed calls and texts from Alice and Stuart and one that might have been from work. I would check them later, maybe.

My mother picked up almost immediately. 'Pauline?'

'No, Mum, It's me.'

'Vanessa! Oh, I thought it was going to be your aunt. Where are you? Have you heard from her at all?'

'I'm with her at the moment.'

'You are? Where?'

'We're . . . we're at a service station.'

'A service station? Why? Where? What on earth is going on? Do you know anything about this man she warned me about?'

'Has he come to the house?'

'He did! He demanded to be let in! I said that if he didn't make himself scarce in five seconds flat then I'd call the police. I dialled the number and put it on speaker and let him hear the voice for himself. He made a swift exit. What on *earth* is going on, Vanessa? I've been at my wits' end!'

'It's OK, Mum—'

'Oh! Is that it? Is that all I get? I get some mystery call from my sister about a mad man who might come to the house and then I hear nothing for hours, and all I get is *"it's OK"*? Vanessa—'

'Mum, it has never been more important that you accept what I'm saying. Pauline and I are fine and there is nothing to worry about—'

'Don't you dare patronise or placate me! I am your

mother and you will explain exactly what is happening *this instant!*'

'OK!' I said. 'OK. Fine. That man thinks that Pauline and I know the whereabouts of someone he's looking for. Someone he wants very badly.'

'Who?'

'I don't know! That's the point. He turned up, very threateningly, with this barking mad idea, and we couldn't persuade him otherwise.' I must have been talking to my mother. 'Barking mad'? I never said 'barking mad'.

'Well . . . well why does he think this? Where did he get this mad idea?'

'I don't know that either! But somehow he did. And Pauline thought it would be a good idea to head out of town for the day until he's gone.'

'Why didn't she just call the police?'

I decided to use one of the many bees that my mother kept in her bonnet against her. 'You know what our police are like.'

'True, I suppose. Although that makes me feel a bit less secure myself.'

'I'm sure the threat is enough to get rid of him.'

'So how did the two of you come to be at a service station together?'

'Pauline was going to pick me up from the train station anyway. I've been up north sorting some stuff out, for a friend. She rang and asked if I'd booked my train ticket and I said no, and she said she'd meet me halfway.' It wasn't the most foolproof of cover stories, but I hoped against hope that it would be enough.

'Right. So . . . you're both all right, then.'

'Yes, we're fine. And you are too?'

'Well . . . yes, I suppose. I just wish somebody had told me all this earlier!'

'It's all been a bit rushed.'

'I really think we should go to the police. I take your point about them being fairly useless, but if we can't go to them in times of danger, then what hope is there?'

'If this man turns up again, we will call them. But honestly, that could make it all much more complicated than it deserves to be. I don't want our lives disrupted by this nutter any more than they already have been.' Another well-deployed bee from the bonnet. Mother did so hate having her life disrupted.

'Well. All right.'

'Cool. Anyway, I'd better go. My food's getting cold.'

'All right. When will you be back?'

'I'm not sure, soon. We'll keep you posted.'

'You'd better. And you'd better take care as well.'

'I will. You too. Love you, Mum.' I couldn't remember the last time I'd said that.

'Well, I . . . I love you too.' Awkward, but kind of nice. I hung up and headed back to Mark and Pauline. 'All fine. Tourneaux turned up at the house but she got rid of him.'

'Great,' said Pauline, visibly sagging with relief.

'Any advance on next moves?' I said. 'I really don't think we should go back to Llangoroth.' I felt bad thinking that way, like it was OK to leave my mother there, but not for us to go back.

He's not going to want to draw more attention to himself, though, I thought. *He won't hurt her.*

But he would hurt Mark.

'Maybe we should go to yours?' asked Mark.

'In London? We could . . . it's a long way to drive . . . and . . .' And I lived with Stuart.

My phone rang. A number I didn't recognise. Not even thinking that it would probably be the most obvious person, I answered. 'Hello?'

'Hello, Vanessa.' Tourneaux.

I froze. 'What do you want?' Pauline and Mark stared at me, instantly knowing.

'You ran rings around me earlier. Well done. Clearly I underestimated you. It won't happen again.'

'How did you get my number?'

'It wasn't difficult.'

'My mother said you went to our house. How *dare* you. If you—'

'I would never have hurt her. And I don't want to hurt you or your aunt. I just want the boy.' I could tell that he wanted to hurl furious abuse down the phone at me for evading him earlier, but he was being polite and measured to get me to co-operate. Somehow this quiet, personable voice was worse.

'Well,' I said. 'You're not having him.'

'I will find him. And if necessary, I will go through anybody who stands between us. So I'm making you a one-time offer. You and your aunt go home. Leave Mark to his own fate. And you'll never hear from me again. I'm not in the business of hurting innocent people.'

Green jacket, I thought.

Whatever kept trying to warn me . . . it had warned me about him.

'Abandon him,' said Tourneaux. 'And neither of you will get hurt.'

'Why do you want to hurt him? He's done nothing to you. He's done nothing to *anyone*.'

'Let me speak to him,' said Mark. I shook my head and he scowled.

'That's not your concern,' said Tourneaux.

'It most definitely *is*. He's my friend and you want to . . . what? Lock him up? *Kill* him?'

'Mark Matthews has no business walking this earth. There's a reason he's the only one left.'

That took the wind out of my sails. 'The only one?' I said, in a tiny mouse voice. 'Did you kill the rest?'

'They were dealt with humanely by like-minded individuals.'

'*Like-minded individuals*, eh? Mates of yours? Who do you work for, anyway? Some cult?'

'I work for everyone. Everyone with any interest in preserving the purity of—'

'*Anyway*,' I interrupted breezily, trying to sound as blasé as possible to achieve maximum piss-offage. 'This has been lovely. But these nails aren't going to file themselves, so if there's nothing else?'

'You'd better watch your lip, girl—'

Mark grabbed the phone and practically snarled down it. 'Listen here, you *cunt* . . . hello? Hello? Fuck. He's gone.' He looked at me and then at Pauline, whose eyes had widened. 'Sorry,' he said, looking very bashful. 'I'd never normally say that word. He's just . . . rubbed me up the wrong way.'

'Oh, I agree with the sentiment,' said Pauline, mildly. 'He is definitely the worst swear word anybody can think of. It's just a shame the worst swear word most people can think of is a word meaning vagina.'

Mark blushed. 'Yeah, sorry. Um . . . so. I'm the last of whatever the hell my kind is and Tourneaux wants to kill me? That's the headline?'

'If we're being blunt,' I said, 'yes. And he also said that if Pauline and I abandon you then he'll leave us alone.'

'I'd take him up on that offer if I were you.'

'Certainly not,' said Pauline.

'Well,' I said. 'Sort of certainly not.'

'What do you mean?' asked Pauline.

'I mean, I'm certainly not going to abandon him,' I said. 'But you're going to abandon us.'

'If you think that, then you've got another—'

'Pauline,' I said. 'I love you. I adore you. We both do. And what you've done for us has been above and beyond the call of any kind of duty. But the less of us there are, the more of a chance we stand of getting away.'

'What do you mean? I'm slowing you down?'

'No,' I said. 'That's not what I mean, not at all. I was just trying to come up with a crap excuse, rather than being honest and telling you that I don't want anything to happen to you. But sod it. I'll just be honest. I don't want anything to happen to you. And something very bad might well happen to you if you stick with us.'

'Vanessa—'

'She's right,' said Mark. 'I know that you're the adult, Pauline. And that you feel responsible. But Tourneaux is after *me*. And I couldn't stand it if you were hurt because of me.'

'Oh, but it's fine for me, is it?' I said.

Mark gave me a look.

'Sorry,' I said. 'Bad joke, poor timing. Read the room, Vanessa.'

He shook his head, but couldn't resist smiling. 'I'm so, so grateful for you helping me out, Pauline,' he said. 'I couldn't have got through the last few days without you.'

'This is ridiculous!' said Pauline. 'I appreciate your concern, I'm very touched, but I cannot let you two face this madman alone! I'm a grown woman! I can make my own choices. If Vanessa stays with you, then so do I.'

'I'm an adult too, Pauline,' I said. 'Unbelievably enough. It's our choice. We're going back to London.'

'If he got your phone number, he'll be able to track down where you live,' said Mark.

'I know plenty of places we can hide out.' That was at least fifty per cent lie. 'Please go back to Llangoroth, Pauline. I will keep in touch. Tourneaux will leave you alone. All he cares about is getting Mark.'

'Vanessa . . .'

'*Please*, Pauline,' I said. 'Please. For me. For us. Take us to the nearest train station and then head home. Be safe.'

'Please,' said Mark.

Pauline looked from me to Mark, then back to me, then at the table. She shook her head very slightly. 'I . . . your mother . . .'

'Knows nothing about what's really going on,' I said. 'And it stays that way.'

'But if anything happened to you. I . . . I'd never forgive myself.'

It was on the tip of my tongue to joke that if anything did happen to us I forgave her in advance, but I knew it wasn't the right moment. Maybe I was finally learning. 'Nothing will. We're going to figure this out and we're going to beat that arsehole. And we'll both be fine. I promise.'

'You can't promise—'

'I just did.' I put my hand on hers and squeezed it. She squeezed mine back, two sharp crystal tears dripping down her cheeks.

'You always were a stubborn, infuriating, *impossible* child,' she said. 'You were bloody *born* that way.'

I smiled. 'Start as you mean to go on, innit.'

There was a town about twenty miles in the right direction where we could get a direct train to London. Pauline drove us. No-one spoke. I thought frivolous thoughts to keep myself occupied, like how glad I was that I'd been too pre-occupied to pack properly last week and that most of my stuff was still at home rather than at Pauline's. It made me almost not think about how I was going to explain Mark to Stuart.

When we got to the station, my aunt pulled me aside and pressed an envelope into my hand. I started to open it but she shook her head. 'Not now,' she said. 'When you get back. All right? Promise?'

'Promise.'

She insisted on buying our tickets and we both hugged her fiercely on the platform. I didn't cry, though, which was strange. Maybe I was just cried out. I felt like I must have cried more in the last five days than I had in about five years.

'Thank you so much,' I whispered. 'I'll keep in touch.'

'Bloody right, you will.'

'Love you, Pauline,' said Mark. 'Thank you. I'll keep her safe.'

Ha, I thought, *we'll see about that, tiny boy.*

'I love you too.' Pauline kissed him on the forehead. 'Just

as impossible in your own way as she is. What a pair. See that you do keep each other safe. Or I'll be having words.'

The train arrived and she pushed us away playfully. 'Get on before I change my mind and come with you.'

Another train. We found a seat and looked out of the window. Now that there was a pane of glass between us I saw Pauline begin to cry, and I felt guilty for leaving her, and scared, and I missed her like we'd already been apart for months. I almost thought I might cry after all, but I forced myself not to. She waved and we waved and the train started to chug and I sat back in my seat.

I looked at Mark.

He looked at me.

Now what?

CHAPTER SEVENTEEN

'YOU DIDN'T HAVE to come with me,' said Mark.
'Yes, I did.'

'OK.'

I stood up and stretched, which made me feel momentarily better. 'Back in a minute.' I wandered up the carriage to the toilet, locked myself in and looked in the mirror.

'All right,' I said. 'This sort of worked before. A bit. I need you now, other me. More than ever. *Come on.*' I stared at myself, tensed, concentrating, nearly staggering from the effort, woozy with the headrush bubbling up through my brain. No mysterious second reflection this time, though. No visions.

I tried a different tack, relaxing, allowing my imagination to fill in the blanks, willing myself as gently as possible to see something, someone, out of the corner of my half-closed eyes, a suggestion that might obligingly materialise. But my head hurt too much and I already knew that it was silly. This vision me, whatever she was, was not a magic eight-ball, or a genie I could summon for information whenever I wanted.

'Bollocks,' I muttered.

I sat back down and Mark smiled at me, as though this was a normal train journey. I smiled as well. I thought about saying something, then thought about waiting for him to say something. It felt like talking needed to be done. But it also felt like we'd talked too much. Like we'd done nothing but talk, when we'd not been crying.

I wanted to reassure him. Comfort him. Ask him about all the new information, what he was thinking, what he was feeling. He was the son of someone not quite human. Maybe the last of his kind in the world. And he just sat in his seat, looking out of the window, like we were sacking off a boring day at school and going to the seaside. I wondered if his species, whatever they were, all had this kind of temperament. If they only lost it under very special circumstances.

Like finding out your father never wanted you.

That the mother who did want you died before she could name you.

That you were alone.

He's not alone, I thought, so savagely that I wondered if he could see it in my face, or maybe even hear it. But he wasn't looking or listening. He was watching the world, mulling things over in that specialist brain tank of his.

Screw talking and planning and worrying, at least for a bit. What would happen would happen. I got two dreadful teas from the trolley and sat back and made myself relax, watching things unwind and unroll, motorways winding through soft hills, lopsided field patterns, the constant randomly generated jigsaw-puzzle projection. Greedy sheep, which made me think of home. Oblivious cows, which made me remember a conversation I'd once had at a festival with an extraordinarily wasted young man who had promised me that if I ever got close enough to a cow to look into its eyes, *really* look, I'd see something quite special, that it was like looking into the eyes of a beautiful girl.

I laughed out loud at the memory and Mark raised an amused eyebrow. 'Funny times?'

'Funny time.' I told him the story and he laughed as well. It was wonderful to hear him laugh. Genuinely laugh.

'That's a good one,' he said. 'Special breed.'

'The most specialest.'

'Speaking of special breeds . . . remember Mount Doom?'

'How could I forget?'

'Well. It has been a while, technically.' He was getting used to the idea pretty quickly.

'I s'pose.'

Mount Doom, or the Hill of Doom, or the Trek of Doom, so-called because by the time you got to the rave at the top you felt like you'd undertaken a seriously epic quest and were too exhausted to stand, let alone get monumentally shit-faced. Especially if you'd been carrying all the booze, which I had been.

'You were a great help getting up that mountain,' I said.

'"I can't carry it for you, Vanessa",' said Mark, in his best West Country Hobbit voice.

'"And I can't carry you either",' I shot back, in my own, significantly better West Country Hobbit voice.

'I was carrying things of my own.'

'Oh yeah? Like what.'

'You know. Regret. Other heavy burdens.'

I laughed and sat back in my chair, remembering this particularly insane party, luxuriating in the warmth of the memory. We'd heard about it third . . . no, *fourth* hand, and somehow persuaded Laura's older sister to drive us. She hadn't been impressed when we'd finally found it, after nearly an hour's drive through a pitch-black wilderness of country lanes and sinister fields, following some spectacularly vague directions forwarded to us from a friend of a friend of a friend.

'You can find your own way back,' she'd said as we piled out of the car, bursting with keenness. 'I'm not missioning out here again.'

'Fair play,' Laura had said. 'See you in a few days!'

It had been me, Mark, Luke and Laura. Fifteen years old. Younger than the rest of the partygoers by several years, utterly overwhelmed, but also feeling about as cool as it was possible to feel. Although that had been nothing compared to how cool we'd felt telling everyone at school about it when we'd gone back in on Monday.

Or had it been Tuesday?

I fall against Mark, my eyes nearly rolling back in my head, trying to focus on the light creeping over the brow of the distant hills. He puts an arm around me. 'You all right, bro?'

I mumble an affirmative, blink several times and breathe deeply, deeeeeeeeply, letting the tingle pass through my cells, supercharged yet ultra peaceful. I look over at the two Ls. Luke's pretty much passed out. One too many somethings. He's fine, though. Laura is rolling a cigarette with a look of concentration you'd expect to see on the face of someone defusing a nuclear bomb, sticking her tongue out, one eye comically wide and supremely bonky, the other screwed tightly shut, brightly coloured woolly hat askew. I'm utterly entranced by how special she looks. What a totally gorgeous mess. What would her mum say. Would she feel as proud as I do?

'Maybe we should get going soon?' says Mark. 'It's . . . like . . . day.'

'There'll be people here until tonight,' says Laura. She has to

moisten her lips after every couple of words. 'Probably tomorrow. These things go on for days. And that guy Gary told me we could hang around.'

'Gary . . . who was that?'

'The one who played the really horrible set.'

'All the breakcore? I actually really liked that.' I crane my neck to look at Mark. 'If you want to get going, I reckon I'll come along.'

'Cool.'

'Laura?'

'Reckon I'll hang about,' says Laura. 'Luke's going to be useless for ages anyway. And I'm still quite keen. Reckon I might go and buy some speed off that guy.'

'What guy?'

'The um . . . the one who . . . who has all the . . . the speed.' She giggles.

'You are a dangerous weapon.'

'I'm fuckin' Excalibur mate.'

'Hold on a sec,' says Mark. He gently dislodges me, gets up and wanders out of sight.

'Off for a walk together, eh?' says Laura, resuming the Herculean task of rolling her cigarette. It's her third attempt. I predict that there will be a fourth. At least. 'Togetherrrrrrr.'

'Shut up,' I say, trying to look grumpy. 'I'm not in the mood.' I am in the mood.

'Hokaaaaay. I fucking love you.'

'I love you too.' How many times have we said that to each other tonight? Fifty? A hundred?

Mark returns about ten minutes later with a full bottle of water, a full pouch of tobacco, some Rizlas and a lighter. All stuff I came with and have since lost. 'Supplies,' he says. 'We might be doing a lot of walking before we find someone who'll pick us up.'

'Someone might be leaving now,' I say. 'We could see about blagging a lift.'

'Yeah, cool.'

I hug Laura. 'See you Monday.'

'Monday? Yeah, likely. See you on fucking Friday, mate.'

I laugh, lean over and give Luke a kiss on his silly forehead. He grunts in his sleep, gurning away sweetly.

Goodbyes done, Mark and I start our fourth walk of the night down this godforsaken hill. As we stumble, I stare out into the distance. I have no idea where we are. Literally the middle of nowhere. The sun washes over the fields, my brain blurring from so many hours of kaleidoscoping lunacy, and I feel like I can barely remember what the world is like. If it's even there anymore.

What if it isn't?

'What if the world ended?' I say. 'While we were up there?'

'Ended?'

'Yeah. What if we get back to town and it's deserted? Everyone gone? Some disaster? Or just . . . like . . . everyone disappeared?'

'At least we won't have the embarrassment of going into the Spar looking like death. They always look at you like they know.'

'They do know. But they won't be there anymore.'

'Wow. All the sausage rolls in the shop . . . ours. For free.'

'No more world. We were up here getting wasted and dancing and talking bollocks and having fun . . . and the whole time the world was ending. We had no idea.'

By the time we get to the bottom of the hill I've almost convinced myself. After all, there was no phone signal up there, *nobody could have warned us. The quiet is adding to it, sort of eerie but also beautiful, soft summer morning wind and the lazy twitterings of early birds. Like the human world could quite easily have collapsed while we were out of our heads. I almost like the idea. If this had been the last party ever, it was a hell of a rave to go out on.*

As if on cue, after a long period of silence – technical issues, analysed haphazardly by unsteady people seeing triple – someone fires up the decks and ghastly hardcore begins to blaze. Morning, campers.

'Looks like we got out just in time,' says Mark. He smiles at me and I almost kiss him right there and then, because at this moment I love him more than anything, more even than I usually love him.

Because we feel like the last two people in the world.

Maybe we are.

I hugged the memory to me, relishing the way it filled me up with such lovely sparks, although it brought sadness too, a soft and shivering regret. I could remember looking at Laura while she rolled that cigarette, how bloody stupid and wonderful she'd looked, how much I had adored her. I could feel what I'd felt, like the memory was a physical thing, a drug of its very own. And that had gone now.

I promised myself that once all this craziness was over, if we got through it, I was going to seek her out and try to mend things.

It was probably way past too late.

She'd probably tell me no, and be justified in doing so.

But I would at least try.

We ate chocolate and above-average baguettes from the

trolley and talked about everything that wasn't important, but which was also the most important stuff we could have talked about. We took it in turns to remember parties, comparing how off our tits we'd been, what the music had been like, who had said the funniest thing, who had lain on their back and made elephant noises, how many boys had dressed as girls and who had looked prettiest wearing make-up. We compared winter days, the way frosty stalactites hung from this tree or that tree, or how much more difficult the snow had made it to get to somebody's house, although we'd always got through it. If there was a party to get to, we got there. We compared summer days and forest raves and the memories of cosmic conversations. We talked about sitting round bonfires singing along to whoever had the obligatory guitar at that particular moment, muddling our way through Jack Johnson and Red Hot Chili Peppers songs, passing round warm boxes of wine. We talked about the world ending while we were getting high.

I didn't talk about how far behind me it all felt.

How partying and getting wasted had been so integral to youthful frolics but were now things I smiled fondly about rather than got unreasonably excited for.

How it had consequences you never considered when you were burning brightly in the thick of it.

I didn't talk about what to do next.

I just talked to my friend, the way we'd always talked.

Until he said, 'We don't know how much I'm going to change.'

I didn't know how to respond, so I said nothing.

'I haven't had another spasm, but I could have another one any minute. I don't know. We don't know. I don't know if I'm going to shrink or grow or get weird powers or what.'

I shook my head. There was also the little matter of me. What had Mr Matthews said? That the people around Mark's kind could be affected? The people that loved them, that they loved?

I imagined that included me.

'But,' Mark said, 'being with you makes it a hell of a lot less scary. Thank you.'

I smiled. 'That's what I'm here for, you numpty.'

'I know.'

I said 'numpty' again because I suddenly didn't want to get sentimental. I didn't care how much he was going to change.

And I didn't care if Tourneaux was armed, how angry he was, how badly he wanted Mark.

He wasn't having him.

That was it.

CHAPTER EIGHTEEN

L ONDON GHOSTED INTO view, all jagged diagonals
and grime and shine, bleached and smoky against the dull
yellow evening.

'I've never been here before,' said Mark, watching the concrete peaks rear up. 'It's pretty big.'

'It is.'

I'd done some calculations. Even if Tourneaux had
managed to get his tyres fixed super quickly and somehow
immediately knew we were heading to London and drove at
a hundred miles an hour all the way, he'd still be a way from
the city. We definitely had time to get to my place so I could
grab some stuff. Then to Alice's.

'Will she ask questions?' Mark asked, as we got off the
train.

'Probably.'

'What will you tell her?'

'I don't know.'

I held his hand as we hurried through a hundred little
tsunamis of people, all single-mindedly focused on their des-
tinations, on what they were going to have for dinner, on
who they were meeting, on how pleased they were that they'd
downloaded *Sonic the Hedgehog* to their iPhone. I wondered
how many of their lives were at risk right at this moment, or if
they only had drug-resistant bacteria and ecological apocalypse
and terrorist attacks to worry about, like normal people.

A Tube and a bus and a walk, and there was my building. The building. Stuart's building. Whatever. Inside, up the stairs, and there was the door. I felt as though the last sanity in the world was lurking behind that door and I wished, selfishly, unfairly, that it was just mine. I wanted to hang out with Mark in my own flat. It was a silly thought, but it burned.

I reached into my bag for my key and the door started to open.

Icy water rushed through my veins.

He was here already.

Tourneaux had beaten us to it.

He was going to kill both of us.

I was halfway through turning to warn Mark when the door opened fully and Stuart stepped out with a bag of recycling in his hand. He blinked when he saw us. 'Um . . . hi.'

My metaphorical jaw hit the floor. 'Oh! Um . . . Hi Stu.'

'I couldn't get hold of you.' He was trying to act normal, but there was a frost lurking. 'Wasn't sure when you'd be back.' He looked past me to Mark. 'Who's this?' Now the frost bit, hard.

It made me angry, even though it shouldn't have. *Think*, I thought.

'This is Mark,' I said. 'Old friend.'

' "Old"?'

'From back home,' said Mark. 'In Wales. She . . . used to . . . babysit me.' The way he said the words, it was like they'd never been introduced to each other.

'Right.' Stuart nodded. 'And . . . you've come for a visit.'

'He's thinking of moving down,' I said. 'Going to college. So he's looking around. I bumped into him back home. Said he could stay for a bit.'

Stuart didn't believe a word of this. I knew the signs. He nodded again. 'OK. Well. Have fun with that. I'll take this out. Then I'm going to meet Jeff.'

'Cool,' I said. 'I . . . um. You . . .'

'What?'

'You shouldn't come back.'

'Pardon?' The temperature dropped again.

'I mean . . . not yet. It's not safe.'

'Not *safe*? Vanessa, what the hell are you on about? You vanish for days, I barely hear anything, now you turn up at our flat with some teenager and tell me not to come back?'

'Sorry,' I said. 'It . . .'

'Let's go back inside and you can tell me what's going on,' said Stuart. Because that's what normal people did.

'Stuart, really—'

But he'd already turned around and gone back inside. I looked at Mark and said *sorry* with my eyes. He looked . . . was he *amused*? I thought I could just about read amusement. Little shit.

Then again, at his age, I probably would have found it funny too.

Stuart put the kettle on, which annoyed me. This was not a cosy chat. We weren't having tea. Except why wouldn't he put the kettle on. Because we always had tea when we talked. Or when we sat quietly. Or when we did anything. He didn't *know*.

'Stuart,' I said. 'Seriously. I . . . I can't explain what's happening. But in a couple of hours this flat won't be safe.'

'OK. So why are *you* here, if it's not safe?' I knew he didn't believe me.

'To grab some stuff and head out again.'

'And who's the kid? Really?'

Mark had obviously sensed that it would be prudent to steer entirely clear of this conversation, so he'd shut himself in the living room. I envied him. 'He's an old friend,' I said.

'An *old friend*? He's what, fifteen?'

'Sixteen. And no.'

'No what?'

'No, he's not some kind of severely fucked-up rebound.' *You would if you could,* I thought, although now was so far beyond the time for that kind of independent thinking that it was all I could do not to punch myself in the head. Plus, I felt as though it would take several PhDs in sociology, gender relations, law and theoretical time displacement to work out exactly how wrong the possibility was, on a scale of 'ill-advised but understandable lapse in judgment' to 'fetch me my pitchfork, lads, we got ourselves a paedo'.

Stuart made a face. 'That's not what—'

'You know that's *definitely* what you were thinking.'

'Well, put yourself—'

'In your shoes, yes, I know. It looks bad. It looks bad and weird and what the hell is going on and I wish I could tell you but I can't.' I ran my fingers through my hair. 'Stuart, please. I'm so tired and there's loads to—'

He banged his fist on the table, which made me jump. Stuart never banged his fist on anything. 'Vanessa, for *God's sake*! I'm tired too! In case you've forgotten, we bloody *broke up* a few days ago, after quite a long time together! Maybe you've moved on already—'

'I *haven't*, it's not that, it's—'

'Look, whether you have or not, you *owe* me an explanation, all right? I'm not trying to play the victim here. I know that things between us have been . . . not right. And it's both our faults. But that doesn't matter. Right now, you just owe me the courtesy of telling me the truth. Don't fob me off. All right?'

I looked him in the eye, feeling my lip curl in that sulky movement I wished I'd grown out of. 'Fine. When I was younger I had a friend called Mark. A close friend. He disappeared when we were sixteen. Vanished without a trace. And it messed me up. I never told you about it.'

'Why—'

'I *never told you about it*. That's all. Moving on and stuff. A few days ago, he reappeared, out of nowhere. Hadn't aged. As if nothing had happened. I went home to look after him. And now someone is after the two of us.'

Stuart was lost for words. He looked at the window. At the fridge. At the floor. Back at me, then away again. Then he shook his head, picked up the recycling and walked past me.

'You wanted the truth!' I said. The front door slammed. Stuart didn't slam doors. I was doing a grand job today. I stood in the kitchen feeling stupid. And guilty. And *angry*.

I opened the living room door and drew breath so sharply that it hurt my lungs. Mark was lying face down on the floor, panting, wings sprouting from his back. Huge and white, their feathers criss-crossed with tiny, intricate blue veins, they had ripped straight through his T-shirt and hoody.

'Fuck!' I fell to my knees next to him. 'Mark! Mark! Can you hear me?'

'Yes,' he whispered. 'I'm just in . . . quite a lot of pain.'

'Can you sit up?'

'Probably . . .'

I helped him to sit up, positioning him so that the wings

weren't touching the ground or anything else. They smelled hot and . . . *powerful* . . . and they kept twitching. Mark's eyes were screwed tightly shut, but he was smiling. 'You're smiling,' I said.

'Mm.' He spoke in a grimace, but the smile gave it a strange flavour.

'Um . . . can you, like . . . can you move them?'

His brow creased and the wings flexed slightly. 'Um,' I said. 'Mark . . . you have wings.'

'Yes.'

'Why didn't you call before?'

'Well . . . you two seemed to need some time alone.'

'You absolute—'

'And also I was in so much pain that I couldn't really form sounds.'

He stood up hesitantly and I moved to help him, but he shook his head. 'No. Let me . . . let me do it myself.' His eyes were still closed and he walked two unsteady paces, then stood still. He took a deep breath and opened his eyes, and with a majestic *whoosh* his wings completely unfolded, spreading like those of a huge bird of prey. The wingspan must have been six feet, getting on for seven.

I cried out in surprise and, despite myself, a kind of delight. 'Mark. *Mark*.'

'I know.' He turned and looked at me. 'I know.'

'How do they . . . how do they feel?'

'I don't know . . . it's like . . . it's like having another pair of arms, sort of. Just . . . growing out of my back. And they're bigger. And . . . they're wings.' He flapped them experimentally. I stood up and walked slowly around him in a circle, marvelling, entranced as he moved his new wings. I

217

kept trying not to think the thought that was filling my head. *He looks like a—*

Mark grinned at me and flapped them again. The living room was a twilit wood, leaves swooning down all around us, shivering as they fell.

He looks—

'You look like an angel,' I said.

And then he grabbed me and kissed me and the whole world, sofa, trees and all, seemed to vanish for a while.

I'd like to say it was the most awe-inspiring, ecstatic, life-affirming kiss you can imagine. That it was a perfect summation of our entire friendship, all the years I'd missed him, the impossible excitement at his reappearance, the love I'd always tried to pretend wasn't there. That time itself stood still and the universe re-shaped itself around us, that we came back changed. It wasn't like that, though. It was a nice kiss and it made me feel a bit horny, but it also made me think too much, so I pulled gently away.

'I . . . I don't know about that,' I said.

He looked like he knew what I meant, but decided to be contrary, just for the sake of it. 'Why? Because I'm sixteen and you're twenty-three? It's not that massive a gap.'

I'll be twenty-four before long, I thought. *Before you're seventeen.*

When I was sixteen you were nine.

Except he wasn't. When he was nine, I was nine.

When he was sixteen . . . *first* sixteen . . . I was sixteen. But now . . .

'That's not what I meant,' I said. 'You know that's not what I meant. Although . . . it is a slight issue.'

'Is it?'

'A bit.' I sat down. 'No, it's . . . it's because even if we were sixteen together and the last seven years hadn't happened, I don't know if us kissing would be a good idea. That's why I never kissed you then.'

He did know what I meant, although he didn't say anything. I knew he knew what I meant, because it was the same reason he'd never kissed me before either. Wasn't it?

'For God's *sake*, anyway!' I said. 'You just sprouted *wings*! And someone wants to kill you! This is not the time *at all*.'

'Do they look sexy, though?'

'Oh shut up.'

'Seriously, bro, do I look sexy?' His look was so Puckish I couldn't decide whether I wanted to hit him or kiss him again. Maybe both. In whatever order.

'Shut up, Mark! And put them away.'

'Put them away?' He laughed.

'*Can* you put them away, do you think?'

'I don't know. I'll try. I mean—'

'Good. Try. I'm going to go and pack some stuff.' I left him in the living room and drank a very cold glass of water before heading to the bedroom. I dug out my old suitcase, completely covered in laminated tickets and stickers, and packed some clothes, some spare toiletries, my laptop and a few odds and sods. As I was closing the suitcase, I remembered the envelope that Pauline had given me and delved into my bag to find it. There was a folded piece of paper inside.

I unfolded it and gasped. It was a cheque for a significant amount of money. I held it for a moment, staring, struggling to comprehend it, although in hindsight it was screamingly obvious. Then I tucked it into my purse and buried that in the bag. It would either help us hide out for a bit, or alternatively, if we could sort all this bollocks out, it would cover my last round of bills before moving out.

That made me think of Stuart. There was fixing to do there. Serious fixing.

I took out my phone and quickly called Pauline to tell her we were safe. She said she'd got back and had found no sign of Tourneaux. Thank God. I thanked her for the cheque and said I couldn't accept it, because I had to say that. She said I'd accept it and be grateful or I wasn't her favourite niece anymore. I said OK and that I loved her and she said she loved me too and that she shouldn't have said I was her favourite and that I wasn't ever to crack that one out with Isobel for the sake of cheap one-upmanship. I promised that I wouldn't.

I returned to the living room, hoping that Mark had put his wings away, because of course they made him look sexy. Luckily he had.

'Wow,' I said, walking around behind him to see. He'd taken the ruined hoody off but kept the T-shirt on. I could see his back through the huge rip, completely smooth, the redness of the skin the only clue that something might lurk beneath. 'Was it . . . difficult?'

'No. Not really. I wasn't really sure what I was telling the wings to do, how I was telling them, but they . . . they just seemed to know.'

'Right, we . . . shit. Hold on.' I ran back to the bedroom and grabbed an old sweatshirt of Stuart's from under a pile of my own dirty clothes, and a unisex T-shirt of mine. Part of me thought that giving Mark one of my own T-shirts to wear might be a tad inappropriate in light of recent developments, and that giving him anything of Stuart's was definitely entirely inappropriate, but a more dominant part thought that all other parts should shut up until further notice.

Except, no. As stupid as it was, I couldn't give him Stuart's clothes to wear. That wasn't cool. So I grabbed my least girly hoody – which was still purple – took it back to the living room and tossed it to Mark, along with the T-shirt. Then I very deliberately turned around while he changed, taking out my phone.

'Where the *fuck* have you been?' said Alice, by way of a greeting.

'Hey Al bear. I'm fine thanks, how are you?'

'I've heard pretty much nothing from you! I was worried!'

'Please, Alice, I've just had to deal with this from Stuart, I could do without it from you.'

'OK, but—'

'*Alice.* You know we had that really hammered chat once, and you said that no matter what I needed, however weird or difficult, you would be there for me? And I said the same to you?'

'I dimly recall something along those lines, although you might be paraphrasing . . .'

'Well, I need to come to your place right now with an inexplicable friend. And maybe stay for a bit.'

'Where are you now?'

'At the flat. Just about to leave. If you're home?'

'I'm home. See you in a bit. I'm not sure what I think of the word "inexplicable" though.'

I could probably explain to Alice. She wouldn't storm out and slam the door.

'We'll see,' I said. 'Love.'

'Love.'

I hung up and turned around. Mark had changed and was looking at me expectantly. I wagged a stern finger at him. 'Right, you. No more talk of kissing until further notice. OK?'

'Yes ma'am.'

'Don't call me that.'

'Sorry.'

'Yeah, you will be.'

CHAPTER NINETEEN

THANK FUCK FOR London. Thank fuck for the grubby bus stops and downturned mouths, the endless centipedes of impatient cars, the fumes and the food and the fact that it was a miracle that human beings were able to live here. Thank fuck for procedures like Oyster cards, such stolidly earthbound routines. So earthbound that I could actually feel vaguely normal as Mark and I travelled across town to Alice's place, even though every second threatened a further spillage of impossibilities out of my head and into the world. Every now and then I had to blink away the mirage of a murmuring tree where there shouldn't, *couldn't* be one, or a dream-like mist of dying leaves, or sometimes reanimated leaves flying back up to their welcoming boughs, *ah, children, you're home, why did you stay away for so long*. Occasionally I would spy myself staring sadly back at me, from the middle of the road, from a bus, from a shop window, from an enormous billboard, and then I would blink and it was just a stranger, a girl nodding along to private music or resting her head on a friend's shoulder or watching inscrutably from within the pristine confines of a perfume advert, or a boy with nervous, twitching knees, or an old lady sighing.

It was a good job this sudden torrent had come now, back in the smoke. London made these waking dreams avoidable. I could laugh them off. I could feel like a part of this world, but an anonymous one, a cell, which suited my purposes much better than Llangoroth. That place, my home, my origin point, was so exposed. Everyone knew everyone. Everyone had a finger in every other pie, stakes in other people's gossip, investments that went back decades. You couldn't walk around semi-conscious, your body enjoying the world's space, your mind enjoying your brain's, without somebody speaking to you. You couldn't ignore them without it getting back to your Mum. 'Why did you ignore so-and-so? They said you were walking around like a zombie! Are you all right? Are you ill?' You certainly couldn't put your hood up and walk the streets with your hands in your pockets listening to Burial, as I had been known to do, like a massive 21st century wanker.

You were a part of things in Llangoroth – you were an organ. A beating, bloody fragment of soul, to be monitored and interfered with. To be commented upon. To be missed. Down here you were just a microbe doing your bit, your tiny infinitessimal part, keeping the place running. If you fell out, you would be instantly replaced. Normal service would be resumed. Normal service wouldn't even stop, not for a second. Nobody would be any the wiser.

Here you were not special.

I was not special.

Perhaps counter-intuitively, I found this comforting. It made travelling with a winged boy seem much simpler. Cos who knew what other weirdness was going on out there, unnoticed.

We hopped off the bus and headed up the street towards Alice's building. 'He's going to find us at some point,' said Mark.

Ah yes. The psychotic man.

'Maybe I could just fight him?'

'Wings or no wings,' I said, 'you very recently got your arse handed to you by some country bumpkins. I don't see you holding your own against a gun-toting nut job who wants to cleanse your kind from the face of the Earth.'

'Cheers, mate.'

'No worries.'

Alice hugged me hard when we got to her flat. I could smell Chinese food. 'So glad to see you,' she said.

'You too.'

She narrowed her eyes in Mark's direction. 'Hello.'

'This is Mark,' I said.

They shook hands. 'Hi, Mark,' said Alice. 'You're . . .'

'Young?' Mark nodded. 'Yeah.'

'He's Mark,' I said, as she showed us into her unbearably stylish flat. '*Mark* Mark.'

Alice blinked, as if she didn't quite grasp what I'd said. Or as if she grasped what I'd said, but knew that it made no sense. '*Mark* Mark.'

'Yes.'

'No. Not—'

'Yes, possible,' I said. 'Well . . . no. Impossible. But . . . happening. Please can I have a cup of tea?'

'*Mark* Mark? Like, *your* Mark? Mark who . . . who did the . . .'

'Yes,' I said. 'Tea? Please?'

Alice suddenly looked severely mentally fatigued. 'Um . . . OK.' She went through to her little kitchenette.

Mark turned to me. 'Is this a good idea?'

'Telling her? Yeah. It's fine. She'll be fine.'

'*What the fuck?*' Alice practically shrieked from the kitchen.

I smiled sweetly at Mark. 'Sit down, boyo. I'll handle this.'

I handled it. It wasn't the easiest thing ever but I handled it, and the three of us sat down and had tea. Alice couldn't take her eyes off Mark. I decided to keep the wings under wraps for now. I didn't want her brain doing the blue screen of death on us.

'Sorry,' she said, as he looked away, embarrassed. 'I don't mean to stare. It's just . . .'

'It's fine,' said Mark. 'Don't worry.'

'So this guy.' Alice managed to force herself to stop looking at him. 'Tourneaux. He's genuinely dangerous. True believer.'

'Think so,' I said.

'And good at tracking?'

'I don't think you need to worry,' I said, appalled at how unconvincing I sounded.

'Oh, that's all right then. Cos I suppose he couldn't possibly look on Facebook and see that we're good friends who live fairly near one another . . .'

'My privacy settings are really good.'

Alice gave me a look that could have curdled a pregnancy. 'Are you fucking being fucking serious right now.'

'Yes. No! I mean . . . look, it's just . . . he told me that he didn't want to hurt anyone. Else. Apart from Mark. Sorry, Mark.'

Mark shrugged.

'Whatever he's doing,' I said, 'and *whyever* he's doing it . . . he thinks he's in the right. True believer, like you said. He's doing it for a cause, however screwed up that cause is. So I think, in his way, he's probably sort of honourable.'

'Speaking as a journalist,' said Alice, 'that sounds an awful lot like conjecture.'

'Well, obviously that's because it's complete conjecture. I

am relishing my new role as an Olympic-level straw-grasperer.'

Alice smiled. 'Nessie, you don't need to get defensive, or make up words. And don't worry about me, either. I've twatted a few unwanted males in my time.'

'So have I.'

'I know, I know, you're a badass too. What I mean is, I'm sure a deranged crusader won't be too much of a stretch.'

'I did kind of run rings around him earlier.'

'Which has probably pissed him off beyond all reason,' said Mark.

'Cheers, mate.'

'No worries.'

'Thinking about it,' I said, 'might be an idea to de-purple my hair? Means I'll stand out less.'

Alice nodded. 'Yep. I'll do it for you in a bit. Any thoughts on an alternative colour?'

I was momentarily struck by an image of the other me, the mirror me, and it plunged my body into a well of deep, dark cold.

'Black,' I said, doing my best to ignore the chill.

'Good plan. I have the technology.'

'Cool. Um, *alsooo* . . . you know journalism? The thing you do?'

'The course we did together for three years?'

'Yep.'

'Rings a bell.'

'You were always much better at it than me. All aspects. Especially research.'

'Not—'

'*Not* the time for false modesty. You were much better. You got a First.'

227

'And you *should* have got one.'

'Yeah, but only because I was good at writing. I was rubbish at actual journalism, hence—'

'*Anyway*,' said Mark.

'Sorry,' I said. 'Basically, we need to find out more about this guy. The internet didn't cough up much. Anything, in fact. And I'm not sure what else to do.'

'Vanessa,' said Alice. 'Did your internet research consist of you googling every vaguely connected word you could think of for a couple of hours and then giving up?'

'I didn't *give up* as such . . .'

'Tell you what,' said Alice. 'Let *me* do some research. The internet doesn't begin and end with Google, you know.'

'OK. Well . . . can I help?'

'You know how we fell out when we lived together?'

'Yeah.'

'Remember the only *other* time we fell out?'

'For fuck's sake!' Alice snaps. 'Do you want to fail?'

David looks at the floor, sulkily.

'Well? Do you?'

'No. But that doesn't mean you have to be such a bitch.' He gets up and walks off, leaving his bag, his pile of library books and his laptop. Alice runs her hands through her hair, eyes more manic than I think I've ever seen them.

'Alice?' I say. 'Maybe—'

'No. No. We have three days to get this bastard thing done. I don't have time for that cretin to act like a fucking . . . cretin!'

'Alice . . . I want to do well as well. But—'

'If you want to do well then let's do fucking well!' She turns around and goes back to her computer, breathing heavily.

I vaguely consider going for a walk as well, but I know that when we call it a night she'll be calmer and apologetic. Possibly apologetic enough to buy me a mojito. So I look back down at my book.

'I work better under my own steam,' said Alice. 'If you write down all the stuff you know, then I can organise it and get on it. But by myself would be better. I hate having to shout. Especially at you.'

Mark sniggered and Alice turned the full force of her immaculate left eyebrow on him. 'What was that?'

'Nothing,' he said. 'Going to the toilet.' He got up and walked out of the living room.

'He's kind of yum,' said Alice, in a low voice, when Mark had gone. 'Y'know. For a tween. Picking up where you left off?'

'No!' I knew she knew. But I had to pretend. 'He's sixteen and I'm twenty-three.'

'And I bet you've been repeating that in your head and out loud ever since he reappeared.'

'Please, Al bear.'

'OK. But you know I'm right.'

I grunted.

'I'm *definitely* right.'

'There's something else you need to know,' I said. 'Before he comes back.' Quickly and, I thought, impressively succinctly, I explained about Mark's otherworldly attributes and what little we knew of his mother. 'You can add that to your research pile.'

I could tell Alice was on fire with questions – who wouldn't be, to be fair – but Mark had returned from the toilet so she just nodded. 'Yeah. Write everything down and I'll get on it later. I'm not at work until the afternoon tomorrow so I can do some in the morning too.'

'Thank you.'

'Yeah,' said Mark. 'Thanks.'

'No problem, sugars.' Alice clapped her hands. 'Wine.'

We de-camped to the bathroom with wine so that Alice could get started on my new hair. It was a testament to the trust we shared that I was happy for her to drink and dye. I even felt myself relax a bit as she did her thing. 'How were the SWLC?' I asked.

'Really good, actually,' said Alice. 'They're on a big trans-inclusion drive at the moment. I'm going to help them organise a march.'

'Cool.'

'They also had a lengthy tangent on how asparagus makes your wee smell funny.'

'Does it?'

'Apparently. I hate the stuff so I wouldn't know.'

'Fair dos. Fascinating. Equality, asparagus and piss. Good old SWLC, fearlessly exploring the no man's land between high and low culture.'

'Um, what's the SWLC?' said Mark.

Alice and I giggled. 'Super Woke Lesbians Club,' said Alice. 'Which we *really* shouldn't call them.'

'OK . . .'

'Basically it's a crew of incredibly right-on uni friends of Alice's,' I said, 'who all happen to be lesbians. They talk about politics and social issues and stuff. Usually over cocktails.'

'They're your friends too,' said Alice.

'Eh, not really. I mean, they know who I am and I know

who they are. I can't keep up with them, I never could. So much *theory*. They use words like "praxis" in conversation. I swear you only invite me so you can enjoy my symphony of confused faces.'

'Pretty much.'

'Anyway,' I said, 'they're all super lovely, crusading for justice and so on. I'm one hundred per cent on their side. But they can be *super* serious. Which makes me laugh. Because I don't take anything seriously. Because I don't care about anything.'

'You're so un-woke you're practically in a coma,' said Alice.

'Practically dead.'

'Such a bad ally.'

Mark looked like he was having trouble processing all this. 'So "woke" is . . .'

'You know,' said Alice. 'Woke. Like, card-carrying social justice warrior.'

'Registered feminazi,' I said.

'Chartered libtard snowflake,' said Alice.

'Signatory to the PC Killjoy Act,' I said.

'I have no idea what either of you are saying,' said Mark. 'I don't think we had any of this stuff in my day.'

'I'm *so* sorry for my gauche young friend, Alice,' I said. 'You'll have to forgive him. Where we grew up, heteronor-mativity was the only game in town. And there were like two non-white families within a hundred-mile radius. He's probably still getting used to you.'

Alice nodded sympathetically. 'And I'm only semi-brown.'

Mark went red. 'Leave me alone.'

Alice finished my hair and we returned to the living room to drink more wine and talk more rubbish. Amazingly, I managed to forget about Tourneaux, until Alice stood up dramatically and announced that it was time to do research.

'Are you sure you're OK to do this?' I asked, giving her the list I'd written out.

'Yes. You two can sleep in my room.'

'But—'

'No butting. I've got a sofa in my office. I can sleep there. There's more bedding in the wardrobe, one of you can have my bed, the other can make one up on the floor. You'll forgive me if I don't do it for you.'

'It's fine.' I hugged her and kissed her cheeks. 'Thank you so much.'

'Don't be a dick. If I was on the lam with an impossible boy you'd be the first person I'd ring. Not that you'd be any help.'

'You're right, I probably wouldn't be. Thanks for le cheval noir as well.'

'Think you mean cheveux,' said Mark. He'd always been inexplicably good at French, even though he never did any work. 'Cheval means horse.'

'I know, you big swot. Crap French. It's sort of our thing.'

'Oh.'

Alice chuckled. 'Go to bed. I'll let you know if I find anything.' She patted my head and trotted off to her study with the remains of the wine.

'You can have the bed,' said Mark, when I came back into Alice's bedroom, teeth brushed and pyjama'd up. He'd assembled his bed on the floor and was now standing in the middle of the room with his shirt off, wings fully extended, taking it in turns to move the right and then the left.

'All right, Topless Tim.' I stood and watched him. He winced with every other movement, but it already seemed to be getting easier for him. 'You didn't have any problem . . . um . . . getting them out?'

'No. Just . . . thought. Not even that. You don't really *think* about unfolding your arms when they've been folded, do you? You just . . . unfold them. It's like that.' He flapped both wings in unison. 'Hurts a bit but it's not so bad.' He drew his wings in so they were folded in against his back, then extended them again. They made a *whoosh*, which momentarily drowned out the ocean breeze filtering through the cracks in the walls.

'Are you sure?' I said. 'About the bed?'

'Well, what's the alternative?' he asked, slyly.

'You in the bed and me on the floor,' I said, pointedly. 'Don't try and do flirting, Mark. It doesn't become you.' Not even shirtless with his wings out.

He made a squiggly face. 'Sorry.'

'So you should be.'

'Your new hair looks good, by the way.'

'Flattery will get you nowhere. Seriously.' I got into bed and watched him for a little longer. After a minute he turned to face me, closed his eyes and drew the wings right back down so that they disappeared inside. There was no noise when they vanished, which sort of surprised me. I think I was expecting a really disgusting sound. But no. They were just gone, absorbed, and he was wingless Mark, breathing very deliberately to ride out the pain. Then he put his T-shirt back on, switched off the light and got into his bed on the floor.

I lay with my eyes open for a minute, wondering who was going to speak first. I guessed it would be him.

'I've been thinking,' he said, slowly. Bingo. 'It's pretty obvious how I got here. To now, I mean. From then.'

'Mm?'

'Well, I did it, didn't I? Without realising.'

'You transported yourself through time?'

'Must have done. I'm . . . I don't know. Manifesting my power or something.'

I laughed despite myself. 'Would that these wings were time wings.'

'Eh?'

'Sorry. I was just referencing something you couldn't possibly have seen for my own amusement.'

'Cheers, mate.'

'No worries.' I thought about what he'd said. It made sense, of a sort. 'Why now, though? Why would you come here?'

'Well I didn't do it on purpose, did I? It was a mistake. Like young Superman sneezing and accidentally destroying a barn.'

'Maybe you could feel that something bad was going to happen.' The fuzzy darkness was suddenly full of that scene that might have been. Mr Matthews sobbing, beating his son to the ground.

'I don't remember that.' He knew what I meant, even though I hadn't said it. Was that his power? Had he always been able to do that?

'Maybe it was deeper than remembering,' I said. 'Like, subconsciously you knew something awful was going to happen to you. And you made yourself disappear.'

Mark didn't speak.

'I know asking how you are is stupid,' I said. 'All the stuff with your dad. Your mum. Your wings. I know summing up how you are would be impossible.'

'But you're going to ask me how I am.'

'Yes.'

'Go on then.'

'How are you?'

'I'm fine.'

'I knew you were going to say that.'

'Ha. Thanks for asking, though.'

'No worries.'

After another pregnant minute, he asked, 'Do you think that might be it? That I . . . that something deep down, deeper than human, down where . . . wherever the wings come from . . . just knew I was in danger? Panicked and sent me here?'

'Maybe, possibly. It's . . . I don't think it's just you, either.'

'What do you mean?'

'What your dad said. About how your mum, you, your . . . your kind, if that's not a horrible way to put it . . . can change the people around you. I think he's right. Ever since you reappeared, I've felt different. I've been . . . seeing things. Feeling things. Not premonitions, exactly.' I could see the words I'd written in my notebook, the words I'd thrown away. The words that weren't mine. They were there, floating in the air in front of me. I blinked them hurriedly away. 'Hints, maybe. I don't know. And some things that were just . . . weird. And scary.' For a second, maybe less, the other me flashed into view. And I remembered the smell of the leaves as they died on that road in the country, just before Mark had fallen.

And risen.

'And some that were beautiful,' I said.

Sometimes I feel as though I could just walk straight in.

Not swim, not straight away. Walk into the sea until it's over me, completely over me. Until I'm part of it. And then I swim, I swim straight down, and there's a new world down there. A luminous forest. Soft bubble mountains.

'It's like . . . like you're changing me.' I was talking more than I wanted to. More than I should have been.

'I'm sorry,' he said. 'I don't mean—'

'No. No. Not sorry.' I was suddenly aware that he was kneeling beside the bed, looking at me. Golden leaves and white feathers were falling from the invisible space above the ceiling, fluttering down, dancing intricate waltzes. They brought a hot and cold smell with them, a mixture of sea air and flesh and fresh, damp earth. The trees at the foot of the bed creaked and a moon bigger than the world made eyes at me.

'Not sorry,' I whispered.

CHAPTER TWENTY

I WOKE EARLY. Mark was still asleep and I quietly got up and went to the bathroom, and then to Alice's study. She was at her computer with a half-full cafetière next to her, one hand on the mouse, the other clasped around a cup.

'Morning,' I whispered.

She jumped and turned around in her chair. 'Oh, hey Nessum.'

'I was going to see if you wanted a coffee, but your house elf beat me to it.'

'Sounds like him. Obsequious little shit.' She beckoned and I sat on the edge of the sofa that filled nearly half of her cramped office.

'I hope you haven't been awake all night,' I said.

'Of course I haven't. I was looking until I couldn't keep my eyes open, then as soon as they opened again I got back on it.' She glanced at the clock on the wall. 'Blimey. Nine o'clock. I didn't think you did early.'

'Dunno what you mean. Find anything?'

'A bit.' She opened a few tabs and did some scrolling, glancing at the notes she'd made on a legal pad. 'Bits and pieces about sightings of people with wings, dotted across decades. Same sort of frequency as sightings of werewolves and vampires. Which . . . by the way?'

I raised an eyebrow. 'Are you serious?'

'Sorry. Thought it was worth asking. Um . . . yeah. So

they're mostly attributed to optical illusions or religious fervour. Lots of people have claimed to have had visitations from an angel, who then proceeded to tell them a bunch of shit they already knew or could easily have found out, as if it were in some way divine.'

'Careful, you're beginning to sound like me.'

Alice sipped her coffee. 'The day I become as intolerant as you is the day I embark on a torrid affair with Richard Dawkins.'

'You could probably convert him.'

'Ha.' Alice smiled. 'You know, you should have a crack at it.'

'At Dawkins?'

'Ugh. No. Basic tolerance. I still go to Midnight Mass with my fam at Christmas. I love that shit.'

'Try casually mentioning the fact that you have been known to enjoy the company of girls as well as boys at one of those events,' I said. 'See how tolerant they are of *you*.'

'*Anyway*. We digress. I found a couple of references here and there to people who believe the sightings were real, although not angels exactly. Sort of . . . halfway between human and angel. But therefore impure and either actively evil or just too disgusting to be allowed.'

'Is it a specific group that thinks this?'

'Not really. There's no name or website or anything. And I came across the same school of thought in connection with Christian, Islamic and most other beliefs. So it's not some even more mental offshoot of the Westboro Baptists or anything like that, as far as I know.'

'Just general non-affiliated nutcases.'

'Quid each in the Not Woke Jar for "mental" and "nutcases".

But yeah. Non-affiliated. So nothing about Tourneaux or his people I'm afraid. *But*. There was one thing. One little essay on a blog.'

'Whose blog?'

'No name. The blog's called Weird, Sister. General randomness and strange happenings, UFOs, Bigfoot and such like. Some 9/11 conspiracy crap. And a lot of faerie porn, for some reason.'

'Sounds like a reputable source.'

'Agreed, but interesting anyway. Have a look.' She moved aside so I could read.

'It's easy to forget in this day and age, when we have become so comfortable in our routines, in our technical and moral superiority, in our arrogance, that we are not the beginning and end of the human paradigm. Far from it.'

I shook my head. 'I instinctively distrust anybody who chucks the word "paradigm" around.'

'Same,' said Alice. 'But read on.'

'We are one step on a ladder that stretches from the murky depths of the past to an uncertain, unrecognisable future. And we may not even be a definitive link. I came upon this thought when reading of the little-known legend of winged people. Humanoids graced with wings of such angelic ferocity that primitive and, unfortunately, unreliable witnesses mistook them for harbingers of godly providence. And I tried to bring my scientific lens to bear. As you, dear readers, know, I try to cast aside the lead weight of scepticism and cynicism and shine a bright light on the world beyond the box.'

'The box is there for a reason,' I muttered.

'I thought first of flightless birds. The ostrich. The penguin. They have their vestigial wings, the tools that once bore them

from edge to edge upon the thermals, but they have simply run out of use for them. Their destinies lie not in the sky but on the ground. Could the same not be said for humans? Of course, the size and strength of wing needed for a full-size human to fly as gracefully as the hawk is an evolutionary impossibility. But perhaps flight was not their purpose. Do animals not artificially increase their size to ward off predators? Might ancient humans, still bubbling in time's great cookpot, have been blessed (or cursed) with appendages not necessarily as useful as they appeared to be? Might they have been a marker of superiority and nothing else? And might, therefore, the more numerous and inferior wingless have taken it upon themselves to stamp out these pretenders? It is a tragic thought – we humans use a fraction of the potential contained within us. Perhaps, had they been allowed to survive, the winged ones might have helped us to unlock the true potential within? Perhaps we will never know? I leave it to you, dearest reader, to decide.'

'Too many rhetorical questions,' I said.

'Definitely,' said Alice.

'Also, "dearest reader" is the worst.'

'Agreed.'

'This is the best evidence we can find? In the whole world, the only vaguely relevant thing is some DMT-fried crackpot?'

'I know it's a parade of cringe,' said Alice. 'But, you know. There might be a couple of points in there.'

'I don't know,' I said. 'Maybe . . . or maybe we're just not going to find anything. It's just too amazing. Too incredible. Too rare.'

'Too incredible for Wikipedia.' Alice shook her head. 'Scary.'

'But,' I said, slapping my forehead. '*But. But!*'

'Rocking some explosive *buts* there, love.'

'Books!' I said. 'I didn't even think about books. I just . . . Jesus. What an idiot. What an absolute 21ˢᵗ century idiot.'

'It had occurred to me to use the library,' said Alice. 'I vaguely remember them, from the before times. I used to love the uni library, actually. But I'm not a member of one now.'

'It's not hard to join up.'

'No . . . but you'd need a pretty major library to find stuff that's almost completely absent from the internet.'

'Yeah. And I don't even know where I'd start. Mythology? Evolutionary biology? Where?'

'I'd start by going to a library.'

'Cheers, Sarky McGee.'

'You're welcome. There's got to be one nearby. I can't believe I don't even know where.'

'Maybe you're not the Queen of Research after all.'

'I could look on the internet for you.'

'Fuck the internet, dawg. I'm going to find it by *walking*. Back to the old school.'

'Mental. Anyway. I'm one hundred per cent definitely bookmarking Weird, Sister. Some of the funniest shit I've ever read.'

'I'm going to have a shower, then I'm going to go out and find a library, among other things. Mark's still asleep and I don't want to wake him. If he gets up while I'm gone, tell him I won't be long.'

'OK.' Alice shook her head. 'You know . . . Mark . . . I'm going to *have* to write some poems about this.'

'Figured you would,' I said. 'And I bet they'll be fifty thousand times better than any poems I could write about him. You jammy bitch. Not content to be a better journalist than me, you just casually stroll in and whoop my ass at poems too.'

'Shut up. Your poems are really good.'

'Thanks. But they've never made a room full of drunk strangers cry.'

'That's because you've never performed them to a room full of drunk strangers.' Alice shook her head. 'I know how many times I've said this to you, and I know it still refuses to sink in, but I'm just going to keep saying it. You're a sick writer, mate. You always were. You just need to get your arse in gear and do it properly. You need to let yourself be awesome.'

She *had* said that a lot. But for the first time, I wondered if maybe she was right. I nodded and patted her shoulder. 'Thanks mate. Really. I'll get on that. After I've found a library. And saved my friend from a madman.'

'OK,' said Alice. 'It's a deal. Love.'

'Love.'

I meant to find a bank and then a library, but ended up wandering for a bit. I liked this area. It was near Waterloo and had a nice mixture of eccentric pubs and small shops. The commuter rush had ebbed and the sun was already getting pretty hot. I could almost have been enjoying a normal day off work.

Except that every now and then I could see my face where it shouldn't have been. On mannequins, on humans, in intricate graffiti and random spills of light. My face, watching me, although she was no longer sad. She didn't seem to be warning me anymore. She was just . . . watching.

I walked all the way to Waterloo and then towards the river, where I had a coffee and watched some boats, remembering younger me, alone and stupid, years ago, staring down at the water, watching her cigarette disappear. I had a brief, wry chuckle, then jumped as my phone rang.

It was him.

'What do you want?' I growled.

'Ah, good. I just wanted to check it was you.' Tourneaux hung up. Moments later he was standing next to me. 'Would have been terribly embarrassing if it hadn't been, eh? Sorry that you wasted your time changing your hair. Although I do prefer the black to the purple.'

I didn't say anything.

I didn't want him to see me shake.

I didn't want him to hear fear in my voice.

'I have to hand it to you,' said Tourneaux. 'You're making things much more difficult for me than I expected.'

It was broad daylight. Surely he wouldn't—

'But I'll find where you're staying,' he said. His tone was so conversational. He was having *fun*. 'I'll find where you're keeping him. You'll take me there.'

'No I won't.'

The facade fell away. 'Listen to me, you stubborn little *bitch*. You know nothing of his kind. You know nothing of my mission. And you know nothing of pain. I'm an expert on all three. And if you don't want me to make things *very* unpleasant for you—'

'*He's just a boy,*' I said, although I only half believed it. 'Why do you—'

'His existence is an affront,' said Tourneaux. 'It is our *shame.*'

'Did you kill his mother, too?'

'Where is he?'

243

'Fuck you.' I turned to run but he grabbed me and spun me around and hissed into my face, spraying spit. His breath stank.

'*You're going to tell me where he is, or—*'

'Hey. What's going on?' A man in a suit had stopped by us, concerned.

Tourneaux looked straight at him. 'Nothing,' he said. 'Kindly move along.'

The man looked at me. 'Are you all right?'

Should I answer? I thought. *Should I get him involved?*

I knew I shouldn't, but I didn't need to say anything anyway. It was obvious.

The man turned back to Tourneaux. 'I think you should let her go.'

Wow. This was not like London at all.

'Leave,' said Tourneaux. 'Now.'

'I think you'd better—'

'Last warning. Get lost.'

The man moved to separate us, but Tourneaux was too quick. He let go of me, grabbed the man's arm and broke it with a snap that made vomit bubble in the base of my throat. The poor man was in too much pain to even scream, he just dropped to his knees, clutching his wrecked arm, and Tourneaux drove his knee savagely into the side of his head. The man slammed into the ground and I ran, tears in my eyes and sick in my mouth. I could hear Tourneaux pounding behind me.

He'd lost it.

Completely.

If he'd ever had it in the first place.

I made it to the Tube station, vaulted over the barriers

and ran down the escalator, ignoring the yells of the guards. They didn't catch me but they must have caught Tourneaux, because when I chanced a look behind me he wasn't there. I kept running, though, and didn't stop until I'd boarded a train. I collapsed into a seat and made a huge effort not to break down, hearing the snap of that poor man's arm in my head, amplified by a thousand.

I had to make sure I lost Tourneaux.

I texted Alice to tell her what had happened, then made a detour of nearly an hour, travelling north on one train and taking a zig zag of buses and Tubes back down south. I didn't go back to the original station, or even to Waterloo, but to a tiny middle-of-nowhere station. It seemed as though I'd spent the last week going from nothing station to nothing station. From there I took a bus and got off ten minutes' walk from Alice's. The whole time I was travelling I kept looking around, checking behind me, convinced that Tourneaux was going to appear at any moment, but he didn't. Even when I got back to Alice's I felt sure I would open the door and find him there, standing over Mark's mutilated body, ready to kill me too . . .

But Mark answered the door, alive, smiling. He even looked surprised when I leapt on him, hugging out the fear. 'Are you OK?' I asked.

'Fine. How are *you*? Alice said Tourneaux found you?'

'Yeah. He's . . . he hurt a guy. He's not playing anymore. Where's Alice?'

'She had to go to work. She said she won't be back until nine.'

I realised that I'd forgotten to put Pauline's cheque in the bank.

And to look for a library.

They both seemed like silly things to think about now.

'I don't know what to do,' I said. 'I don't . . . we can't stay here. Alice is my best friend. It won't take him long to work it out. I don't know how he even managed to find me earlier . . . he must have known we were somewhere near Waterloo . . .'

'Is there anywhere else?' Mark asked. 'Anyone?'

There wasn't. No-one like Alice. No-one who would understand.

'I don't think so,' I said.

'OK then. Well . . .' Mark looked away from me, out of the window.

'What?'

'Maybe we should just wait. Fight.'

'What, set up booby traps all over Alice's flat? Go *Home Alone* on his ass?'

'Maybe? Or just wait and . . . you know. Jump him.'

'How many times do I have to remind you about those kids? Fighting him is not an option.'

'If we're both ready, it could be. Element of surprise. We beat the crap out of him, tie him up, then you tell the police he broke in.'

'I tell them?'

'I'll hide. Keep things from getting complicated.'

I shook my head. 'I don't like it. Just waiting for him to appear. And I don't like turning Alice's flat into a battle-ground. And . . .'

'And what?'

'He'd kill us,' I said. 'You didn't see him attack that guy. It was brutal. Effortless. We wouldn't stand a chance.'

Mark breathed deeply. 'So . . . what do we do?'

'I don't know . . . we could find a pub that has rooms? Or . . . a Travelodge or something? Just for now?'

'But we can't just keep running away forever . . .'

'I know! I *know*! Fucking hell.' I sat down and closed my eyes. 'We can't fight him. We'd have to . . . you know. And I can't do that. Neither of us can.'

Mark didn't seem to know what to say to that. I sympathised. 'I'll make you a cup of tea,' he said.

'No. Don't. Come over here.'

He came over and sat next to me.

'Give me a hug while I think.'

He put his arm around me and I put my head on his shoulder, closed my eyes and didn't really think.

I was almost halfway towards considering coming up with a plan when my phone rang. The acidic spike of dread that immediately pierced my stomach told me it was Tourneaux, but then I checked and it was only Stuart. For a second I considered not answering, but I knew I should.

'Sorry Mark. Give me a sec.' I got up and walked over to the window. 'Hi.'

'Hi.' Cold.

'How are you?'

'Just seeing if you and your friend were going to be around later at all. I was planning on spending the evening at the flat.'

'OK. I . . . we won't be there. We're at Alice's.'

'Thought so. Doesn't matter. Better for you to . . . I don't know . . .'

'Stuart, it's not like that.'

'Vanessa . . . you know how I feel about you.'

I wasn't sure I did, but for simplicity's sake I said, 'Yes.'

'But I think maybe it just wasn't meant to work.'

'No.'

'That boy . . . I'm not going to ask. It's none of my business what you do now. Just . . . be careful.'

'It's not—'

'Not my business.'

'That's not what I was going to say.'

'I know. But it's not my business. Whenever you're ready, we can sort out the bills and stuff and you can move out, or I can move out, or whatever's easiest.'

I wondered if I was going to cry. 'Stuart . . . the flat's not safe.'

'Oh for God's sake, Vanessa. Not this again. It's *fine*. I imagine you had a heavy weekend back home, yes?'

'No!' Amazing how much like 'yes' I could make 'no' sound.

'So you're probably feeling a bit paranoid . . .'

Oh, you patronising shit. 'Stuart, *please*.' I felt certain that he should have been able to hear it in my voice, understand that something was genuinely terribly wrong.

Maybe he could. Maybe he was just ignoring it on purpose, to spite me.

'It's fine,' he said. 'I'll see you soon. We can chat properly. Or something.'

I sighed. I wasn't going to get anywhere. There was no point. 'Fine.' Tourneaux knew I'd know better than to go there. Maybe Stuart would be safe?

'OK. Well . . . see you.'

'See you.'

I hung up. Not five seconds later the phone rang again, and I answered without looking. 'Oh what now?'

'Vanessa?'

'Dad?' I nearly fell over. 'Um . . . hi. Sorry. I thought you were someone else.'

'Are you all right?'

'I . . . I'm fine.'

'Sorry, is this a bad time?'

'Um . . . not a great time, sorry. I'm just on my way out . . .'

'Oh, OK. Well . . . it doesn't really matter. I just wanted to . . . say hello. And say . . . um.'

'Dad? Are *you* all right?'

'Well . . . I . . . I was looking at some pictures this morning. Old photos. You, me, Izzy, your mother. Feeling a bit . . . I don't know.'

'Nostalgic?'

'Sort of. The good and bad kind, you know?'

'Yes.'

'So I just thought I'd say that . . . I love you. If that's all right.'

'Of course it's all right!' I said, even though I wasn't entirely sure this conversation was really happening. 'I love you too.' It sounded a bit strange coming out of my mouth, as it had with Mum, but still nice.

'Thank you. Well . . . I'll leave you to it. Would be nice to have a proper chat soon.' Everybody seemed to want to have a proper chat with me. Why?

'Definitely,' I said. 'Take care, Dad.'

'You too. Bye.'

'Bye.'

I hung up and turned to Mark, shaking my head. 'What?' he said.

'Synchronicity.'

'Synchronicity?'

'Stuff. Stuff is too weird. Too weird for me. Fuck stuff. Stuff's ridiculous. Let's go to a Travelodge.'

CHAPTER TWENTY-ONE

T HE INTERNET ON my phone was playing up so I used Alice's computer to find Travelodges in London. There were two in Tower Hill, which felt like a safely random destination, so we grabbed our stuff and headed out. It was risky going out in broad daylight again so soon, but riskier to stay at Alice's. I texted her quickly before we left, saying thank you and sorry and I'd call her and maybe she should stay out as late as possible tonight, just in case. Then off we went, hoods up, stopping briefly at a bank to deposit Pauline's cheque.

I'd stayed in a Travelodge once before and they weren't exactly luxurious, but they were nondescript and probably quite hard to sneakily break in to, even if you were a murderous nutter. I even managed to get away with not giving a name. Thank God for sloppy procedures.

When we got to our room Mark went straight to the window and stared out at the city. His back glowered at me.

'Whassup?' I said, too cheerily.

'Nothing.'

'Call it a hunch, but I think you might be lying.'

'Well, obviously a lot. But I don't do ranting.'

'It can be quite cathartic. Maybe you should give it a try.'

'Maybe later. What's the time?'

'Three.'

'Give me a couple of hours and maybe I'll do a rant.'

So for a couple of hours I made use of the tea and coffee making facilities and read a book I'd pilfered from Alice, while Mark moved steadily around the room, brooding. As fun afternoons go, it wasn't up there with the best of them, but I still had to restrain myself from laughing a couple of times. Mark just looked so funny, wandering around in a grump.

It got to five, then half five, then six, and I went out to a nearby shop and bought supplies, which we ate in silence. Then it was seven. Then . . .

The sea presents itself to me and I just walk straight in. I don't need to swim. I just walk, until it's up to my knees, up to my waist, up to my chest, over my head. Until I'm part of it, breathing water as though it's the cleanest air ever to pass through my lungs. Now I swim. I swim straight down, and there's a new world down there. A luminous forest. Soft bubble mountains. Fish of every colour, shimmering between light patches, like an ancient emperor's treasure cast overboard. Crystal spires gleaming, people swimming in and out of them . . . no . . . not people.

Angels. Winged kings and queens and princes and princesses, so bright and beautiful that I feel a soft stab in my heart. Naked against the warm, forgiving, remembering sea, I open my arms to join them and—

I woke up with a mumble. It was significantly darker now and Mark was at the window again. It took a couple more mumbles before I could say anything coherent. 'What time is it?'

'Not sure.'

'Didn't I ask you to wake me?'

'No. You just fell asleep.'

'Oh. OK.' I got up and looked at my phone. Half nine.

'Have you just been staring out of the window the whole time?'

He didn't answer.

'Mark.'

'What?'

'Talk to me.'

He didn't turn around. 'I don't want this,' he said.

'I know.'

'I don't want to be in the future. I don't want to be some kind of . . . freak. I don't want *these*.' He extended his wings suddenly and violently, tearing his T-shirt and making me jump. 'I don't want to know things,' he said. 'I don't want to know that my dad never wanted me, or that my mother died giving birth to me. I don't want to run and hide from some psychopath. *I don't want any of this.*'

He turned around and his eyes almost glowed in the darkness. 'But I do want you.' Maybe his eyes *were* glowing. They certainly seemed bluer than they'd ever been. Had they even been blue, before? I couldn't remember. I thought he was going to come towards me, but he didn't. He just stood there, an angel against the black. 'And I can forget about everything, *everything*, all this shit, this madness and horror and pain, I can forget about all of it. So long as I have you.'

I looked at him.

He knew I wanted him too.

Of course I did.

But . . .

But there was always a *but*.

And I couldn't ignore them.

My phone rang. 'Don't answer it,' said Mark.

'It might be important,' I said.

He bristled visibly at that. *As if he's not important,* I thought. *Stupid child.* The thoughts were unnecessarily harsh, but they helped to snap me out of the moment. I couldn't be in that moment.

I might never leave it.

Stuart was on the phone. What did *he* want?

Oh well. If the moment had been on life support before, it was stone dead now.

'Hello?' I said.

'Vanessa.' His voice was hoarse, stretched, distorted with pain. 'You need . . . you need to go to the police . . .'

'What? Stuart? What happened? Are you all right?'

'I . . . yes . . . I'm . . . *ah* . . .'

'Stuart, where are you? What's happened?'

'Came back to the flat . . . there was a guy here. Blonde hair . . . green jacket . . .'

Tourneaux.

'Stuart—'

'He said he was looking for you. Said for me to tell him where you were, or . . .'

'Oh God . . .'

'I said he should get out before I called the police . . . but he attacked me. He . . . he was strong. Really strong. He broke my arm . . . some fingers, I think . . .'

I drew in a harsh, painful sob. 'Oh God, Stuart, I'm so sorry . . .'

'I *told him, Vanessa.*' He was crying now, crying that was half physical agony and half a guilt that I could *feel,* even from here. It made the phone heavy in my hand. 'I said you were at Alice's . . . I'm so sorry . . . he was so . . . he broke another finger . . . I couldn't . . .'

'It's OK, Stuart, it's OK.'

'He knocked me out once I'd told him. I only just came to
. . . he was here about an hour ago . . .'

It took less than an hour to get to Alice's from there.

Alice would be home by now.

Oh God.

Oh God, no.

Not Alice too.

'Stuart,' I said, 'I have to call you back. I'm sorry, I'm so,
so sorry. But I have to see if Alice is all right.'

'It's OK . . . it's fine . . . I'll . . .'

'Call yourself an ambulance. As soon as I hang up, you call
an ambulance. And the police. Tell them everything. I'll . . .
Stuart, this is all my fault, I'm so sorry. I have to call Alice
. . . I'll call you back when I know she's OK . . .'

'It's OK, Vanessa.' Even through his pain and guilt, I could
hear the strength that was in Stuart, the strength I'd loved.
'*I'm* sorry . . .'

'I'll call you back.' I hung up. Blind, horrific panic was
flooding through me, scalding, freezing. Mark looked at me.
He didn't need to be told what was happening.

I rang Alice's mobile.

It rang and rang.

Rang.

Rang.

Rang.

No answer.

Oh God.

I let it ring far too many times. 'She's not answering.' I
rang off, feeling like I was going to fall apart, disintegrate. 'Oh
God, she's not—'

My phone rang and my heart lurched. I answered. 'Alice? Alice, I—'

'Your friend is very pretty.'

Terror nearly overcame me. I had to physically fight the urge to hurl the phone away and be sick.

'Listen to me,' said Tourneaux, his voice horribly, terrifyingly mild. 'I left your boyfriend alive. But if you don't do exactly as I say, I might not be so kind to your pretty friend, Alice. I can do terrible things to her. And I can make them last. Understand?'

'Yes.'

'You're going to come to Alice's flat. Alone.'

'Alone? Don't you—'

'*Alone*. You're going to tell Mark to stay exactly where he is, or you and your friend are dead. You're going to come here and then you are going to lead me *personally* to wherever you and Mark are hiding. If you don't carry these instructions out *exactly* . . . Alice dies. Well. Eventually she'll die. After a lot of pain. And then Mark, rather than dying quickly and honourably as I offered before, will die slowly and agonisingly and humiliatingly. In front of you. I don't think I need be any clearer than that.'

'No.'

'Leave now.' He hung up.

'Vanessa,' said Mark. 'What's going on?'

'He has Alice,' I said. 'He's going to kill her. I have to go.'

'You can't—'

'I *have* to! He nearly killed Stuart! He's going to kill her! I have to go. And I have to go on my own.'

'Vanessa, this is *insane*! He'll kill *you*!'

'He won't. He needs me to find you. I'm going to go to

Alice's and make sure she's safe. Then I'm going to bring him back here, where you will be waiting. I'll knock three times. You have to be ready for him.'

'I'm not letting you go alone . . .'

'*Yes you are.*' I grabbed my bag, pocketed my phone and threw my jacket on. I walked to the door but Mark barred my way, spreading his wings.

'I'm *not* letting you go,' he said.

I looked him in the eye. 'He's hurting my friends. He might kill Alice. I'm going. And you are staying here. You have to be ready for him.'

He looked back at me, furious and defiant and so caring.

But he knew.

And he knew what I meant by *be ready.*

His wings drooped and he moved aside. I kissed him once, lightly, heavily, and left.

I lurched through the night, hot and black and blue, blinking furiously, thinking grounded thoughts, trying to stop myself from floating away. As I walked I rang Stuart, and when he answered his damaged voice stabbed me in the heart.

'Are you all right?' I asked.

Of all the stupid questions.

'I've . . . called an ambulance,' he said. 'They'll be here soon. Is . . . is Alice OK?'

'Yes,' I lied. 'She's fine. Did you call the police as well?'

'Yes.'

'Stuart, I have to ask you something horrible.'

'What?'

'Please don't tell them why he attacked you. Don't tell them what he was looking for. Say . . . I don't know. Say he got the wrong address and when you confronted him he lost his rag. Don't say he was after me or Alice.'

'But . . .'

'Stuart, *please*. It's too important.'

'OK . . . Vanessa . . . what's happening?'

'I'll explain when it's over. I promise. I'm sorry I've been so crap. I'm sorry for everything. I've got to go now. I'm—'

'Don't say you're sorry. I—'

'OK. But only if you don't say *you're* sorry.'

'OK. I love you.'

I paused, then said 'Bye', even though I'm sure it would have made him feel better to hear it back. At least a little bit better.

It would have been a lie, though.

I crossed over the busy road, the cars as indistinct and unthreatening as distant clouds in my numb, hyperactive state, and headed down a concrete cut-through that I hoped would get me to the station a bit quicker. It was empty and smelled awful, like hold-your-nose awful. There was something oddly familiar about it, although I'd definitely never been here before.

Halfway along, my phone rang.

It was Alice's number.

I stopped dead. 'Alice? Is that you?'

'Um . . . who else would it be?'

'Are you all right? Has he done anything to you?'

'Who?'

'Tourneaux!'

'Vanessa, I don't know what you mean, but I've just got back to my house and it's been burgled.'

'What do you mean, you've just got back?'

'I mean I was delayed at work and I've only just got back

and the place has been broken into. What did you mean about Tourneaux?'

My body went from very hot to very cold in a matter of nanoseconds. 'He . . . he's not there?'

'No. You think it was him?'

'It must have . . . but he said . . .'

Very, very cold.

Very, very still.

'Vanessa?'

I tried to speak but couldn't.

Then someone came up behind me and knocked the phone out of my hand.

Someone spun me around and secured me in some kind of martial arts grip, pulling me against him and trapping both my wrists.

Someone who loomed like a vampire, magnified by fear and by the dark.

Tourneaux looked into my eyes and he could see everything. My fear. My anger. My soul. Everything. And in his, I could see nothing.

'You made that a bit too easy, I'm afraid,' he whispered. 'Leaving your web history on your friend's computer. Tut tut.'

Oh God.

He pulled me even closer, so our faces were right up against each other. 'I know exactly where to go,' he said. 'But I thought the two of you would be easier one-on-one rather than together.'

I wondered if I was going to wet myself.

Even if he hadn't completely overpowered me, even if he hadn't been stronger in every way, I was too petrified to fight.

It was over.

'I want you to understand, before I kill you,' said Tourneaux. 'I am doing a duty. Mark and his kind are the missing link, the misstep between the glorious beings we once were and the impure, imperfect people we have become. They are the evidence. The physical manifestation of our shame. A snapshot, if you like, of humanity as we fall. And they must not be allowed to live.'

Where was I?

Where was the other me?

Why hadn't she warned me?

Now, of all times?

Why?

'*Why?*' I whispered.

'It is my duty,' said Tourneaux. 'He is the last of his kind. In a way, I am the last of mine. The last person who knows the truth. The *real truth*.'

'But . . . b—'

'I'm sorry to have to do this. Genuinely. I'm sorry for all the terrible things I've had to do in order to complete this mission. But you are too dangerous. Already, he has started to change you.' He wasn't looking at my face. He was looking at the air around me. 'I can see it, you know. What he's doing. His influence. It's all around you. Like a halo.'

'*Please* . . .'

'It can't be allowed,' he said. 'It's not meant for us. And . . .' Suddenly he looked different. There was something in his face.

Regret?

'And I feel that it is kinder,' he said. 'For you. To go first. You already lost him once.'

Kinder . . .

'I will make it quick for Mark. You have my word.'

Did I believe him?

Why now, of all times, had I given up?

He moved me around so I was facing away from him, keeping his hand over my mouth. My wrists came momentarily free, but still I couldn't move.

He pulled something from his coat.

Brought it around.

Plunged it into my stomach.

CHAPTER TWENTY-TWO

T HE PAIN WAS intense, so intense. It bubbled up in my throat and mouth, choking me, forcing me not to scream. Tourneaux kept his hand over my mouth until he was sure no noise was going to come, then loosened his grip and turned me round, gently, almost kindly, so he could see my face. Look into my eyes. He watched with the strangest mixture of emotions, so strange that I couldn't begin to interpret them.

I looked down at the knife. I stumbled backwards. I fell against the wall. Bleeding. Shaking.

Somehow far away.

'I'm sorry,' said Tourneaux.

'I'm sorry,' said Tourneaux.

I noticed a fly on the opposite wall.

'I'm *sorry*,' said Tourneaux.

'I'm sorry,' said Tourneaux.

Each time he said it, it was a little slower. A little deeper. Like someone was steadily slowing the tape down. Someone above us, holding their finger on it, on this scene, bringing it to an aquatic crawl.

'I'm sorry,' said Tourneaux.

I slid down to the floor.

'I'm sorry,' said Tourneaux.

I looked up at him, then away. *'I'm sorry,' said Tourneaux.*

I died, and everything stopped. The fly on the opposite wall, rendered gigantic by a lurid splash of lamp post light.

The rubbish fidgeting in the night breeze. The breeze itself. The blood chugging thickly from the knife wound in my stomach.

I was intrigued, though somehow not surprised, to find that I had not stopped. Not entirely. My thoughts, my memories, my awareness, continued to simmer, shiver and spark, except suddenly weightless, un-tethered.

I floated free of myself, becoming a new component in the air above the girl's body, an abstract mass. The five physical senses blurred and combined into something else, a sight that was total and far-reaching, and the dank death smell of the alley that had caught like rotten gas in the girl's nostrils was no longer merely a smell but the *idea* of smell, both the actuality and the concept, exploded, like a schematic rendered in too many dimensions.

I knew I should feel dizzy, but all I felt was absolute calm.

I observed the girl's body. It looked so very small from up here. So temporary. I could see the sticky wound, see *through* it, following the ripples from intention to action to consequence. I knew exactly what could have been done to save the girl, what could have been pressured, plugged, re-attached.

I tried to sigh but instead I rippled, as though I was a patch of water catching a plummeting star, and then there was a sound like all the air escaping from the sky and I was everywhere. Everyone.

I was the girl. Her family, her friends. The boy who had somehow made all this happen.

I was the girl's aunt, her mother, her faraway sister.

I was a different girl, a friend of the one lying dead, sitting alone in her flat, staring at her phone, hugging herself.

I was a different girl again, another friend, distant, lost, drinking a cocktail and feeling unusually thoughtful.

I was the dead girl but younger, living, bright.

I was the girl as she was now, still, dimming.

I was the girl as she might have been, older, a potential future perhaps, impossible now but still flickering valiantly, vainly.

I was everything that each of these people, these women, these girls, this boy, had ever felt and would ever feel . . .

About her.

About Vanessa.

This was what the man had meant, the blonde man in the green jacket, the man standing frozen, a handkerchief in one hand, halfway to the knife in the other hand. What he could see. The halo.

Already, he has started to change you, he had said. Was saying. Would say.

He. The boy. Mark.

He has started to change *you*.

You. Her. The girl. Vanessa.

The name felt simultaneously familiar and foreign, and as I tried to concentrate on it, unpack exactly what it *meant*, what any of this *meant*, I could suddenly see myself, as though from the other end of an immense, dark room. I could see myself, Vanessa, the girl, sleeping next to Stuart. She was wearing that old baggy Simpsons T-shirt. I could see her, so far away. Dreaming away.

Although not far away.

Close enough to touch.

Impossible to touch.

Not impossible—

Something passed between us. Something that travelled the length and breadth of this nothingness of a room. I barely felt it, in my current state, although I knew instinctively what it was.

Sadness.

Grief.

But not mine.

And not hers.

It had already reached her, like the very edge of the sea passing over sand, enough to draw tears from her sleeping eyes, even though she wasn't truly aware of it, not quite yet.

Then the wave hit properly, so hard that she sat up, already sobbing—

And I was shaken back through this dark room, away from her, to the source of the sadness. The grief that passed through me to get to her.

I saw where it came from.

The boy.

Mark.

He was standing in the little alley. The man, Tourneaux, stood between him and my body, Vanessa's body. The body of the girl. I could feel what Mark was feeling. His knowledge, the immediate, unshakable realisation that she was dead.

I saw what followed.

His rage.

It was happening faster than I could see and slower than I could bear, it was happening at all speeds, all speeds flattened out into one speed, because—

Mark howled and something within him exploded. The grief, the sadness and the rage blasted their way out of him, erupting, screaming, burning, a blue invisibility that incinerated Tourneaux where he stood. Before he could make the speech he had planned. The speech I could hear, an echo of before, of now. Before he could even raise the weapon that had killed the girl, or draw the weapon with which he planned to kill Mark, he was just *gone*, erased, eradicated in a brief and agonising flash. I felt his future disappear, felt the path crumble away, felt the cord rip. It *hurt* . . . or at least it felt as close to pain as I was capable of feeling. Such extreme, ultimate violence. The cutting off of a future.

And beneath the pain, beneath the flash, I could see him—

Days ago—

Answering the phone to Mr Matthews—

Beyond—

Backward—

Beneath—

Taught by a tall, stern man—

Indentations in his brain—

Distorting the image—

The image of—

A boy with wings—

Boy with wings—

Little Tourneaux—

Playing in a garden, carelessly—

A boy—

A boy—

Not *the* boy—

The boy—

Mark—

Mark stood where Tourneaux once was, where now there was just his severed timeline, collapsed into shadow.

Mark stood in the alley.

Mark is going to kneel down next to the girl's body and cry.

But I wasn't seeing that now.

I was seeing Vanessa wake up, barely a week ago, in her old baggy *Simpsons* T-shirt, crying, punished by a sadness that wasn't hers. I was seeing her writing hesitantly, bemused at the words that emerged.

Her own murder.

It was happening at the same time that Mark was destroying Tourneaux.

Which was happening at the same time that Tourneaux was killing the girl.

Which was happening at the same time as Vanessa leaving the Travelodge, as Alice calling Vanessa, as dinner with Vanessa's mother, as that trip to the seaside years ago, as Mum and Dad and Izzy and Vanessa having a picnic, as staring up at the stars with Mark, as first cup of coffee, as last glass of wine, as first spliff, as going to work, as quitting work, as first sex as last sex as—

Everything—

It's not meant for us, the man had said.

We were not supposed to change like this.

We were not supposed to see what I was seeing.

I had to tether myself.

Anchor myself to—

Myself.

My dead self.

My dying self.

My earlier selves, living, *crying*—

I need to be inside them—

To feel what they feel—

To make them feel what I—

Feel?

Was I feeling now?

I knew the word I.

I knew that I was me.

I felt it.

And now—

I saw myself, beneath all my other selves, returning home from Alice's flat with new purple hair. She made herself chai tea—

She drinks chai tea for the first time at a tiny, wet festival out in the country, late at night, surrounded by bunting, drooping from the rain but still glowing bravely—

She drinks chai tea for the first time, the second time, the third—

And now, the four hundred and thirty-eighth time—

Each time on top of one another—

No—

No—

Focus—

She stood in her kitchen, drinking chai tea for the four hundred and thirty-eighth time.

She didn't know what was going to happen.

She was linear.

She walked through to the living room. Origin point to destination.

Linear.

She didn't know.

So I screamed at her from the other end of time.

Screamed that she would die.

For a second she saw, and the fear was as cold as—

As—

No—

No, she doesn't see enough—

Losing the—

Connection—

And I rushed away, through Vanessa's life, too many moments to isolate just one—

Back to—

Back to—

Half past three in the morning—

Focus—

Half past three in the morning. Vanessa had been talking to Mark for hours. Mark, the boy, newly returned, newly beautiful and shining and young and confused. They had been talking. Vanessa went to the bathroom.

I couldn't stand next to her. I wanted to stand there and take her by the hand and explain that she had to stay away, she must not fall into Tourneaux's trap, but all I could do was watch the light flicker on and off, watch her shiver at what she was seeing in the mirror, but it didn't make sense to her, it wasn't a message, it was just a black mirror and a featureless doll and blood that wasn't there.

And then, just for a second, or maybe even less, I was there, standing behind her, screaming at her to listen to me, a bloody ghost, and she jumped and spun around and—

And I lost the connection again and was back in the alleyway, watching Vanessa speak to Alice on top of Tourneaux killing Vanessa on top of Mark killing Tourneaux on top of Mark cradling me, Vanessa, the girl, sobbing—

Vanessa—

I was swirling like a snowstorm's fever dream, trying to

find purchase, trying to find matter to grip, trying to find an anchor, but there was nothing, just—

Just Mark cradling the girl's cold body, Vanessa's cold body, *my* cold body, cold but still warm, and the pain he felt was flooding back through me, through what I had become, whatever that was, and I was channelling it, spitting it back down through the chains, through the layers, using all those copies of myself as transmitters, bouncing off Vanessa in the cinema here, where she cried but didn't know why, and then to—

The bathroom, Pauline's bathroom, darling Auntie Pauline's bathroom, Vanessa in the bathroom, staring at the mirror, and there I was behind her, there I was, *me, the girl, the other Vanessa*, the pale *Vanessa*, as *Vanessa* touched her own face, but I was behind her, much further behind, further back and further forward than she could reach, see, know, and I was trying so hard to speak *but I have no words* just something that was like a mind but not the mind that I needed, so all she saw were the pale girl's lips moving moving moving but nothing coming out, and *Vanessa* tried to touch me and the shock reverberated through this collapsing pile of time and I *recoiled* and blood that wasn't really blood spurted and spattered and half of the lightbulbs in Pauline's house exploded and I—

Am in the tip of a Neanderthal's spear, fighting to protect a shape I recognise—

A shape I love—

A shape with wings—

What is this—

This is not Vanessa's life—

How can I see—

And back to Mark, cradling my body, whispering how sorry he was, how sorry, how sorry, how sorry, how sorry, *I love you* he was saying—

The beach, the sea endlessly devouring itself—

The touch of Mark's lips and the shadow of his wings in my living room—

All at the same time—

Time is so inadequate a word—

I don't have the . . . the . . . I *don't even know what I need for this*—

For what I'm experiencing—

I shouldn't have been experiencing this—

This was not a human experience—

Humans did not die like this—

This I knew—

I, this me, knew—

Vanessa did—

I was in America, in the little room that Vanessa always thought was trapped in time —

I fell through it, to Mark's house in Llangoroth, the house he shared with his father—

Pulling Vanessa with me—

From somewhere else—

Tugging at the edges of her mind—

Tugging her from the dream of the little room to the house in Llangoroth—

So she could see Mark's father, hunched over the table—

Feel the—

There was something about this—

No—

Gone—

I was in Alice's bed, Vanessa was in Alice's bed, speaking, and I could hear her without echo, without delay, as clearly as if she was speaking to me now, as if I was telling Mark now, I could hear her say it. *Ever since you reappeared I've felt different.*

It's like . . . like you're changing me.

And we were together on the beach, in the train carriage, in Pauline's spare room, on a country road, sprinkled across time, the residue that falling leaves—

Surrounded by the trees as they crackled over with frost—

Vanessa blinking as a thousand-year-old tidal wave crashed down on *her*—

And I reached out to *her*—

Tapped her on the shoulder—

Said *green jacket*—

The man in the green jacket—

The man I warned me about—

The man I couldn't escape—

Why—

Mark, speaking to me at every second, every minute, every hour between now and then, every version of him speaking in unison—

All of that stuff, from the biggest to the smallest, what is it to that star up there? It's nothing. It's just little things happening. I'm not saying our stuff doesn't matter. I'm just saying that, in the scheme of things, if you compare it to that star up there, or a black hole billions of miles away, or the orbit of an asteroid, or . . . I don't know, the biological processes that make up a plant, or a forest, or the way the moon's gravity affects the tides, or the frequency of whale song, or the rings of Saturn, or the fact that Jupiter has one storm, just one storm, that's bigger than about five Earths and has been raging for hundreds of years . . . all that . . . it doesn't make me feel insignificant. It just kind of puts things in perspective. The universe just gets on with it. So we should try to, as well—

No—

There was nothing more important—

Because if there was—

Then why did I have to warn her—

Why did I *have to do this—*

I was on a train, *Vanessa* was on a train, one of so many trains, all riding the same tracks at minutely different temporal angles. She saw me in the mirror—

I was standing behind her—

She did not jump—

She was no longer terrified—

She spoke to me—

'Hello,' she says.

I wanted to answer, more than anything I wanted to stop the pain, stop the pain that was going to come, but I couldn't—

'What do you want? Are you me?'

I nodded—

I could manage a nod—

Why couldn't I speak—

'Are you trying to warn me?'

Of course, of course, of course—

'You were trying before, weren't you? What's happening? Is it connected? You? Mark?'

It was connected, it was it was it *is*—

'Please. Tell me what's happening.'

Once again I fell away into bleeding, becoming a shiver, and then I was gone—

Watching *Vanessa* die by Tourneaux's knife—

Watching Mark's rage, hyper-charged by an ancient power he didn't understand, tear through Tourneaux, rendering his flesh as insubstantial as dust, less so—

And I heard a voice—

I heard *my* voice—

Calling to me—

'Please,' she calls. 'Come. Come. Come!'

I was there—

I was with her—

'Sorry, but . . . can you tell me?' She was smiling—

She wanted to know—

I wanted to tell her—

But she couldn't hear me. She waved her hand and shook her head and said *no*, no she couldn't hear me, and I felt anger, frustration, amplified by time and repetition, and I clenched my fists and began to bleed and flew away from her—

No—

I could—

I *could* bring her—

Grab her—

Pull her—

Down through the layers—

Years back—

Back here again—

Mark's house in Llangoroth, the little house, and we stood together, Vanessa and I, although we could not see each other, because we could not see ourselves, ghosts as we were, shadows as we were.

We watched Mark come in, walk through us, down the hallway, to the kitchen. Beyond sat his father, slumped at the table. I knew this day.

The day he disappeared.

This event.

This impossible event.

This thing that never happened, that couldn't have happened.

Mark asked his father what was wrong.

His father was hunched over the table.

Shaking.

His father rose.

His face had become a mask, gouged out by pain, by the memories that the feathers brought, the feathers he clutched in his hands, the feathers he found in Mark's bed, the feathers—

The feathers that were so like *Aisling's*—

And just like that I could feel her, somewhere in this tangle, not Vanessa's life, barely even Mark's life, but the connection was still so strong—

I could feel Aisling—

Like a tidal wave—

Gareth Matthews' very own tidal wave—

No—

Must keep hold of this moment—

Gouged out by pain—

The feathers he found in Mark's bed—

The feathers—

From the wings inside Mark—

Extended from his back as he kissed me —

Inside him as he cradled me in the little alleyway—

Inside him as Gareth Matthews lunged and knocked him to the ground—

Burying him in violence—

Burying him in fists—

Screaming—

Both of them screaming—

Me screaming—

In my screaming I lost my grip—

I fell back through the minutes—

To Vanessa and Mark saying goodbye.

Mark shouldering his rucksack and asking what exam it was tomorrow—

Both of them joking, as they always joked.

He walked away from her.

She walked away from him.

I could hear the future—

Mark's father screaming as he beat his son to death—

Beating out the pain—

I felt Mark die—

Felt it echo through the Mark that walked away from Vanessa, that final time—

I screamed—

I grabbed him—

Time folded around us—

I lifted him up, carried him over the event, over his own death, so that it passed meaninglessly underneath us, fading into a maybe, a could-have-been that only I would remember—

I dropped him in the street, the same street I took him from, but not the same street, *not quite*—

Imprecise—

I wasn't supposed to be able to do this—

And I was back in the alleyway, watching him cradle my dead body, and suddenly I understood—

I understood that I would not try and warn Vanessa again.

Because Mark had to live.

So he could change Vanessa.

So Vanessa could die.

So Mark could live.

So I watched. I watched her go about her business, with Mark, watching sadly, knowing what would happen to her.

But I did not try to reach out again.

I passed through moments, through this one, that one, existing in all of them at once, though never properly, but I kept coming back to Mark at this time or that time, back when we were children who laughed and didn't care, like Tourneaux, who was once a child who laughed and didn't care, until his mind had been poisoned, to now, when Mark, he, the boy, my boy, cradled me against him, and I thought of all the ways in which he had changed me, changed Vanessa, changed the girl, ways I understood and ways she didn't, ways I now understood and ways she would. I understood. I knew what had happened.

I could fade away in peace.

I could—

But—

I hear the sound of the sea—

The tidal wave—

What lay beyond Vanessa—

Beyond her life—

But connected—

Through Mark—

I saw a time, thousands of years ago, when those with the

wings were held in high esteem, the very highest. They were few, even then, but they were the best, the bravest, the kindest and most beautiful. They evolved too fast, burned brightly and died out—

They were the most beautiful still—

But I could still understand the pain in Gareth Matthews' face—

As he hurled the feathers—

Memories made manifest—

Memories of Aisling—

Aisling—

Yes—

This isn't finished—

Not quite yet—

I could see her. She brought the sound of the sea, she *was* the sea, at least in part, but she was not a tidal wave. She was so soft, so warm, so old, although she didn't look it. She looked so young.

I saw her clutching her belly, crying.

She was a small lady.

Beautiful.

Her hair was brown.

She looked like Mark.

She clutched her belly and begged Gareth to stay with her.

She lay in the hospital.

The doctor handed Gareth the baby.

The tiniest baby.

Aisling, with a smile, disappeared.

And I rushed through Mark, through the Mark that held Vanessa in the alley, through every version of Mark I knew and every version I didn't, through the newborn Mark . . .

To Aisling.

To her heart, which had stopped beating.

But the carnival of blood and life around her hadn't, far from it, far from it, she was still breathing, even if her chest didn't rise, she was still her, she was still there.

She was still alive.

She just needed time.

But Gareth, crying, didn't know.

The doctor, solemn, didn't know.

The baby, so, so, so tiny, too tiny even for a name, didn't know.

The baby, taken away from his mother.

Me, following.

Gareth, in a little house I didn't recognise, standing over the baby, who kicked his little feet obliviously. Gareth, staring blankly down, his feelings so so so—

The door—

A knock—

And she was standing there, Aisling, standing in the rain, alive, her wings oustretched, a ghost.

Gareth fell back into the house, crying that it couldn't be, that she *died*, that he buried her.

She tried to explain.

Her kind was special.

She wanted to see the baby.

But he wouldn't—

He couldn't—

She was a ghost to him—

He told her there was no baby—

He slammed the door—

The connection *snapped*—

And now she stood on the seafront, her bare feet digging into the damp sand, naked from head to toe, her wings wide and white and so beautiful it burned, tears streaming down her face, down her body. She walked forwards into the sea, walked until she was submerged to her knees, to her waist, to her chin, until her tears and the sea were the same, and she vanished and swam.

Swam to forget.

To escape.

Across the ocean.

And now, whenever *now* was . . .

I felt something.

I was in the little alleyway, in Mark's arms.

And as he held me, at the same time, thousands of miles away, separated by distance but *only* distance, at a New York window attacked mercilessly by the wind and the rain, stood . . .

Aisling.

I flashed between her eyes and Mark's eyes—

Bridging the gap—

Both crying furiously—

Simultaneously—

They both knew why they were crying—

Though not completely—

He cried for me—

She cried for him—

He *felt* her cry for him, although he did not understand —

She *felt* him cry for me, although she did not understand—

And as he held me, so tightly, the grief and the pain and the fury and the love, the twisted, immense, unimaginable mess of it all, flooded through him, searching, finding whatever it was that lived within him, the power, the same power that ripped through Tourneaux—

It passed through me—

Channelled—

To Aisling, crying, so far away—

She staggered from the window—

He's alive.

Mark felt it—

She's alive.

I felt it—

And there was a tugging—

Something tugging me—

Tugging me through infinity—

Tugging me through new images, new memories, new *futures*, Mark and Pauline and the girl, Vanessa, *me*, sitting together, laughing, Alice and Vanessa smiling, *Laura* and Vanessa smiling, their friendship cracked but not shattered, and her mother, Vanessa's mother, smiling, smiling with *me*—

And as they popped up, new bubbles of time, new events, I felt Mark's power, the power that killed Tourneaux, except no, this was its reverse, its opposite, not cold and raging and blue but bright and loving and gold. I felt it—

Tugging me back—

Reversing my wound—

Pressuring, plugging, re-attaching, as I'd seen but been unable to do—

Back to my—

I opened my eyes and they saw Mark's, tearful, anguished, shocked, confused, every emotion happening at once, like my lives, my moments, all on top of one another.

I drew breath, the most wonderful breath I'd ever taken.
'Your mother,' I said. 'She's alive.'
And I knew where she was.

EPILOGUE

'**W**ow.'

Mark turned his head. 'What?'

'Look.'

He looked. 'Wow.'

Our first sight of the Statue of Liberty, looming up out of the early murk and transforming what had been a slightly underwhelming morning into something altogether more majestic. I smiled. 'Better than the first time.'

'Yeah?'

'Definitely. The first time I saw her . . . I don't know, I think I'd kind of set myself up to be disappointed. So I ended up being disappointed. But this time . . . phwoar.' I laughed. 'Sexy.'

Our cab driver said nothing, which was pretty amazing. I think it was the first New York cab I'd ever taken whose driver hadn't tried to talk my ears off. I'd assumed that being garrulous was a prerequisite for the job.

As we sat and let him guide us into the bosom of the city, my hand moved to the space on my stomach where the knife wound should have echoed, reduced to an ugly scar and a lingering pain. Where now, months later, there was just smooth skin.

I know Mark noticed the movement. He always noticed. But he never said anything. It wasn't something we really talked about. Just like we hadn't really discussed Tourneaux in much detail. Mark seemed content to believe that the guy had been truthful with me, about being the last one who knew. And he had sort of seemed like the type to tell a doomed girl the truth.

So we could rest easy, right? The danger was gone. There were no others lurking out there in the darkness.

I wanted to believe it, but somehow I couldn't quite let myself.

Maybe that was just part of being a grown-up.

'Be cool if she had wings,' I said.

'Who?' said Mark.

'Lady Liberty.'

'Oh yeah. That would be good.'

'Maybe one day.'

'Or maybe we could re-design her completely,' said Mark. 'Make her into one of those sky-scraping lesbian fairies of yours.'

I giggled and the cab driver's eyes definitely flickered to the rear-view mirror. They didn't look amused, which made me want to laugh more.

I'd booked us into the same little hotel that Alice and I had used when we'd come years ago. I recognised the old lady who greeted us, although I didn't think she remembered me. Probably definitely not. She'd have encountered fifty thousand guests since me. I'd not encountered any little old lady hotel proprietors since her.

She led us up to our room and we threw our stuff down and made coffee, both exhausted from the flight. Mark hadn't slept. I had a little, but my dreams had been odd, as they often were these days. Not even dreams, really – they were memories, sometimes mine and sometimes not, far too clear and precise, like I was stepping into the past rather than viewing it through a foggy lens. Sometimes I thought I saw the future, but those visions were much harder to hold on to, usually impossible, for which I was grateful. It was discomfiting enough to wake up with the borrowed knowledge of things that had already happened.

I hadn't felt any other changes.

Not yet, anyway.

We got breakfast at a diner nearby and I scoffed all of mine and most of Mark's. 'You'll get fat,' he said.

'Probably. Will you still be my friend if I do?'

'Yeah. I won't fancy you, though.'

'I don't fancy you anyway, mate.'

'What if I get my wings out?'

'Not in public, dear.'

He did this from time to time. He didn't push, of course. Mark never pushed. Just . . . hints. A look, a casual comment, to let me know he was still there. Still waiting. And every time I smiled and batted it away.

I wasn't trying to tease him.

There was just so much thinking still to do.

I had to know that it was right.

It was too important not to be sure.

'Are you ready for this?' I asked. Stupid question.

'Born ready.' Stupid answer.

He had written the address on a piece of paper, which he had been taking out of his wallet roughly once every fifteen minutes, scrutinising it with such intensity that I half expected it to burst into flames. Now we stood, looking up at a tall bronze apartment building, the first hint of sun visible behind it. I knew the building. I'd seen it before, attacked mercilessly by the wind and the rain.

I couldn't believe we were finally here.

I wondered what Mark was thinking.

'Elevator?' I said.

'Stairs.'

Made sense. More time to think. To prepare for something that you couldn't ever prepare for. We walked up several flights of stairs that smelled of old lives and emerged on the eighth floor. Brown carpet struggled away in either direction and Mark headed slowly for the end of the hallway, stopping outside a door.

The door.

Her door.

'Ready?' I said again.

He didn't answer. He just folded the piece of paper and put it in his pocket, and his left hand found mine.

With his right hand, he knocked.

THE END

ACKNOWLEDGEMENTS

M ANY THANK YOUS due, as always, to Chris and Jen at Salt and to Ben Illis for essential editorial guidance and the general shepherding of this book into physical, commercially available form.

Thanks to Catherine Dunstan, Rafi Mohamed, Anna McKerrow, Lu Hersey and Emily Martinelli for valuable feedback, you all helped to make this a stronger story.

Thanks to all the usual suspects for support, morale and gentle piss-taking. If any of you think you see yourselves in this book, yeah you're probably right, it's you. Nah, not really. Well, maybe. Kinda.

And finally (but hopefully not finally), thanks to everyone who reads what I write. Bit pointless otherwise.

NEW FICTION FROM SALT

RON BUTLIN
Billionaires' Banquet (978-1-78463-100-0)

NEIL CAMPBELL
Sky Hooks (978-1-78463-037-9)

SUE GEE
Trio (978-1-78463-061-4)

CHRISTINA JAMES
Rooted in Dishonour (978-1-78463-089-8)

V.H. LESLIE
Bodies of Water (978-1-78463-071-3)

WYL MENMUIR
The Many (978-1-78463-048-5)

ALISON MOORE
Death and the Seaside (978-1-78463-069-0)

ANNA STOTHARD
The Museum of Cathy (978-1-78463-082-9)

STEPHANIE VICTOIRE
The Other World, It Whispers (978-1-78463-085-0)

RECENT FICTION FROM SALT

KERRY HADLEY-PRYCE
The Black Country (978-1-78463-034-8)

CHRISTINA JAMES
The Crossing (978-1-78463-041-6)

IAN PARKINSON
The Beginning of the End (978-1-78463-026-3)

CHRISTOPHER PRENDERGAST
Septembers (978-1-907773-78-5)

MATTHEW PRITCHARD
Broken Arrow (978-1-78463-040-9)

JONATHAN TAYLOR
Melissa (978-1-78463-035-5)

GUY WARE
The Fat of Fed Beasts (978-1-78463-024-9)

NEW BOOKS FROM SALT

XAN BROOKS
The Clocks in This House All Tell Different Times
(978-1-78463-093-5)

RON BUTLIN
Billionaires' Banquet (978-1-78463-100-0)

MICKEY J C ORRIGAN
Project XX (978-1-78463-097-3)

MARIE GAMESON
The Giddy Career of Mr Gadd (deceased)
(978-1-78463-118-5)

LESLEY GLAISTER
The Squeeze (978-1-78463-116-1)

NAOMI HAMILL
How To Be a Kosovan Bride (978-1-78463-095-9)

CHRISTINA JAMES
Fair of Face (978-1-78463-108-6)

This book has been typeset by
SALT PUBLISHING LIMITED
using Neacademia, a font designed by Sergei Egorov
for the Rosetta Type Foundry in the Czech Republic.
It is manufactured using Creamy 70gsm, a Forest
Stewardship Council™ certified paper from Stora Enso's
Anjala Mill in Finland. It was printed and bound by
Clays Limited in Bungay, Suffolk, Great Britain.

LONDON
GREAT BRITAIN
MMXVIII